WOUNDED

A BROOKSIDE ROMANCE

ABBY BROOKS

Cover design by Michele Catalano Creative.

Dedication

To Bill.

Chapter 1

BAILEY

"Have you seen him naked yet?" Lexi Stills, my best friend since the first grade, leans forward, resting her elbows on the table in the crowded hospital cafeteria.

"Seen who naked yet?" I ask, feigning confusion.

Lexi purses her cherry-colored lips. "Liam McGuire, you ass." She picks at the crust of her sandwich and pops a bite into her mouth. "You know, the super-famous singer who just happens to have been admitted here at Grayson Memorial."

"Oh yeah. Him." I shrug, playing it cool just to drive her crazy.

"Yeah, *him*." Lexi stops chewing and lifts her eyebrows. "So?"

"So, what?"

"Have you seen him naked?"

Laughing, I sit back in my chair and scrape my

spoon around the sides of my yogurt cup. "Nope. No hot nude scenes with famous musicians for me," I say, even though it's kind of a lie.

Liam has a habit of leaving his hospital gown open and I've seen his ass more times than I can count. I just don't feel like opening that particular can of worms with Lexi right now. Of all the fangirls in the world, she might be the fangirliest and I'm not in the mood for the slew of questions that will follow the admission that yes, I have seen his ass, and yes, it really is as magnificent as she thinks it is.

"Don't give up hope." Lexi looks so crushed I almost tell her the truth. Almost. "I think he's staying here one more day," she says. "After that, I bet they ship him right back to Los Angeles for some kind of plastic surgery miracle only someone that rich and famous could afford." She rakes a hand through her honey-blond hair, pulling little wisps back off her face. "It's such a shame. The accident and all that. I wonder what will happen now that he's all scarred up."

"Maybe he'll learn some humility. That man is every bit as bad as the tabloids make him out to be."

Lexi rolls her eyes. "Only you would be immune to the awesomeness that is Liam McGuire." She balls up her napkin and throws it onto the table next to her mostly eaten sandwich.

"So, how's Gabe?" I ask, carefully enunciating my words so she knows I'm changing the topic now and have no intention of letting her change it back. Being

Liam McGuire's nurse is bad enough. He doesn't need to become the sole topic of every conversation on top of it.

"That boy is going to be the death of me." She's trying to sound exasperated, but the look of sheer adoration gleaming in her eyes ruins the effect. "He's as hard-headed as he is sweet. Do you know what he said to me yesterday?"

"I haven't the foggiest." Lexi's stories about her five-year-old son Gabe never disappoint.

"He was playing with his truck on the table and then he looks at me, as serious as can be, and says he's going to need me to talk to him before I find a husband because he wants to make sure the guy's truck is good enough for me."

I laugh as we stand and gather our trash. "Sounds like he's already on his way to being more man than boy. A little bossy, a little protective, and interested in his truck above all things."

Lexi lets out a long sigh. "Lord help me," she says, looking towards the ceiling as if expecting an answer.

The hospital cafeteria is busier than I've ever seen it. Ever since word got out that Liam McGuire is holed up here, we've had an influx of oddly difficult to diagnose illnesses and injuries. Phantom pains and coughs that seem way more serious at home than they do once the patients arrive here. There's even paparazzi hanging out at the front doors.

Paparazzi.

In Grayson, Ohio.

They scurry forward like a swarm of ants every time the doors open, cameras flashing madly, calling out Liam McGuire's name like a battle cry. When they discover the infamous pop star isn't coming out to show off his new badass scar and flash his so-charming-it-should-be-patented smile, they collectively groan and retreat as if to lick their wounds and prepare for the next time those doors swing open.

Lexi widens her eyes at me as she throws her trash in the bin. "Can you imagine how much attention you'd get if these people knew you're one of his nurses?"

A little strum of panic tangles up with my lunch and bounces around my stomach. "You keep your mouth shut, you hear me?" Lexi loves the spotlight. Me? No thank you.

"Fine," she says, pouting. "But you're throwing away an opportunity here. This could be your fifteen minutes of fame."

I link arms with my best friend and we saunter out of the cafeteria. "Nah. I'm saving my fifteen minutes for something way better than this."

"You say that now, but I bet when you're old and gray you'll realize you squandered an opportunity here."

"I'm glad to see you have so much faith in me. That you think the best I'm ever going to be is a nurse to some spoiled brat of a pop star."

"I have more faith in you than you have in yourself, you dingbat," Lexi replies as we arrive at the nurse's station.

"Of course, his call light is on." I let out a little growl of frustration. "When *isn't* it on?"

Lexi shakes her head. "You are the only female between the ages of fifteen and one hundred to be upset because she has to spend too much time with Liam McGuire."

"I doubt that," I say before I head down to his room at the end of the hall.

I don't know if it's because he's been famous since he was fourteen and all the attention spoiled him, or if he's just got asshole in his genes, but it only takes a minute or two of being around the guy to get my hackles up. I don't care how good looking he is or how well he can sing, if you're ugly on the inside, you're ugly on the outside.

Although, for as much as I can't stand the guy, there is a small part of me that does feel a little bit sorry for him. A very small part. And just a tiny little bit. I mean, the guy survived an accident that may or may not alter the course of his life. His tour bus swerved off the road just outside of Grayson and rolled over a few times. Everyone survived, although after seeing pictures of the bus, I don't know how. The thing was just a garbled piece of twisted metal and broken glass.

Liam suffered a concussion and a wicked gash that runs from his hairline to his chin that should have taken his eye but didn't. All the doctors keep muttering about how lucky he is, but I don't know if they've really thought it through. For a guy who makes his living off his looks, an injury like that is probably devastating. I don't think I could be human and *not* feel a tiny bit bad for him.

But like I said, just a tiny bit.

BAILEY

The security guards stationed outside his room smile and stand as I come near. I know they do it out of politeness, but it unnerves me every time. I want to throw up my hands and remind them I'm just me.

Gary, a tall man with one hell of a potbelly, holds up a hand. "Why don't you hold off a beat?"

Just as I open my mouth to ask why, a loud crash sounds from inside the room.

"Damn it, Brent! I am not going back to LA. End of story!" Liam's words come blaring out into the hallway, with the hushed response of Brent—his manager— low, oily, and too quiet to understand, following quickly after.

I give Gary a weary nod and then smile at Josh, a much younger and thinner version of his partner. "Has he been like this all day?" I ask.

Josh lets out a low whistle. "This is an improvement."

Great. Liam is a challenge when he's on good behavior. When he's in a mood? It's just bad all around. "Wish me luck," I say as I prepare myself to enter the lion's den.

"I'll cross my fingers for you." Josh smiles a little too widely, the space between his teeth glaring at me like a jack o'lantern carved by a five-year-old.

"And where the *fuck* is that nurse? I hit the call button an hour ago!"

I cringe. "There's my cue," I whisper, squaring my shoulders and adding steel to my spine before entering the room.

Liam is up and out of bed, the alarm on his IV pump beeping away. "Took you long enough." He glares at me and folds his arms over his chest. "You need to make this machine stop beeping. Now." I can tell by the way his hospital gown flutters at his waist that it's open in the back. Good god. Does the guy have any modesty?

I roll my eyes and bite my tongue as I hit the alarm mute button. A quick investigation shows me that the cord has been pulled out of the wall. "These things have a really short battery life." I bend to plug the thing back in. "You shouldn't pull the cord out of the wall or the alarm will go off like this," I say, twisting to look him in the face and give him my best *don't mess with me or I'll cut you* look.

Liam sets his jaw and scowls, looking unfortunately sexy despite his shitty attitude. "Yeah, well, I can't sit still anymore because I'm losing my mind in here. That thing's going to have to figure out how to hold its charge longer."

Right. Because that's even a possibility.

I hold my tongue and study Liam. His auburn hair is bleached blond and somehow, even in the hospital, is swept back away from his face and gelled to perfection. Both ears are pierced and he has enough tattoos to make me wonder what exactly he's trying to prove. The bandage covering half his face does very little to take away from his looks, and even I can admit he's gorgeous.

Well, that is, until he opens his mouth and ruins everything.

Keeping it professional, I put on my blandest smile and stare up at him. "Since I'm here, I'll go ahead and check your bandage. Please have a seat, Mr. McGuire. I'll get the things I need and be right back."

He glowers down at me. "I'd prefer to stand."

I stifle a growl. He's such a petulant child. If this is how they treat people out in Los Angeles, I'm more than happy with my simple life here in Ohio.

"And I'd prefer not to have to climb up on a chair to do my job."

He glowers down at me, determined to get his way.

This guy has no idea what he's getting into. I put my hands on my hips and shift my weight back to my heels, lifting my chin to stare him straight in his face. There's no way in hell I'm standing on a stool to change his bandage. If he wants to see which one of us has the widest stubborn streak, I am more than ready to dig in my heels until he backs down.

Brent, the manager from hell, saunters toward us, his hands outstretched as if to avert the war he sees brewing on the horizon. "Come on, Liam. Do you really want to have to wait for this girl—"

"Woman." I glare at Brent.

"Whatever." He waves a manicured hand at me. "Do you really want to wait for her to find a stool?"

"Nope," I say. "I will most definitely not be finding a stool. You'll take a seat so I can do my job and go check on my other patients."

Liam and Brent's jaws drop in unison and I turn on my heel to leave the room. As soon as I'm out of sight, I pause and blow a puff of air out from between my lips.

"He is such a pain in the ass," I say to Gary and Josh.

Josh gives me a thumbs up, a cheesy grin lighting up his face. "You're doing amazing."

The guy means well, but his awkwardness just adds fuel to the fire of frustration in my belly. I return his thumbs up, looking decidedly less enthusiastic than he did, and head off in search of the supplies I need. When I come back into Liam's room, Brent is still talking a mile a minute.

"When that bitch comes back—" He looks my way as I walk in, a greasy smile sliding across his face as if he wasn't just talking about me.

I raise my eyebrows to let him know I heard, but bite my bottom lip to keep in the response that's stomping its way up my throat. They can think whatever they want to think about me as long as I never have to see them again once they check out of the hospital tomorrow.

"Shut up, Brent," says Liam, and for the first time since he was admitted here, I feel like thanking him.

Liam meets my eyes, and, taking extreme care to exaggerate his movements, he grabs his IV stand, turns, and crosses the room to sit in an armchair, stretching the power cord to its limit.

Yes, his hospital gown is open in the back.

No, he's not wearing anything under it.

I am more than certain he thought he'd embarrass me by giving me a view of his admittedly magnificent backside, but he's going to have to try harder than that if he wants to unsettle me. I'm a nurse, for heaven's sake. I see people's butts all the time. If he's looking for a flustered girl with red cheeks, he's looking at the wrong woman.

"Thank you," I say as I come to stand at his side.

Liam stays silent as I pull on a pair of gloves. I pick at the edges of the tape around the gauze and he turns to look at me.

"Eyes front, please." I don't meet his gaze. The last thing I want to do is give him another reason to complain about something.

He flops back in his chair, ripping the bandage from his face with the movement. The thing dangles from my hand and I stare at it in surprise. So much for being gentle.

"See?" he says, flaring his hands and glaring at Brent. "She won't even look at me. Can you think of any other time a female has been this close to me and not lost her fucking head trying to get my attention?"

Being rude back won't get us anywhere, but he's got one more chance to be an ass before I won't be able to keep my mouth shut anymore. I'm strong, but I'm not that strong.

Brent waves a hand in my direction. "She is obviously not in your target demographic." His gaze sweeps over me, assessing and dismissing in one smooth movement. "She's too old and not nearly trendy enough to matter. If I were you, I would take it as a good sign that she's not trying to engage. This is not the kind of girl you're looking for."

I dab antibiotic ointment on his wound, biting the inside of my lip so hard I taste blood. "I'm right here," I mutter.

Liam shakes his head and pulls away from me. "Holy shit, Brent. Do you ever shut the fuck up?"

I lean in with my ointment and Liam waves me

away. "They're all going to act this way." His dark eyes flash as he gestures towards me. "You and I both know that my brand is all about sex. The body. The face. No one cares what I sing as long as I look good doing it." He rests his ankle on his knee and looks me full in the face. "Be honest. You can barely stand to look at me. You're not going to like my music as much now that I look like this."

"All I want to do is change your bandage so I can check on my other patients. As your manager suggested, I'm not in your target demographic." I almost tell him I never liked his music in the first place, but I swallow the words. Two wrongs don't make a right and just because he's an ass doesn't give me a reason to be awful in return.

"What the hell happened to you?" Liam stares me right in the face and laughs. "It looks like you swallowed something nasty. Face all screwed up. Nostrils flaring. Not your prettiest look, sweetheart."

So much for being professional.

"First of all," I say, my words carefully carved from ice and stone. "I didn't swallow something nasty, thank you very much. I just get a little sick to my stomach being around you. Second of all, I can barely stand to look at you because you're an asshole. And third of all, I never liked your music. You can rest assured that's not going to change now." I put a finger on his dropped jaw and turn his head towards the wall. "Now, if you'd just keep your face pointed that way, I can get you bandaged up and get out of here."

Liam does not look at the wall like I just asked him to. He brings his gaze right back to me and there's a flash of emotion on his face that I recognize. It's only there for a moment, one tiny little millisecond of feeling, and then it's gone. Whisked away with a sniff of his nose and a shake of his head. But it doesn't matter. I saw it and I recognized it for what it was.

Despair.

Brent goes off like a windup toy, a slew of words sliding from between his overly balmed lips.

"Holy fuck, Brent. Shut up," Liam says without looking away from my face.

Brent does not shut up. "This is ridiculous, Liam." He pinches the bridge of his nose and smooths back his perfectly shaped eyebrows. "I don't know who she thinks she is, saying those things to you, but we'll have you on the first plane to LA as soon as I get my assistant on the phone. And you..." He levels a finger at me. "You can rest assured that I'll have your job for this."

Liam sighs and closes his eyes. When he opens them again, they're trained on mine, and for the first time since he's been here, he looks real. "You might be the first person to ever be honest with me in my whole life."

A million sarcastic remarks want out past my lips.

Little caustic things, venomous revenge for every awful thing he's said to me over the last couple weeks. A minute ago, I would have let them fly in a glorious display of self-righteousness. And in all honesty, I'm not convinced he still doesn't deserve a solid dose of the truth. But that look in his eyes. The despair. I can't say any of those things after seeing that.

I finally settle on: "I'm sorry."

"I might be, too," he replies. And then he blinks and the moment's gone. "Now, finish whatever it is you're doing to my face—" he waves a hand over his cheek and turns away from me, "—and get the hell out of here."

"Gladly." I bite off the word, instantly sorry I didn't let my sarcasm fly when I had the chance.

I've never liked Liam McGuire. His music is vapid. Soulless sound designed to showcase his sex appeal. Combine that with the ridiculous headlines smeared across the tabloids—the temper tantrums, the womanizing, the utter asshattery—and you can bet that I've considered him a scourge on this Earth for the better part of a decade. But seeing that despair in his eyes just now? That bothers me. This guy has everything money could possibly buy, a lifestyle that anyone would be crazy not to lust after, and yet he still knows the cold, dark, empty pit of hopelessness. There's something profound there. I'm just too pissed off to dwell on it.

I gather my things and leave the room. Liam and

Brent start in on another argument as I pass Gary and Josh, pausing to blow a puff of air past my pursed lips once again. Whatever it is that Liam's dealing with that hurts him like that, I'm sorry for him. I really am. But I sure will be glad when they ship his spoiled ass back to LA.

Chapter 3

LIAM

"Hang up the phone, Brent."

Brent hunches around the thing and turns his back to me. Assuming I didn't speak loudly enough for him to hear, I raise my voice to better make my point. "Hang. Up. The. Phone. Brent."

"Hang on a second," he says to his assistant on the other line and then pulls the phone from his ear, waiting for me to speak, impatience tightening the space between his eyes.

I didn't tell him to put his assistant on hold. I told him to hang up the damn phone. I stare him down, drumming my fingers on the armrest of this tacky chair, eyebrows lifted. Waiting.

With a heavy sigh and a shake of his head, he puts the phone back to his ear. "I'll call you back in a few minutes. You better have a way to get him out of this backwoods shithole, sooner rather than later." He ends the call and slides his phone into his breast pocket.

"I'm not going back to LA."

Brent scoffs. "Yes, you are. We've got consults scheduled with four of the best plastic surgeons in the world—*in the world,* Liam. You're going to come out of this just fine. Better than ever, even. PR is already putting out fires in the media, calling bullshit on any story that claims you're hurt."

"But I am hurt." I turn my focus towards the window and the cluster of buildings soaking up the sunshine on the other side of it.

"They don't need to know that." Brent waves his hands through the air, grabbing my attention again. "To clarify, we're admitting that you've been injured. You know how women are. If we can generate sympathy for you, a little worry about your safety and well being, they'll be so worked up by the time you get back on stage that half the audience will orgasm the minute they see you. We're just denying the allegations about an injury to your face."

"Allegations. Are you shitting me right now?" I point to the bandage. "Does this look like an allegation to you?"

"As soon as we get you out of surgery, that's all they'll have. Allegations." Brent waits for me to reply, but I've got nothing to say to him. He starts pacing excitedly, his polished shoes squeaking on the sterile floor. "We'll have a tour scheduled the minute the doctors clear you to travel. Wait. No. Maybe it's better if we hold off. Really drag it out. Leak a few stories about how hard your recovery has been. You know, really get those sympathetic engines revved up." He smiles so widely his face might crack. "We're going to make so much money off this accident."

His eyes are glassy with adrenaline and I hate him for it. Our bus rolled into a ditch. People are hurt. Like seriously hurt. There's a chance one of the groupies isn't going to walk again. I'm hopped up on so much pain medication I can't always see straight. And he's busy planning a comeback tour and counting the money.

I look the bastard right in the eyes. "I'm not going back."

"Bullshit."

"You know it and I know it. My career is over. They get one look at this scar..." I can't even finish the thought. "I don't want sympathy selling tickets. I want my music selling tickets."

Brent lets out a puff of air and laughs. "It's never been your music filling the seats, Liam. You and I both know that or you wouldn't be so concerned about what happens if people see that scar." He softens his tone and uncrosses his arms. "Come home. Talk to the surgeons. We'll drop the sympathy stuff and focus on getting you back on your feet."

He says that but he doesn't mean it. Brent will say anything to make me stop fighting with him. Next thing I know, I'm doing the very thing I didn't want to do, saying whatever it is he tells me to say. Smiling for the cameras, strutting around mostly naked in underwear ads. As far as he's concerned, I'm not much more than a trained monkey and I'm tired of it.

I stand and start pacing, yanking on the IV stand until the power cord comes out of the wall. Brent does his thing, talking at me from a million different directions and I do my thing—ignoring him until he goes away.

Of course, there's nowhere for him to go. At least nowhere around here that he would deign to consider up to his standards. He complains about the shitty little motel he's staying at. The lack of decent coffee in the entire state of Ohio. The general basicness of the food and the people. He forgets that I come from a town like this. It's been a long time since I've been home, but my best memories come from a place almost identical to Grayson. All his complaining does is remind me why I decided not to trust him the first time I met him.

The damn IV pump starts beeping at me again, but I ignore it. I can see how it annoys the hell out of Brent. Combine it with the flapping of my hospital gown and the ample view he has of my ass, and his frustration has hit a level where it looks like his face is trying to implode. He's staring at the cord with pursed lips, his meticulously groomed eyebrows so furrowed they look like the unibrow God gave him, wondering if he could get me to stand still long enough to plug it in.

He can't.

I intend to pace until he can't take it anymore and leaves. He can go sit in his shitty hotel room and I can finally get a minute to breathe. Some time to work on the song that won't leave me alone. It keeps playing on repeat in my head, bits and pieces of phrases and a melody so sweet it's like honey on my tongue. I think it's going to be good when it's done, which is a shame because no one but me will ever hear it. It's not sexy enough to fit my brand. I'll just put it with the rest. All the other songs I've written but won't get to perform because the powers that be have deemed them 'too deep.'

No one cares how you feel, Liam, they say. *They just want you to sing songs and shake your ass so they have something to think about when they pull out the vibrators at night.*

Whatever. Fucking assholes.

"Mr. McGuire?" The cute little nurse with the shitty attitude walks back into the room, shaking her head. She takes one look at the power cord trailing behind the IV and points to the bed. "Have a seat."

Thanks to Brent, I'm so tired of arguing, I just do what she tells me without a word, plopping onto the shitty mattress and puffing out my cheeks. I can't figure this chick out. She's cute enough, in a 'real' way. Her blond hair piled high on her head, held there with a rubber band. She probably took all of five minutes to do it, but it works for her. She wears very little makeup, just a little mascara to darken her fair eyelashes, but she's still pretty enough. Compared to the lacquered women I'm used to in LA, she's a breath of fresh air.

When she scrawled her name on the whiteboard during her first shift with me—Bailey with a heart over the i—I thought for sure we'd be fucking in the bathroom by the end of the day. But, turns out Bailey with a heart over the i can't stand me. Imagine that.

Brent pulls out his phone, stabs at the screen with his finger, and puts the thing to his ear. "Tell me you've got those plane tickets," he barks at his assistant.

Bailey meets my eyes and smiles sadly. I know that look and I hate it. She actually feels sorry for me. Me. Liam McGuire. I don't need anyone's pity. Especially not from this tiny hardass of a nurse eking out a living out here in the middle of nowhere. I stand, grabbing the IV stand and yanking the cord out of the wall just as she finishes plugging it back in, and cross the room to Brent. As Bailey gasps and Brent turns to me, eyes wide, I take the phone from his hands and end the call.

"I'm not going back to LA."

"You tell me how you think that's going to play out." Brent steps back and folds his arms over his chest. "Enlighten me."

"I'll stay here."

Brent bobs his head. "And the paparazzi? How will you handle them? You know they're stationed at every single motel in a fifty-mile radius, right? That I have to deal with them every time I leave here and every time I pull up into the parking lot of that trash heap I'm staying in?"

"I'm not staying in a hotel."

"Right." Brent draws out the word, his sarcasm fully engaged. "Of course you aren't."

"That's right. I'm staying with her." I jerk my thumb over my shoulder to indicate bitchy Bailey. "We discussed it last night. After you left." I turn to her, smiling wide. "Didn't we, Bailey?"

She's got three seconds to close her mouth and accept my statement with a smile on her face before Brent calls bullshit. Of all the nurses, in all the world, why did I have to get the only one who wouldn't jump at the chance to have me stay with her?

Brent watches Bailey's reaction and lets out a snort of laughter. "Nice try, McGuire."

I stare at the woman and widen my eyes, only to be rewarded with a jolt of pain through the stitches on my face. I've been talking too much today. My cheek hurts and I'm exhausted. I just want to crawl into bed and sleep. Pull the cheap little blanket over my head and pretend like none of this is happening. Like I'm back in LA in my own bed, sliding between my Egyptian cotton sheets.

"Yeah." The nurse clears her throat, making a whole lot of eye contact with me, and then with Brent. "Yeah, he's staying with me. I just thought we were keeping it secret is all."

She needs to stop looking so baffled by the words coming out of her mouth. Like, now.

"Okay," says Brent, holding up his hands. "I know he's put you in a hard situation, sweetie, but you don't have to cover for him."

Bailey sets her jaw, anger flashing in her eyes. "I'm not covering for him. I was complaining about my patio and he offered to stay here and help me build a new one."

Brent laughs. "I haven't heard you say more than three words to him. You don't even like him. Now you're inviting him to stay in your house? Sorry sweetheart. Not buying it."

"I like him just fine. It's you I can't stand."

Score one for bitchy Bailey with a heart over the i.

"And you," says Brent, pushing off the wall and heading over to me. "Since when do you think you can build a patio? You can't even brush your own hair."

"I sure as shit can build a patio."

Brent laughs again, the condescending little snot. "Because you're so accustomed to hard work and doing things yourself." He shakes his head, crosses his arms over his chest, and turns away from me.

He has no idea how hard I work. The endless touring with back-to-back concerts in different states—hell, different countries—each night. That takes its toll. I barely sleep, but it doesn't matter. I have to get up on that stage and dance and sing and smile whether I feel like it or not. This body, the one they're working so hard to sell, I don't just wake up with it. In between the travel and the performing and the press conferences, I have to find time to hit the gym and hit it hard. I'm no stranger to hard work.

All that being said, if this chick thinks I'm building her a patio, she can think again. Just when I thought she was someone who wasn't interested in getting something out of me, she goes and proves that she's an opportunist like everyone else.

C'est la vie. The world is a shitty place filled with shitty people. Everyone is out to get ahead and no one cares who they step on to get what they want. So, you know, do unto others and all that. I'll use this nurse to get Brent out of my hair. Maybe take a beat and let my face heal in peace. And after that? Who knows? Maybe Liam McGuire will just fall off the map. Go out on a high note rather than ride my career all the way to the bottom.

Because let's be serious, if I don't have my face and my sex appeal, then I have nothing at all.

BAILEY

What in the world is happening right now? Did I really just invite Liam McGuire to stay at my house in exchange for building me a patio?

Why, yes. That's exactly what I did.

It's not like he's actually going to stay with me. Obviously, he's looking for a way to get his manager out of his hair. But, the guy is so used to taking what he wants, to spouting nonsense and having everyone nod their head in star-struck silence, I couldn't help but add the bit about the patio in there. He put me on the spot? Well, I put him on the spot. All's fair in love and war. Right?

Except there isn't any love here. None at all.

So, what's that leave us with? War?

Holy shit. What have I done?

As Liam argues with his manager, standing in a

pool of sunlight streaming in through the window that's turning his hospital gown all but transparent, I soothe myself with the knowledge that I haven't really done anything. I mean, let's get real here. Liam wants to stay with me as much as I want him to stay with me. So, like, not at all. But as Brent goes to work belittling the guy, I see more and more little flashes of sadness and anger on Liam's face. He hides it well, wrapping it all up in disdain and irritation. Not many people would catch the nuance or notice the difference, it's just that I'm particularly clued in to people hiding pain. I can't stand it. No one should hurt and feel like they need to hide it. The deeper you bury emotions like that, the more destructive they become until it all explodes in one big dramatic event.

"You're right about one thing," I say, interrupting Brent in one of his condescending tirades. "Liam's going to have to fly under the radar and that's not going to happen with him looking like that." I gesture to the highly styled, pierced, and tattooed man with his ass hanging out of the back of his hospital gown.

Brent feigns shock. "Finally. Someone's making some sense around here."

"So," I continue before he goes on. "You have to go buy him some clothes." I turn to Liam. "And you'll need a haircut. Maybe even go back to your natural color."

Liam's jaw drops, but I push forward.

"I don't know what to do about the tattoos." I

chew on a fingernail and study his arms before turning to Brent. "How recognizable are they to his fans?"

Both men blink at me in silence.

"Alright, fine. You guys think it over, but I have work to do." I move as if to leave the room.

Brent takes one last look at the stubborn set of Liam's jaw and sighs. "Fine. You're right. He's going to have to blend in a whole lot more than he does now. I'll call his stylist and get her flown out here. I don't know what to do about the tattoos. His fans will notice and recognize them." Brent reaches for his phone and I stop him.

"Nope. No stylists. Nothing fancy. You guys will just make him a different version of what he already is. If he's hanging around here, he's going to need to blend in, not stick out."

For as certain as I sound about all of this, there's a steady strain of 'what the hell am I doing' running through my head. But, I'll be damned if I spend any more time listening to these men argue. If they can't figure out which of them is in charge of this situation, I'll take the choice right out of their hands.

"You," I say, pointing at Brent. "Go to Walmart—"

"Walmart?" Brent looks horrified.

"Yes. Walmart. Buy him jeans. Shirts. Probably long sleeves if he plans on leaving the house. It's summer, so that will suck, but at least the tattoos are covered. He can have short sleeves for when he's at my house. Get him a bottle of hair dye, as close to his natural hair color as possible—"

Now it's Liam's turn to look horrified. "I'm not using store-bought dye on my hair."

"Then you're not staying with me." I square my shoulders and head to the door, fighting laughter at the absurdity of this conversation.

"Wait," they say in unison.

"I'll go to the store and get him some clothes." Brent looks so dejected I'd feel sorry for the guy if he wasn't such a pain in the ass.

"And some hair dye." I look pointedly at Liam and he nods.

"And the dye," echoes Brent.

"Great. You," I say, pointing at Liam. "Get in bed and stay there. If I have to come in here and plug that machine in one more time, the deal is off. You," I say to Brent. "Nothing fancy. *Normal* stuff. Understand?"

To my surprise, Liam crawls into bed and Brent starts fishing in his pocket for his keys. Overwhelmed by it all, I turn on my heel and walk out of the room, making a beeline for the nurse's station and praying that Lexi is there.

It must be my lucky day because there she is, leaning on the counter, reviewing an EKG report, a pen stuck between her cherry lips.

"You cut Gabe's hair, don't you?" I ask as I arrive beside her.

"Hello to you, too," she says without looking up.

"And yes. I do it myself because he's too young to know if I do a bad job."

"So, theoretically, you could cut a man's hair."

Lexi looks up, squinting at me. "What's going on with you?" Her eyes go wide. "Are you sweating? Why do you look like you're trying not to throw up?"

"I did something," I suck in my lips and stare my friend in the face.

"What did you do?"

"It's probably nothing more than a cover story. As soon as Brent leaves, we'll go our separate ways and nothing will come of this..." I trail off, the shock over what I've just done setting in.

"Who's Brent? Who needs a cover story?" Lexi flares her hands and leans forward, waiting with wide eyes as a family passes in a flurry of balloons and stuffed animals. "Details, Bay," she whispers when they're far enough away not to hear.

"Liam McGuire may or may not be staying with me for the foreseeable future."

The pen drops from her fingers and clatters to the counter. "Shut. Up."

"I don't even know how we got here." I cover my mouth with my hand.

"I thought you couldn't stand him." A smile pulls at the corners of her lips. "You bitch. You've been keeping secrets from me." She leans in. "How long have you been fucking him?'

"God no! It's not like that at all." A doctor comes

out of room and looks up, startled by my raised voice. I smile sweetly and shrug an apology, waiting until she's out of earshot to continue. "He doesn't want to go back to Los Angeles," I say, lowering my voice. "His manager's an ass. And now he's staying with me. Or not. I'm not really sure. And maybe he's building me a patio."

"A patio?" Lexi stares down the sterile hallway toward Liam's room. "How in the hell did you go into the room of a patient you hate and come out with a houseguest who might be building you a patio?" She licks her lips. "And why didn't I get assigned to his room? I mean, I would die for an opportunity like this."

I put my back against the counter and look up at the ceiling, squinting into the fluorescent lights. "He's probably not staying."

"You can't wish it true, babe. Besides. Maybe it'll be good for you. Maybe you'll have a chance to loosen the chains on that chastity belt you've been wearing ever since Tyler..." She trails off, an apology already making its way onto her face.

I hold up my hands and give her a look. There's no reason for Tyler to be anywhere near this conversation and Lexi knows better.

"Sorry." Lexi straightens. "I just worry about you."

I brush away her concern. "I'm fine." But nothing about Tyler is a laughing matter and of all people, Lexi would be the one to know. "So, you'll cut his hair?" I ask after a minute.

"Whose hair?"

"Liam's."

"You want me to cut Liam McGuire's hair?"

I nod. "Will you do it?"

"Are you kidding me? Can I keep some of it?" She nods as I grimace. "I'm totally keeping some of it."

"You're weird, Lexi."

The rest of our shift passes quickly. The horde of fans faking injury and illness keeps all of us on our toes, making it hard to give time to the people who really need our attention. Before I know it, my day is just about over and I'm standing outside of Liam's room with Lexi. Gary and Josh study us as we stand there, arm in arm, staring wide-eyed at the door.

"Back for more, huh?" asks Josh.

Lexi is visibly vibrating with energy and excitement. "I can't believe I'm going to meet Liam McGuire!" she says, totally ignoring Josh.

Me? I say a silent prayer that he'll decide to go right back to LA and continue being a rich bastard out there with all the other rich bastards and I can chalk this up as another reason why I need to keep my generous streak in check.

With a decisive nod, we enter the mostly dark room. Outside, dusk settles on Grayson, casting weak shadows across the floor for the little light over Liam's bed to try to chase back outside. Liam's sitting politely in bed, staring at what looks like at least fifty Walmart bags piled up against the wall. They've removed the IV, getting him ready for release tomorrow.

"I think Brent went a little overboard," he says to me with a wry smile.

"Maybe just a little," I say. "Did he get the hair dye?"

Liam gestures to another set of bags crowding the table under the TV. "Among other things."

"I'm Lexi." My best friend steps forward, her hands clasped under her chin. She's so out of her head right now, I doubt she even realizes she interrupted us.

Liam's entire demeanor changes. Gone is the surly man-child and in his place is a warm smile and flirty eye contact. "Hey Lexi," he says, and if sex had a sound, that would be it.

As much as I don't want to be affected by his voice, I am. "Lexi said she could cut your hair. And she promises not to be this weird about it the whole time." I nudge her with my elbow. "Right, Lex?"

Lexi blinks and looks at me, biting her lip. "Right." She swallows and smiles sheepishly. "Sorry."

"No need to apologize," Liam says to her, all sultry smiles and intense eye contact. Then he turns to me, and poof. The surly man-child is back. "Is she gonna dye it, too? Or is that all you?"

Great. So Lexi gets the sweet heartbreaker and I get to deal with the spoiled star. Sure. That makes sense since I'm the one who offered up my house to him in one ridiculous moment of weakness.

"I'm sure you're perfectly capable of dying your own hair." I smile sweetly as Liam scowls.

"But I'll totally do it for you," says Lexi, earning herself another nudge of the elbow. "I don't mind. Not even a little bit."

"Anyway," I say before Liam can reply. "Lexi will cut your hair tonight. You can dye it when we're gone, just like a big boy." I arch an eyebrow at him as Lexi gasps. "I don't work tomorrow, but I'll be here to pick you up. If you're still staying with me. I mean, now that Brent's gone, we can be honest. You really aren't staying with me, right?"

"Oh, I'm totally staying." Liam runs a hand up the back of his neck. "I'm not going back to LA. Not while my face is still healing. Maybe not ever."

"I get that you don't want to go back there. If you and that Brent are any indication of the kind of people in that city..."

"Hey," says Liam, looking genuinely hurt.

This time, it's Lexi who nudges me with her elbow. "Be nice, Bay," she says, looking me full in the face and pleading with her eyes for me not to mess this up.

"Yeah." Liam smiles weakly and I get the sense that I'm looking past the persona and seeing a glimpse of the real man. "Be nice, Bay."

My nickname sounds funny coming from him. I roll my eyes, surprised to find myself smiling. "In all seriousness though," I say, perching on the end of his bed. "Would you be more comfortable in a hotel?" I glance at Lexi who looks horrified. "Maybe we can find a bed and breakfast or something..." I trail off, realizing how desperate I sound. "I mean, let's be real. You and I barely know each other and we don't exactly get along. It's kind of a stretch for us to be roommates."

Liam runs a hand through his hair. "I'm up for the challenge if you are." He holds my gaze and there's something running beneath the surface, something he's not saying but begging me to understand.

"We'll just take it a day at a time," I say, confused by what I think I saw. "You might find that life here in Grayson is too slow for you. And by the time you find a more permanent place to stay, you might really miss LA."

Liam drops his head back on his pillow and his eyelids droop closed. A dark circle stands out under his one visible eye, vibrant against his gray skin. Throughout all the hubbub and craziness of the day, I forgot he's a patient recovering from a nasty injury. He should have been resting, not fighting with me and his manager.

"You look tired, Liam," I say, feeling pretty bad for not taking better care of him this afternoon. "Why don't I bring Lexi back tomorrow, and we can do all the cosmetic stuff after you've had a chance to sleep?"

He peels his eyes open and fights to focus on me. "Actually, can you cut my hair, Bailey? Tonight? I might actually get a decent night's sleep just knowing it's done."

"Lexi will do a better job..." I used to cut my

brother Michael's hair when we were younger, but that was a long time ago.

"I'd still like you to do it." Liam looks ... what? Vulnerable?

I make a face at Lexi and shrug. She gives me a knowing smile, one that says she knows exactly what's going on here even though what she's got in her head couldn't be farther from the truth.

"Bailey will take good care of you," she says and then turns her back to him, meeting my eyes and fanning her face before leaving the room.

"Well come on, then," I say when we're alone. "Let's get this done so you can get the rest you need."

Liam crawls out of bed and I drag the cheap armchair out of the corner so I can stand behind him. Using a pair of surgical scissors I took from the cart and a comb I snagged from his patient care kit, I go to work cutting his hair. I work silently, fighting memories of Michael sitting in a chair for me, my hands in his hair while he wiggled and complained, both of us trying to find our way through a life that no longer made sense.

"Thank you," says Liam, his voice sleepy. "I really didn't want to be *on* for your friend. It was nice of her to offer to cut my hair, don't get me wrong. But you don't expect anything from me and she expects me to be Liam McGuire. I just can't pull it off right now. It's been a long couple days."

"Just as long as you don't expect a miracle out of me. I'm definitely not a stylist from LA."

Liam sighs and leans back in the chair. "And that's why you're perfect."

I watch as he takes another deep breath and lets it out slowly, his shoulders relaxing.

"Is it hard?" I ask. "Being famous?"

"You have no idea." Liam rubs a hand on his thigh. "It's a lot of work. And a lot of being what everyone expects you to be. Sometimes I go days without ever having a minute to myself to just look tired or..." He trails off and shrugs. "Whatever it is people do when they're not being watched."

"But the money's got to be nice." I comb through his hair, lifting it for the scissors.

"Money isn't everything."

I can't help but let out a little laugh. "Says the guy who has enough to have everything he needs and then some."

"Says the woman who has no clue what it's like to have people say that about you." His shoulders drop as he sinks further into the chair. "Don't get me wrong. I do recognize how blessed I am. It's just tiring. I'm sure I'll survive." His tone of voice shifts, the sound of his persona sliding back into place and covering up the tiny glimpse of the man behind the image.

I finish the job lost in my thoughts, my disdain for Liam eroded by the tiny peek of what it's like to be him. It really makes me wonder what the rest of his life is like? Not the stuff we see splashed over the tabloids, but all the behind-the-scenes stuff? When does he ever get to relax? After I finish cutting his hair, he looks so exhausted I offer to color it for him, too.

When everything's said and done, I survey the results. All in all, I didn't do half bad, if I do say so myself. The darker hair color sets off his eyes, and the stubble showing up on his cheeks highlights the strength of his jaw and cheekbones. He looks way less like a boy and way more like a man. I'm sure what I just did would be damn near sacrilegious to his fans, but I'll chalk it up as an improvement.

Liam falls asleep before I even finish pulling the covers up around him. I check to make sure he has a glass of water on his bedside table before turning off the lights and leaving the room with as many of the Walmart bags draped over my wrist as I can manage. I'm so lost in my thoughts, the hour-long drive home passes without me realizing. And, while I imagine Liam sleeping heavily after the day he's had, I can't sleep at all. My mind is on fire, spinning in circles over this stupid arrangement. Hours pass while I toss and turn, and I'm up and out of bed before the sun breaks above the horizon. I'm going to have a complete stranger living in my house for who knows how long. A complete stranger who's so famous half the world will be on my doorstep the moment someone notices him.

Chapter 5

BAILEY

When I get back to the hospital in the morning, Liam is up and dressed in his Walmart clothes, looking almost like a normal man. Well, as normal as a man that good-looking ever can.

"What do you think?" he says, opening his arms wide as I walk in the room.

I nod my approval. "Not bad."

"Not bad?" Liam looks down at the jeans that hug his ass just a little too perfectly. "I look damn good and you know it."

"I know you're a cocky ass," I say with a little laugh. If we're going to be living together, we need to figure out how to be in the same room without wanting to kill each other.

"Well yeah. That too. But when you look this good..." Liam gives me one of his most winning smiles and I roll my eyes to cover up the little smile that plays across my lips in return.

"How are you feeling this morning?" I ask. "You look like you got a good night's sleep."

Liam nods. "I did. And I needed it." He licks his lips, uncertainty flitting through his eyes. "No bandage today." There's a question flickering across his face as he awaits my judgment.

"I see that." I bob my head and shove my hands in my back pockets. "Looks like things are healing pretty well." Oh my god. Kill me now. This conversation couldn't be more awkward.

Liam looks just as uncomfortable as I feel. "You look nice, too. I mean, for Ohio."

"For Ohio?" I raise my eyebrows and lean against the wall, folding my arms over my chest.

"I mean..." Liam rolls his eyes, and looks away before dragging his gaze back to me. "Whatever. That came out wrong."

"Yep. It sure did." I laugh again, taking way too much satisfaction in seeing him look so uncomfortable. "Here. I thought this might be a good idea," I say as I pull one of Michael's old ball caps from my purse and hand it to him. When he pulls it on, the effect drops my jaw. Well, almost. It takes the discipline of a monk, but I manage to keep my lips clamped together through the sheer force of my will. He didn't shave again today and with the ball cap pulled low over his eyes, he looks ... good. But I'll be damned if I let him know that.

"Take out the earrings," I say, gathering the rest of the Walmart bags.

"Good call." Liam pulls the earrings out of his ears and drops them in the wastebasket. "I've always hated those things but my fans love them. And what they want always wins out over what I want." He says it so matter of factly, I feel another little jab of sympathy for the guy.

"You good to go?" I ask. "All discharged and everything?"

"Yep. Lead the way." Liam gestures towards the door.

I stoop and gather the rest of the bags. "Just so you know," I say when he doesn't look even remotely concerned about helping me with the cumbersome load. "I don't mind carrying these for you today because you're still gathering your strength. But as you finish healing, you need to realize that you're not in LA anymore and I'm not one of your *people*. I'm not your porter, your maid, or your butler. You're going to have to start doing things for yourself."

Liam looks flabbergasted. "Geez, Bailey. You don't have to be a dick about it."

"Me?" My eyebrows hit my hairline. "I'm the dick?"

Liam laughs, a warm sound, like sunshine on my face. "I mean, here I am, injured. Barely able to stand. And you go off on me because I don't have the strength to carry a few bags of clothes. That's harsh." He winks and I roll my eyes, laughing.

"Whatever," I say as he tries to take a few bags from me. "Oh, no." I pull my arm away. "I wouldn't want you to hurt yourself." I give him the sweetest look I can possibly muster and head out of his room, surprised to find myself almost enjoying his company.

The walk through the hospital to the front door is our test drive. If we can get through here without drawing attention, we might be able to get past the paparazzi waiting for us outside. We make it to the entrance without issue and I pause, take a deep breath, and let it out slowly, staring towards the blinding light streaming through the glass doors.

"You ready for this?"

Liam takes a few bags out of my hands. "I know how to handle myself in front of the cameras." He gives me a look that borders just enough on condescending to irritate me. So much for enjoying his company.

"That's just the thing. You *aren't* supposed to pull attention. We don't want any cameras pointed our way."

"Don't worry, Bailey. I got this." Liam pulls his hat low and links elbows with me, before pushing out the front door.

"Don't look at them," I remind him.

"Nope," he whispers. "If you don't gawk, they'll smell blood. Stare at them like you've never seen anything more amazing." And with that, we step outside. I do my best to stare as the crowd rushes forward but damn, my heart's racing. I swear we've got a big neon sign with his name on it flashing over our heads. Most of the photographers look dejected and turn away within seconds, but one or two cover their eyes and squint in our direction.

As we head towards my truck, I keep praying they'll lose interest but they don't. They step off the curb and follow us into the parking lot, spurred on by each new furtive glance over my shoulder. I need a way to distract them. To hide his face. To keep anyone from wondering if they might possibly recognize him.

"Don't look back," he whispers.

"They're still following us."

"That's because you keep looking back."

"You told me to look at them," I hiss.

"Once. You did that. Now let's focus on getting out of here."

I lead him to my truck, but the one or two photographers have turned into four or five and more are stepping off the curb and heading our way. Desperate, I grab Liam by the shoulders, spin him so his back is to them, and reaching up on my tiptoes, press my lips to his.

He freezes, his eyes wide open and staring into mine for a few shocked heartbeats. But the shock only lasts a second. Closing his eyes, Liam kisses me so deeply, so fervently, I forget everything. My blood hums through my veins and I sigh into him, my body softening against his. He drops the Walmart bags to the ground, sliding his hands over the curve of my waist, pressing them into my lower back, drawing me close. After a few delicious seconds that might as well be an eternity, I pull back, stunned, and look up at him.

"They were getting close," I murmur.

"And you thought that would make them stop?"

Flustered, I stammer around an explanation as my cheeks grow hot. "I didn't have time to think."

Liam chuckles and bends to grab the bags, artfully positioning himself behind me. I peek at the crowd and thankfully, they seem fooled by our kiss.

Me? I'm not sure what just happened, but we most definitely crossed a line. Hell, we didn't just cross it. We stomped all over it, tap dancing the thing right out of existence. However long this guy ends up staying with me, I can't let that happen again. He may be a spoiled ass, but Liam McGuire knows how to work magic with that mouth and I refuse to be one more person caught under his spell.

Chapter 6

LIAM

Bailey looks flustered. And the fact that she's flustered is flustering her even more. Her cheeks have gone pink and her eyes are wide and round. They're an interesting shade of blue that might be green. I never really noticed them in the harsh light of the hospital, but out here in the sunlight, they're fascinating.

"Come on, hot lips." I smile down at her as her cheeks burn past pink and into bright red. "Let's get out of here before we draw their attention again."

She grabs the bags I dropped and leads me to the passenger side of a dinosaur of a pickup. Rust spots pepper the body of the truck, but when she hauls open the door, the interior is immaculate.

"I've got storage bins in the back. I'll put your bags in there so they don't fly out." She glances at me, barely meeting my eyes before she looks at her feet. "Get in before someone sees you."

I climb into the passenger seat, trying to get acclimated to the roughness of it all. It smells faintly of gasoline or oil, some heavy smell that I don't equate with Bailey at all. She's trying to cover it up with a vanilla air freshener, but it's not working. It just smells like a girly mechanic in here.

While she climbs into the bed of the truck, hauling up the bags of cheap clothes Brent left for me yesterday, I flip down the sun visor and study my face in the mirror. The doctor took the stitches out today. Told me things were healing nicely and that I was very lucky without ever looking up from the chart in his hands.

I stare at the pink scar, raised and swollen, a vicious gash from my hairline to my chin. The accident is a blur. I remember the squeal of the tires, a crunch of metal, and then the whole world going topsy-turvy. I remember screaming and pain so hot I could see it. I remember smelling blood and fire, and that's all there was until I woke up in the hospital.

They say I should be dead. That I have every reason to be thankful. I keep thinking they're full of shit. My life is in shambles. My face—the only reason anyone cares about me at all—is ruined. What exactly do they think I should be thankful for? Being alive? What good is living when I'm about to lose everything I've spent the last fifteen years working for?

The driver's side door opens with a groan and Bailey climbs in. "All set?" she asks as she yanks the thing closed and slides the keys into the ignition.

"Your truck stinks." I flip the visor closed and put on my seatbelt.

She scrunches up her nose. "Thanks?"

"Do you have a boyfriend or something? It smells manly in here."

Bailey brings the engine to life and yanks the gearshift into reverse. "This truck used to belong to my dad."

Nothing in her demeanor makes me think that topic is up for further discussion. I watch her maneuver the truck out onto the road. She looks pretty adorable, being as tiny as she is, trying to manhandle a vehicle this big. We drive for a long time and the buildings fade away until they disappear altogether, replaced by long stretches of cornfields and blue sky. If I thought Grayson was small, apparently it's the big city to her. She lives in an even smaller town about an hour away called Brookside.

Gravel crunches under the tires as she turns into a long driveway. Bailey's home is old and reminds me of the truck. She's done her best to take care of it but it's still falling apart around her. The porch is clean and she's got flowers blooming in the beds, but the paint is chipping and the windows look drafty. The house has the same feeling as the pickup, where she tried to mask the scent of a mechanic, like the former occupants still own the place more than she does.

The front door opens right into the living room with the kitchen directly behind it. To the right is a small den filled with bookshelves and a piano that devours the majority of the space. It's sitting right under a window that looks out towards the woods in the back.

"Do you play?" I ask, nodding towards the den as we pass.

Bailey shrugs. "A little."

She points out the bathroom on our way down a short hallway to the bedrooms. And when I say *the bathroom* I mean the only bathroom. I don't know how in the world I thought this was ever going to work. When I invited myself to stay here, I imagined a much larger space, more like what I'm used to in LA. In my mind, we would be in our separate areas of the house and would never really have to interact.

"Here we are," she says, gesturing to a closed door near the end of the short hallway. She stares at it for a split second longer than she needs to and then opens it up to reveal a sparsely decorated room with a twin bed and a desk under the window. I peer into it, grimacing.

"It used to be my brother's. Michael." She leans against the doorframe. "He moved out a few years ago. I just haven't found anything to do with this room since."

"You used to live with your brother?"

"I grew up in this house. When my parents died, I inherited it. Michael lived with me until he graduated."

I nod, staring at the bed. And I thought the one at the hospital was uncomfortable.

"Your stuff is in the truck," she says, pushing off the wall. "Feel free to get it and make yourself at home. Or not. We can talk later about how long you're actually staying here." She points to a door across the hall. "That's my room. You're welcome everywhere in the house except in there, understood?" And with that, she walks into her room and closes the door, leaving me to stand awkwardly in the hall.

I was right. The bed is worse than awful. I've been awake since before sunrise, just hoping that if I pretended to be asleep long enough, I'd finally drift away. No luck. I heard Bailey get up and mess around on the piano. She definitely downplayed her ability yesterday. Her music is beautiful. I almost got up so I could be in the same room to listen, to take more of it in, but that woman just plain doesn't like me. I guarantee the second she realized I could hear her, she would stop playing.

Now she's banging around in the kitchen, and the

smell of coffee and sausage wafts down the short hallway and into my room. After the last few weeks of hospital food and weak coffee, I am in the mood for something tasty and extra caffeinated. I hop out of bed and stretch, run a hand through my hair, surprised to find it short. Of all the crazy-ass shit I've done, this might be the craziest.

I slide open the closet, or at least I try to. The door catches on something and I wrestle it open only to find myself staring at nothing but empty space. Right. I was the one supposed to bring in my clothes yesterday. I suck in my lips and stare at the pile of yesterday's clothes on the floor near the bed.

Fuck it.

I'm not getting dressed just to get undressed again. I wander down the hall and out into the main room of the house wearing nothing but my boxer briefs. "Morning," I say to Bailey, lifting a hand as I pass. For as much as she was banging around in the kitchen just moments before, she's utterly silent now.

"Morning," she says, just as I walk out the door.

The sun shines down on me from a clear blue sky and the lush grass tickles my bare feet as I cross the yard. I take a deep breath as I hop up into the back of her truck. The air is clean and refreshing, such a change from the smog and pollution back home.

"Just what in the world do you think you're doing?" Bailey's standing on the porch with her hands on her hips, a spatula sticking out of one fist.

"Getting my clothes."

"In your underwear?"

"There's no one here to see me. And even if there were, I've been on billboards in Times Square wearing less than this."

Bailey scowls and pops a hip. "I'm someone."

I pull a lid off one of the bins and fish out the bags of clothes hiding inside. "Huh?"

"I'm someone. You said no one is here to see you. But I'm someone. And I'm here. And I see you."

I straighten and lift my chin. "And you like what you see, don't you?"

Bailey shakes her head and walks back into the house without a word. I can't remember the last time someone wasn't falling over themself to make me happy. It's either refreshing or a pain in the ass, I haven't decided yet. I grab the rest of the bags out of the bins, drop them in my room near the bed, and get dressed in a random pair of shorts and a short-sleeved shirt before heading into the kitchen and taking a seat at the table. Bailey's at the stove with her back to me, her ass looking scrumptious in a tight pair of jean shorts.

"I like my coffee black, my eggs with a three-to-one ratio of whites to yolks, and my sausage in link form. Preferably made out of turkey."

Bailey turns, her eyebrows raised and her mouth open. "The coffee is over there." She points to a coffee pot on the counter. "Mugs and plates are there." She points to a cabinet. "The eggs are fried and the sausage is pork and comes in patty form. Do with it what you will. If you want anything other than what I have here, you're welcome to call a cab and buy some groceries." She carries a plate and mug of coffee to the table and sits across from me while I stare at her in shock.

"Right," I say, biting off the word and pushing my chair away from the table. I can't remember the last time I served myself, and I make my irritation evident as I fling open cabinets and plop plates and forks on the counter.

"Listen," says Bailey when I sit back down at the table. "You put me on the spot with your manager and for some reason I rolled with it. You can stay here until you figure out what you're doing, but you're on your own. I'm not one of your *people*." She takes a drink of her coffee, eyeing me over the rim of her mug. "And I wasn't kidding about the patio." She puts the coffee down with a light laugh and shake of her head. "Okay. That's kind of a lie. I mostly just said the first thing that came to my mind, but the way I see it, you owe me. Big time."

"I'm not building you a patio."

"Well, you're not staying for free. You can either be useful or get the hell out." She finishes her breakfast, rinses the plate in the sink, and then turns to face me. The sun streams through the window and gleams in her hair. It tugs at a memory, my mom laughing at something I said back before she moved us out to LA. She was always so beautiful when she laughed.

Bailey squints at me, a question in her eyes. "I have to go to work," she says, ignoring whatever she saw on my face. She levels a finger at me and smiles. "No parties while I'm gone."

Chapter 7

BAILEY

I pull up in front of my house, worn and weary after three days' worth of twelve-hour shifts. My arms weigh at least one hundred pounds each, my thoughts come burbling up to me as if through thick mud, and the whole world feels itchy, scratching against my senses like the worst kind of wool sweater. All I want to do is get in my house, collapse on the couch, and sleep for at least a year.

The evening air swelters around me, another weight on my tired shoulders, making the climb up the few stairs leading to my porch downright tedious. I slide my key into the lock and swing the door open, sighing at the blast of cool air brushing past the sweat at my temples. It's a long drive from Grayson to Brookside, especially in a truck without air conditioning.

"Hey." The voice comes from my left, Liam, prone

on my couch, wearing nothing more than a pair of athletic shorts.

All my hopes of a relaxing evening alone come crashing down around me. I don't know how I forgot that I have a roommate who constantly gets in my way, but I did. So much for sitting around in my underwear, binge-watching Gilmore Girls on Netflix, and eating nothing but a pint of ice cream for dinner.

"Hey." I drop my purse on the ground and sigh, offering Liam a weak smile.

"Wow." He pushes himself up on an elbow so he can see me over the back of the couch. "You look rough."

"Thanks?" I make a face.

He grimaces, looking almost apologetic. "You just look really tired. No need to get all offended. Damn, Bailey. Don't be so sensitive."

"Oh, right. Because everyone likes to be told they look like shit." I walk around to the front of the sofa and make a shooing motion for him to move his legs. "Besides. Do you really have any room to talk?" I ask as I drop onto the seat, letting my head fall back and rest on the back of the couch. "You're the one laying down in a living room, no lights on or anything, wearing the exact same thing you rolled out of bed in."

"Whatever. Like you even know what I wear to bed. You're already gone by the time I get up." Liam pulls himself up into a sitting position. "Here." He gestures with his hands. "Pop those feet up here."

I roll my head along the back of the couch and eye him suspiciously. "Why?"

"Because I give fucking awesome foot rubs, that's why."

"Oh, hell no. That ain't happenin'. I've been on my feet all day and just spent an hour in that sauna I call a truck." I shake my head. "Believe me, you do not want anywhere near these things right now."

Liam shrugs. "Suit yourself," he says and gives his attention back to the television. "Have you seen this?" He indicates the documentary he's got paused on the screen.

I study the faces, looking for anything familiar in the grainy footage from the seventies. "I don't think so."

"What Happened, Nina Simone?" Liam stares at me like I should know what the hell he's talking about.

"Huh?" I am way too tired to think clearly and his question makes zero sense.

"That's the name of the documentary." Liam looks at me like I'm an idiot. "Nina Simone? Piano player? Singer?" When I continue to draw a blank, he drops his jaw. "I Put a Spell on You? Feeling Good?"

I blink, trying desperately to understand. "Oh!" I laugh, nodding as my sludge covered brain finally connects the dots. "Those are song titles."

"There we go. I knew it had to be in there somewhere." Liam reaches for his phone and I'd be a liar if I said I didn't take the moment to appreciate the muscles in his arms and back. With effort, I drag my eyes away from him. The last thing I need is for his ego to notice me noticing him.

"Right," I say, rolling my eyes. "My bad for not immediately recognizing the name of a documentary I've never seen about a singer I've only barely heard about."

"She's amazing." Liam pulls up YouTube on his phone. "Here," he says, scooting so close to me his thigh presses against mine. "Just listen to this."

He selects a video, hits play, and listens—enthralled—as a song that's more familiar than I realized starts playing.

"Oh, yeah." I close my eyes and nod my head to the opening riff. "I know this one."

He pauses the video. "Of course you do. It's amazing. Now, shhh. Don't talk. Just listen." He starts the video over again and closes his eyes as the music moves through him.

I watch him instead of the phone. The tiny smile that plays across his face. The way his breathing deepens, as if he's breathing the melody into his bones. My mom used to look that way when she played the piano. And I probably look that way when I play, too.

Liam opens his eyes and catches me staring. "What?" He draws his eyebrows together and shifts away, creating space between us. I don't know if I'm glad he's not touching me anymore or if I miss the contact. The fact that I'm confused dredges up a little ball of frustration in my stomach.

I smile as I tuck myself into the corner of the couch, kicking off my shoes and curling my feet up underneath me. "My mom used to say music is something that gets in your soul. That all people appreciate music but there's a lucky few who get to live it. She lived it, I think." I drop my gaze to my hands, feeling her loss more than I have in a long time. "Looks like you do, too."

Liam presses a finger to his lips and squints at me. "So, the constant touring? All the platinum albums? None of that was enough to make you think I live and breathe music?" Liam gestures with his phone, widening his eyes. "But you watch me listen to one song and that's the tipping point?"

"A lot of people exist in lives they didn't build for themselves." I scooch to the edge of the couch, trying to gather up the energy to stand.

Liam gazes at me, his eyes locked on mine like he can see right past all the things I want him to see to all the things I really am. "Wow," he says after a few seconds. "That's deep." He laughs and whatever I thought I saw in his eyes fades until I have to wonder if I imagined it.

Suddenly desperate to put some distance between us, I stand with a groan and wander into the kitchen. Under normal circumstances, I'd make myself a dinner with little to no nutritional value and eat it in front of the TV. Maybe I'd play the piano after soaking in the tub. But, with Liam here, none of those things seem appropriate. I just can't be that relaxed around him.

"Have you eaten?" I call to him. "Any chance there's leftovers?"

"Nope." There's a rustle of movement as he stands. "Wanna go out or something? I am in desperate need of a change in scenery." His tall frame fills the doorway, his presence preceding him, his energy permeating the kitchen. I feel crowded before he even enters the room.

I lean against the counter opposite him, putting as much physical space between us as I can. "Are you sure going out is a good idea? What if people recognize you?"

"I can't spend the rest of my life hiding in your living room." Liam runs a hand up the back of his neck.

"At least we agree on something," I say. For some reason, I find the look of shock on his face utterly hilarious and bite my bottom lip to keep myself from laughing at him.

"Do you know how many women would kill to have me spend the rest of my life in their living room?" Liam pushes off the wall, shaking his head and looking way more amused than offended.

I turn away from him and reach into a cabinet for my dad's favorite coffee mug, needing the comfort and familiarity of the old, chipped handle right now. "I'm not most women."

"You can say that again." Liam crosses the room,

his bare feet slapping lightly on the cheap tile. "So? What do you think?" he asks, leaning against the counter beside me. "You ready to go out and get crazy?"

"I'm too exhausted to get crazy." I fill the mug with water from the tap and take a drink, watching him over the rim.

"But that exhaustion is exactly why you need to go out," he says, hope lighting up his face. "Let someone else cook the food and deal with the dishes." He wraps an arm around my shoulder, pulling me close. "Come on, Bailey. Live a little."

I hesitate, more aware of all the points of contact between us than I want to be. "I live plenty," I say, shrugging out from under his arm. "But really, what if someone notices you?"

"They won't."

"How can you be sure?"

"Because," Liam replies, shrugging as if he'd just explained everything in one little word.

"How about this?" I run a hand through my hair, realizing I never changed out of my scrubs and feeling gross. "We stay in and order a pizza tonight..."

Liam's face falls and he looks so crestfallen I almost change my mind.

Almost.

"We can watch your Nina Simone documentary and you can tell me all about what makes her so amazing," I say, offering up the documentary like an olive branch. "And..." I lick my lips. "I promise we'll go out soon. When I'm not too tired to deal with any of the potential fall out if you get recognized."

"Right," he says, his eyes going hard. "All you had to say was no."

"Wow." I take a drink. "Why do I feel like I've walked right into a minefield? We'll go out. Really. Just not tonight."

"I'll believe it when I see it." Liam rubs his hands together, sliding his perfect smile back into place over whatever it is he's got going on in his head. "But if we're staying in tonight, I have a few conditions."

"Conditions, huh?" I run my thumb over the chip in the handle of Dad's mug and tilt my head to the side. "Let me hear 'em."

"First of all, we can watch the documentary, but you have to promise not to talk over it."

I drop my jaw. "I can talk whenever I want to, thank you very much."

"Sure." Liam nods his agreement. "Just not over Nina Simone."

"And your second condition?" I give him a look like a warning shot.

"No pepperoni."

"No pepperoni?" I groan as my stomach growls. "That's just blasphemous."

"What's blasphemous is the fat, sodium, calories, and nitrates in the stuff."

I puff out my cheeks and let air out through my

lips. "What else?" I ask as I put the mug down on the counter.

Liam squints at me, tapping his chin like he's considering something groundbreaking. "This last one is the most important one."

"Did I mention how exhausted I am? Three really long days at the hospital?" I wrap an arm around my waist. "Ringing any bells?"

"I'm getting there. It's just that you have to know. This one is a deal breaker." His eyes sparkle devilishly.

"So," I ask, drawing out the word and raising my eyebrows. "The others are negotiable?"

"Well, no. Not really." Liam laughs. "But this last one is basically the holy mother of conditions and if you agree to it, you have to follow through. No backing out." He levels a finger at me, looking more and more serious by the second.

"I don't back out of things." I lift my chin, a little bubble of defiance growing in my heart.

"I don't know." Liam lets out a long breath. "You look like the kind of person who might be a little wishy-washy."

"Wishy-washy? Me?" I grin, the weight of exhaustion fading in the presence of his good mood. "You have no idea how un-wishy-washy I am."

"I'm still not sold." Liam shrugs and purses his lips. "You know what? It's better if you just go to bed. There's no way you can keep up your end of the bargain. You're just going to let me down."

"Liam!" I step forward, right into his space, and put my hands on his arms. "I'm so positive I can keep up my end of the bargain that I'll agree to it before I even know what it is. You have my word. Now just tell me what it is."

"That's a dangerous game, hot lips." His gaze drifts to my mouth.

Oh, shit.

Is he going to ask me to kiss him?

As heat floods my face and doubt pops the bubble of defiance in my heart, I'm suddenly way less sure that I want to play this game. I know what those lips are capable of. Even when I still hated his guts completely, a kiss from Liam was enough to light a fire in my belly. Now that I might actually like him a little bit, a kiss might ruin everything. I'm not getting myself any more tangled up in this guy than I already am.

But, damn it. I gave him my word, which I take seriously. And after he made such a big deal about me being wishy-washy, I refuse to back down and give him something to hold over my head. I've fought through my fair share of shit and I sure as hell didn't get to where I am by being weak.

My lips part and my eyes go to his mouth as I let out a trembling breath and drop my hands to my sides. If he's about to name kissing me as one of his conditions, then I'll kiss the hell out of him. Maybe this time he'll be the one left reeling.

Liam throws his head back and laughs. "You're too

easy, Bailey. You should play your cards closer to the vest. That competitive streak is way too easy to take advantage of."

Confused and more than a little embarrassed, I cross my arms and take a step back. "Alright then, Mr. Master Manipulator. What did I just agree to? Hit me with this holy mother of conditions."

Liam grins, victory gleaming in his eyes. "You, my friend, are to hop in the shower while I order the pizza. Take your time soaping up those stinky feet of yours, and get ready to enjoy the best foot rub of your life."

"Why do you want to rub my feet so badly in the first place?"

"Because you told me no. I'm not a big fan of that word."

"Whatever," I say, grumbling as I leave the kitchen, smiling despite myself.

The shower goes a long way towards making me feel human again and by the time I find myself back out on the couch with Liam, I almost regret telling him I wanted to stay in.

"Pop those puppies up here," he says, gesturing with his hands and grinning widely.

I shift so my back is pressed against the arm of the couch and put both of my feet in his lap. "This had better be one hell of a foot rub," I say. "After all this build up, I don't know how you're not going to let me down."

Liam grins and runs his hands over the top of my

feet, his touch firm enough not to tickle, but gentle enough to send a wave of goose bumps chasing one another across my skin. I hum my approval, my eyes sliding closed as a smile plays across my lips.

"You really don't know me very well, do you?" he asks as he picks up my right foot and presses his thumbs into my arch. "I'm not in the business of letting people down."

My head drops back on the armrest and I moan as he works magic on my feet, days of stress and tension evaporating under his careful ministrations. Maybe I'm not going to totally hate having him stay here after all.

Chapter 8

LIAM

A firm knock on my bedroom door wakes me up way before I'm ready. I roll over with a groan, pulling the blankets up over my head to block out the sun that's creeping through the slats of the blinds on the window. "Go away," I say around a mouth so dry it feels stuffed with cotton.

"Nope." The bed bounces as Bailey plops down beside me and pulls the blankets down. "You feel like explaining all the boxes that keep piling up on my front porch?"

That's enough to catch my attention. "They're here?" I push myself into a sitting position. "Sweet."

"What's here?" Bailey eyes me. "What is all that stuff?"

I rub my hands over my face. "I bought a few things."

"A few?" Bailey's voice is pitched just a little too high for the pre-coffee phase of my morning. "Maybe you and I have a different definition of that word," she says with a chuckle.

"Bailey. Shh." I show her my hands and close my eyes. "Mornings and I aren't the best of friends."

"Oh, I'm sorry. Am I inconveniencing you right now?"

"What's with all the hostility and sarcasm?" I sniff and rub my eyes. "Is there coffee?"

"I just put on a fresh pot." She jerks her head toward the door. "The sarcasm is just a way of life with me. The sooner you accept that, the better for both of us."

"And the hostility? That just a way of life with you, too?"

"That's still up in the air. Although that foot rub last night went a long way to making me feel better about you invading my space." She stands. "Now, come on. Get up. I want you to see what's out there and find out if you still stand by your word choice." She crosses the room to twist open the blinds, letting in the early morning sun.

With a sigh, I pull back the covers and swing my legs off the edge of the bed. Leaning my elbows on my knees, I put my face in my hands, and take a moment before standing.

Bailey turns around, shock dropping her jaw before

she averts her gaze. "Do you ever wear clothes?" she asks.

I look down at my underwear, confused, before meeting her gaze with one of my most seductive looks. "Do I make you uncomfortable? Is me being an underwear model too hot for Brookside?"

"Just get dressed," she says, trying to look scornful and hide the ghost of a smile twitching at her lips. "And meet me in the living room."

After she leaves, I pull on a pair of shorts and a T-shirt, brush my teeth, and find her waiting for me at the table in the kitchen, sipping coffee out of the same old mug with the chipped handle she uses every morning.

"Good morning, Bailey. How'd you sleep?" I say as I reach into the cabinet for a mug. "See? That's how you're supposed to greet someone when they first wake up."

Bailey sits back and crosses her legs, holding her mug close to her face. "How kind of you to ask. I slept very well, thank you," she says with a grin.

I pull out a chair across from her and take a seat. "So, obviously I bought some stuff." I sip at my coffee, closing my eyes and humming my approval. Bailey makes it strong, just the way I like it.

"What kind of stuff?"

"Does it matter? I mean, it's my money, right? I can do what I want with it."

She shrugs. "Probably."

"Probably?" I set my mug down and lean forward. "What does that even mean?"

Bailey sucks in her lips and averts her gaze. "I mean, yes, you can do whatever you want with your money. But there are a lot of boxes out there and I like things the way they are around here." She tucks her chin, meeting my eyes with difficulty.

"Who says any of the stuff I bought is for you?" Actually, a lot of it is for her. Or, rather, for us. I'll take it all with me when I leave. I'm just tired of using all her old, kind of broken stuff and staring at a bunch of blank walls in my bedroom.

"Fair enough." She laughs, self-conscious. "Sorry. I'm a little weird about change. That was a little intense of me."

"And self-centered," I supply.

"And self-centered." She bobs her head, looking contrite.

"And egotistical."

Bailey narrows her eyes at me. "You should learn to stop while you're ahead."

I hold up my hands, laughing. "Right. Fair enough."

She stands, rinsing out her mug in the sink. "So, what did you buy?" she asks as she dries it with a worn towel.

"A new mattress, for one."

Bailey pauses as she puts the mug back in the cabinet, looking at me over her shoulder. "Excuse me?" Color rises in her cheeks and she looks absolutely beautiful, standing there in her shorts and tank top, her hair gleaming in the sunlight like a halo around her head.

I clear my throat and grab my mug, needing something to look at that isn't her. "Yep. No offense to Michael, but his bed is a piece of shit."

"So, you just bought a new one?" She sounds way more upset than the situation warrants. "What are we going to do with the one that's in there now?"

"Throw it away? You're welcome to keep the one I bought when I leave."

"I can't throw that away." Bailey crosses her arms over her chest.

"Okay." I sit back in my chair. "Then we'll store it or something."

"I can't afford storage."

"But I can."

"And I don't need your money or your charity," Bailey says, squaring her shoulders and lifting her chin.

"Then consider it rent. Aren't you the one who said I owe you? Big time? Maybe this is how I pay off that debt." I nod, satisfied with the idea. It makes sense to me. I have no intention of imposing on her without paying her back.

"What happened to the patio you're supposed to build?"

I laugh. "My strength lies more in my ability to spend lots of money than it does in manual labor. Why don't you let me replace the things that are broken around here?" The more time I spend with the idea, the more I like it. Everything in Bailey's house is old and outdated. The thought of replacing all her worn out things feels good.

"I don't want to replace my things." Bailey speaks through a tight jaw, a river of emotion flowing behind her eyes.

"Well, I mean..." I scoot my chair back from the table and rest my ankle on my knee. "Some of those boxes out there are for you."

"Liam..."

"Come on now. That mug you use every single day? It's got a big old chip in the handle. I bought you a few new ones."

Anger, pain, sorrow, they flash in Bailey's eyes and she swallows hard. "That was my dad's mug," she says, her voice strained.

I watch her fight with the emotions raging inside her and a flicker of understanding flares inside me.

"When did your parents die?" I ask, my voice low.

She turns and clutches the edge of the sink as if she's afraid she might float away. "When I was eighteen."

"And you've lived here ever since?" Things are starting to make sense. The dated curtains in the windows. The ancient couch. The scorched pan she uses to cook breakfast. She inherited all of it.

"I've lived here my whole life." Bailey turns,

forcing a smile onto her face. "Sorry," she says leaning against the counter and swallowing the rest of her emotions. "I'm overreacting."

"I mean..." I hook an arm over the back of the chair. "You might be the first person I've heard of who ever got mad about someone buying them new stuff."

"I'm just not ready to get rid of their things yet." She clears her throat and pushes off the counter, crossing the kitchen to have a seat at the table. "But," she says, her voice artificially light. "That doesn't mean that you can't have nice things and I can't use them while you're here."

"Exactly." I nod, as if that settles everything.

"But, you know..." Bailey trails off, a wide grin brightening her face. "Letting me borrow stuff really doesn't go very far towards paying off what you owe me."

I narrow my eyes. "No?"

"Oh, no." She leans forward, elbows on the table, and runs a hand up her arm. "Not even close."

"I'm not building you a patio. It's just not happening."

"We'll see, McGuire. We'll see." She twists her lips and stares at me and I swear I could fall into those eyes and never find my way back out.

She slaps the table, startling me. "Now. You finish your coffee and meet me in the bathroom. I'll rub some vitamin E into that scar. You'll be good to go in no time, looking like your old, sexy self before you know it."

Bailey stands and heads out of the kitchen, leaving me to stare after her and wonder if maybe I'm going to like living with her after all.

Chapter 9

BAILEY

August fourth.

One hell of a shitty day.

And it has been for the last eight years.

Year after year, anxiety riddles me the week or so leading up to every single August fourth. I snap at people for every little thing. Fight with them for no good reason. I'm a total bitch and I know it. And as much as I feel bad about it after the fact, I couldn't change it if I wanted to. So, I bury myself in work all day only to come home and lose myself to the piano each night. And then the fourth arrives and I implode, folding in on myself to lick the gnarled scars that ache and throb along my heart.

Lexi's there for me every year. It doesn't matter how nasty I get, she won't let me sit at home and wallow in my grief. I know without asking that her mom's watching Gabe tonight, and that Lexi will show up on my doorstep at some point to drag me out of the house. She won't even bother to call first. She never does. She just shows up and marches me out to have drinks with her at Smitty's. Sometimes we sit quietly. Sometimes I get mean. Sometimes—but not often—she manages to make me laugh. Regardless of my behavior, year after year, she's always here for me.

This year, thanks to Liam being in my space, it's the worst August fourth in a long time. He's spent the last week lounging around my house and being in my way every time I turn around. When I want to play the piano, he's in there, dicking around for hours. When I want to come home and relax before bed, he's spread out on the couch, eating chips, and staring at the TV. I barely acknowledge him when I walk in from work at night or when I leave again in the morning. He's a shitty houseguest, but right now I'm a shitty host, and I'm not in the mood to deal with him. Maybe next week, when I'll inevitably be able to think straight again, I'll figure out how to either kick his ass out or into gear.

He's in the den, what used to be my bedroom when I was a kid, playing the piano, when Lexi shows up. She knocks gently before letting herself in.

"Hey you," she breathes and shuts the door against the humid evening air lumbering in after her. "That's nice." She gestures towards the music coming from the den. "Not at all like the stuff he sings on the radio."

I nod, too hollow for small talk.

"Well, come on then. Let's get you out of here before the ghosts get too loud." She maneuvers around the worn couch, one that's been here since I was in grade school. The day my parents brought it home, I worried that our old couch felt abandoned. I was so sad to see it sticking out the back of Dad's truck. I spent days wondering if it was sad, too. Being replaced and thrown away like that after being part of our lives for so long.

Lexi offers me a hand and helps me to my feet. I attempt a smile but it's no good, so I drop it and let her lead me out of the house and into her car. A spectacular sunset explodes in warm shades of gold and pink, streaking up and away from the horizon. I watch as darkness presses down on the light, squashing it until the sun gives up and fades away.

She pulls into the parking lot at Smitty's, the only bar in Brookside worth a damn. "You ready for this? Feel like drinking a little too much tonight?"

I shrug and then nod, letting a long breath out through my nose. "Probably."

Lexi covers my hand with hers and gives it a little squeeze before grabbing her purse and sliding out of the car. I follow suit, humidity punching me in the gut and running away with my breath. The air is so thick it's like trying to breathe through a damp towel, and I can feel a thin sheen of sweat on my forehead.

"Hey. Hold on." Lexi grabs my wrist and turns me

to face her. She smooths back the little wispy curls that have broken free from my ponytail, fighting the natural disaster that is my hair. "There," she says after a bit more fussing. "Much better."

Three beers later and I'm feeling a little more talkative. "I miss them," I say, swallowing hard. "Still."

"I know." She runs a finger along her beer bottle.

"Every year I think it's going to be different. That I've grown up and healed enough for it not to hurt so bad. But I still blame myself. For all of them." I plunge into my guilt, wear it like an old coat, tattered and worn and frayed around the edges, but too familiar to give up. "They'd all still be here if it wasn't for me," I say, peeling back the corner of the label on my beer.

Lexi sits back in her chair and crosses her arms over her chest. "That's bullshit and you know it. Nothing that happened that day was your fault. Not one single thing."

"I could have stopped it. They'd all still be here if I had been a better girlfriend to Tyler." I take a drink. I know better than to fall down a huge hole of self-loathing in the middle of Smitty's but it looks like I'm about to do just that. Somewhere behind me, a woman laughs and it makes me flinch. I take another drink.

Lexi, my bastion of patience and understanding, sighs heavily. "How could you have stopped it, Bailey?" she asks, not sounding quite so patient anymore. "What on earth could you have possibly done differently?"

Her question drops my jaw, a rush of air zooming through my open mouth. "Everything." The word is fire and I hold out my hands, tilting my beer crazily through the air. "If I'd been paying enough attention, I would have noticed what Tyler was going through. I could have stopped it all if I'd just been a better girlfriend."

Lexi leans forward. "We go through some version of this year after year, Bay. Don't you think it's about time to move on?"

I sit back in my chair and scowl across the table. "Fuck you."

My brother Michael staggers over and collapses into a chair beside me, missing most of the seat and clutching at the table to avoid falling straight to the ground. "If it isn't my basket case of a sister and her sidekick, Super MILF."

"Great." Lexi laughs into her hands before running them down her face. "What do you want?"

He leans forward and widens his eyes. "Good to see you, too, Alexa," he says before swiveling his gaze back to me, his eyes swimming in and out of focus until a smile smears itself across his face. "Just thought I'd come join the celebration with my dear sweet sister."

I fold my arms over my chest. "I'm not celebrating."

Michael laughs. "Right." He points a finger at me and drags it through the air to my beer. "Me neither."

"You're not helping, Michael. Are you here alone?

Did you drive?" Lexi scans the back of Smitty's in search of any of Michael's limited list of friends.

"Of course I'm helping. What my big sister needs right now more than anything is family. Especially in the face of such tragic loss." His words are so slurred they're barely recognizable. He raises a glass of what's probably straight tequila. "Happy death-aversary. Thanks for killing our parents." My brother—once a sweet kid with a stupid cowlick that kept his hair sticking straight up from his forehead, the kid I did my best to raise right after ... everything—slams his glass down on the table and sneers at me.

Tears well in my eyes and Lexi pushes her chair back from the table, hauls my brother to his feet, and disappears out the front door into the night, dragging his drunk ass behind her. People stare as I fight to catch my breath. Everyone here knows my story. The whole damn town knows every gory detail. More than they should. More than they deserve. And the best part is that everyone here will tell their friends who will tell their friends and this awful night will be one more scene in the soap opera that is my life.

I swipe at the tears with the back of my hand and glare at anyone still bold enough to look at me. I am not part of their Friday night entertainment, thank you very much. By the time Lexi comes back, I'm halfway through my fourth beer and am probably drunker than my brother.

"I got him a cab and made sure he got in it," she

says, the weight of the evening showing in the slump of her shoulders.

"You know what it is," I say, waving my beer in front of me. "I'm cursed. Everyone I care about ends up broken. Or worse. Tyler shot himself. *He. Shot. Himself.*" I lean forward, elbows on the table. "And I didn't even know he was depressed. We'd been together for two years. How could I not know? And my parents..." I swallow hard and close my eyes, still not ready to talk about them.

"Bailey, you're not cursed."

"And just look at Michael. Do you remember how sweet he used to be? Do you remember how much potential he had? I ruined him." I stare off towards the door after my brother. "I ruined him."

"You were eighteen. Coping with more than you needed to. You kept him out of the foster system and did the best you could."

"And just look how it paid off." I sneer and consider taking another swig of my beer. But I'm drunk enough as it is and as much as I hate August fourth, I'm not interested in paying for it on August fifth.

"You're not cursed, Bailey. You had a lot of bad things happen to you and they just keep on happening, but none of it is because of you." She gives me a weak smile. "Besides, if you were cursed, don't you think it would have hit me by now? You love me and I'm doing just fine."

I make a sound that's meant to be laughter but

since I can't see through the tears in my eyes, it might be a sob. "I do love you," I say. "You're too good to me."

"Nope. Not even half as good as you deserve." She places her hands on the table. "What do you say I get you home and into bed before we give the peanut gallery here anymore to talk about behind our backs?"

I haul myself to my feet, swaying as the world spins in four different directions at once. "Probably a good idea."

Lexi drives me home, not even complaining when I roll down the windows and let the wind come rushing through to dry my tears. It's still humid outside, even as late as it is, but the roaring wind drowns out the litany of grief in my head and the humidity is a small price to pay for the silence. You'd think after eight years I'd be better than this. And most days I am. It's just that August fourth isn't most days. When we pull into my driveway, the crunch of the gravel and the glow of the porch light welcomes me home as it has for all twenty-six of my years. It soothes me at the same time it hurts me. The pain of my loss wrapped up in the familiarity of everyday life.

I roll up the window and turn to my friend. "Thank you," I say and then drop my head into my hand as the word stretches and echoes through the car. What in the world made me think I could drink four beers and be okay?

"No need to thank me. Just make sure to drink

some water and take an ibuprofen before you fall into bed."

I climb out of her car and pat the hood, wave as she reverses out of the driveway, and then drag myself up the front steps and into the darkened house. I hate it here. With their ghosts all around me. Everything just the way they left it. Well, everything except my room and theirs. I couldn't live in either space after they died. My room felt too much the same, too normal. I couldn't sleep in there with my mother's laughter and my dad's smile wrapped up in every single thing I owned.

So, I moved into their room, but that was no good either. The bed sheets still smelled like them. They smiled at me from the wedding pictures on the nightstand, accusing me of stealing the rest of their lives, of ruining everything they built for our family. One day, while Michael was at school, I got rid of it all and moved my stuff into their room. The only things I kept were their pictures. I couldn't throw them away. I just couldn't.

I close the front door behind me and head straight to the piano. Sit at the bench and stare out through the open window and play.

I play for them.

I play for Tyler.

I play for who Michael and I were, and for who we've become. The music rips itself out of me and tears fall from my eyes, dropping on my hands, but still I play.

Before long, I sense movement at the doorway. My fingers slow and then stop, cutting off the melody on a harsh note.

"Don't stop." Liam sounds groggy. "It's beautiful."

"It hurts," I say, sniffing.

"Ahhh." There's more movement and then he's sitting next to me, his shoulder pressing against mine, his sleep-warmed skin almost too hot for me in my agony. "That's why it's beautiful."

I pull my hand from the keys and put them in my lap. "There's nothing beautiful about pain."

"Behind every beautiful thing, there's some kind of pain." Liam puts his hands on the keys, lets them wander around a melody. "I think Bob Dylan said that."

The urge to lean into him, to borrow some strength from his size and his warmth is so strong I almost succumb to it.

Almost.

Instead, I put my hands on the keys and wind my melody around his.

"What's wrong, Bailey?" Liam keeps his voice low, almost a whisper.

"It's just a bad day," I whisper in return.

His fingers chase the melody towards mine. His skin brushes mine and chills rush through my body. I stop playing and stare up at him.

"Why are you being nice to me?"

"Maybe I'm still mostly asleep." Liam smiles, the moonlight streaming through the window catching the scar winding down his face.

Without thinking, I run my finger along it. My touch light, just a whisper of contact. "Does it still hurt?"

Liam leans into my hand, pressing my palm against his cheek, and closes his eyes. "Deeply."

The low rumble of his voice touches the aching part of my soul and I know he's not talking about the scar. I pull my hand away and study his face as he opens his eyes and stares down at me. The space between us takes on a life of its own, shrinking and contracting with each and every one of our breaths. I lean into him, needing contact. Needing sensation and oblivion and a reason to step outside of myself for a while.

"Today's the day they died." I blink several times but don't look away. "My parents."

"How?"

I shake my head and the world spins drunkenly. It hurts to be this exposed, as if my whole body is a raw nerve, our words grinding against it until the pain forces me to cry out.

"I'm sorry," he says, bringing his hand to my cheek and threading his fingers into my hair.

I lean into him and close my eyes, swimming in grief and guilt, desperate to feel anything but the way

I'm feeling right now. I lick my lips. Open my eyes and find him close. So close. He drops his hand from my cheek, his eyes searching my face.

There's a moment. The two of us knowing what's about to happen and trying to decide if we should let it, and then Liam kisses me. His hands slide up my arms and clutch my shoulders. His lips are warm and supple against mine. Our breath fills the room, twining with the rustle of fabric as I bring my hands to his back and grip his shirt in my fists.

I breathe him in. His clean skin and the scent of his cologne are so foreign to me. They're unlike any of the smells that I sometimes imagine still linger around this house, triggering memories with the power to bring me to my knees. Liam is different. Nothing about him reminds me of my past, and there's salvation there. Safety in his newness. In his total lack of knowledge of me from before. I can be anything with him.

Our kiss deepens, the stubble of his beard scraping the delicate skin on my cheeks. I open to him, lean into him, and his tongue darts out to meet mine.

He pulls back but keeps his hands on my cheeks. "Have you been drinking?"

I nod. "It's a bad day."

Liam's eyes burn into mine, moving across the planes of my face. He takes a breath like he wants to speak, only to close his mouth and look away. "I'm sorry, Bailey," he says after a moment. "I don't want this because you're drunk and hurting. And I know, deep down, neither do you."

And then he stands and walks out of the room, leaving me to stare after him, cold in the wake of his fire.

Chapter 10

LIAM

I'm awake before Bailey. After waking to find her in front of the piano, after hearing her play, after that kiss—holy shit, what was that kiss?—I couldn't fall back to sleep. I left the den and crawled into bed, trying to understand how I could kiss her and walk away. She was drunk. Desperate. Ready to give herself to me. And I just walked out of the room without taking any of it.

I tried to pretend I didn't know why for the first couple hours I spent stretched out on my new bed. Tried to imagine how stunned anyone who knew me would be if I told them the story. Tried to come up with a good reason—hell, *any* reason—other than the real one.

But truth is hard to deny and I finally gave in and admitted it.

I respect Bailey Schultz. And the pain I saw in her last night? The pain that ran down her face and poured out of her soul into that piano? I recognized it and I understood it and...

And what?

I kissed her and walked away?

I don't care how true any of that is, I don't understand a lick of it and after a whole night of trying to get to the bottom of what it all means, I gave up and came out to the kitchen to make breakfast. When Bailey gets up, she's going to find a pot of fresh coffee, some scrambled eggs with the proper ratio of yolks to whites, and one hell of a plan to get that patio started. The Internet is a glorious place, and after hours of research and online shopping, I think we're finally ready to get a move on with this thing.

And just why am I suddenly ready to build her a patio when I swore there was no way in hell that was going to happen? I haven't the faintest clue. All I've got is that after seeing her so broken last night, the thought of making her smile has me feeling pretty damn good about myself.

Bailey's routine is like clockwork. On days she has to work, she's out of the house before six. Days she doesn't work? Like today? She sleeps in all the way until seven. I timed breakfast perfectly so it would be hot and ready on the table when she walked out of her bedroom. But as the clock on the microwave ticks past seven-fifteen, and then right on towards seven-thirty, I start to get antsy.

The eggs are shot. No one likes cold scrambled eggs, and with good reason because they're disgusting. And if she doesn't get her ass out here soon, the coffee will be scorched and my grand gesture will be ruined. My good mood dissipates, swallowed up by a cloud of frustration settling around my head like a swarm of gnats. I distract myself by turning on my iPad and opening the tabs of patio ideas I saved somewhere between last night and this morning. This thing is going to be so fucking beautiful when I'm done. She'll have an oasis in her backyard that puts this dump of a house to shame.

Bailey finally makes an appearance just before eight, her eyes swollen and bloodshot. "Morning," she murmurs as she heads straight to the coffee pot.

So much for gushing displays of appreciation on her part.

"The eggs are basically ruined." I gesture towards the pan on the stove. "But please—" I infuse the word with a hefty dose of sarcasm— "help yourself."

Bailey shuffles around the kitchen, scooping a pile of eggs onto a plate and popping it into the microwave. "These are delicious," she says after she's had a seat and made her way through the first few bites.

"They would have been better if you'd been up when you normally are."

Her eyes flicker to mine and she looks like shit.

And she also looks like she's about to launch into some kind of apology about last night. I'm not ready to talk about it. Not in the least. I hold up my iPad as a distraction.

"You're not going to believe the patio I'm going to build for you." I unleash my most winning smile on her and she pauses, her fork hovering just in front of her open mouth.

"Huh?" Bailey blinks. "Really?"

"I've got this thing all planned out. It's going to be fucking magnificent."

She reaches across the table for my iPad. "Let me see."

"No way, hot lips." I ignore the look of humiliation that races across her face. "That'll ruin the surprise."

Bailey puts down her fork and licks her lips. "Liam, look..."

She's going to talk about the kiss and it's my fault for hauling out the nickname, but that doesn't change the fact that I'm not ready to wade through whatever happened between us.

I stand, turning my back to her. "I thought we might go shopping today. They've got most of this stuff at the Lowe's in Grayson."

If she turns me down, I won't be too surprised. She looks like hell.

"Okay," she says. "But I need a shower first."

"Okay?" I whirl, genuinely excited.

"Yeah." She laughs, a sweet sound. "Okay."

An hour later, we're in her stinky truck, making the long drive into Grayson. I can't believe she does this twice a day, especially considering how tired she looks when she finally gets home in the evening. Her twelve-hour shifts sound bad enough, but add on a two-hour commute? No thank you. I keep waiting for her to bring up last night, but she seems to have gotten the message and we're just going to let that be a thing that happened that we never discuss again.

"Do you know how long it's been since I stayed in one place for this long?" I ask, studying the curve of her nose and the swoop of her ponytail. She really puts all those LA whores to shame with her simple beauty.

"Enlighten me." Bailey turns a smile my way and something deep within me answers, smiling in return.

"I seriously hoped you knew because I don't." I watch the sky for a few silent minutes. "It's been nice, waking up when I wanted to. Spending days stretched out on the couch. I can't even tell you how much noise is in my normal day to day."

"I can't even imagine."

"No. You really can't."

She catches the bitterness in my comment and scrunches up her nose. "But I bet your truck doesn't smell funny." She glances at me, her eyes gleaming as the ancient thing rattles and bumps over the road. "So there's that."

"You got me there. None of my cars smell even half this bad."

Her smile fades as she digests what I said. "Dang. Way to rub it in. I've got one stinky truck and you've got a whole fleet of cars." She shrugs and winks, and then laughs.

We pull into the Lowe's parking lot and I resent the long sleeves and ball cap I have to wear to keep my tattoos covered. It's hot as hell and I'm already sweating because Bailey's rust bucket is too old to have air conditioning. I hop out of the passenger seat and the sweltering August heat takes my breath away. Thankfully, Lowe's has the air conditioning set to arctic. The moment we walk in, I stand there, eyes closed, reveling in the cold as a bead of sweat forges a path down my spine.

We wander around the store while I pretend to know what I'm looking at and Bailey tries to sneak peeks at my iPad. She's small, but she's got one hell of a stubborn streak. For as many times as I push her away, she just keeps coming right on back. Finally, after her last attempt comes too close for comfort, I decide to walk around with the thing held over my head where there's no way she'll reach it.

"You look ridiculous," she says, those beautiful eyes of hers dancing in merriment.

"But I'm winning." I tilt my chin and look down at her, hitting her lightly on the arm.

"But *are* you?" she asks. "Really?"

We walk for a few more feet before she stops.

"Seriously though, Liam. I need to see what you

have in mind. Patios can get expensive and I really didn't think you'd ever go through with this." She gives me a look that says *and can you blame me*? "There's a good chance I can't afford what you've got planned."

I didn't even think about the cost involved. "I don't think it's that bad."

"Yeah, well, my checking account isn't that good." Bailey gives me an apologetic smile. "Can I please just look at what you have in mind so we can talk about how much I can actually afford?"

My cellphone starts vibrating in my back pocket. It's sure to be Brent or my mom because they've called three or four times a day since I've been here. I never answer the phone. Just send them straight to voicemail and erase the messages before listening to them. But, right now I'm glad for the interruption, so I hold up a finger to Bailey and answer the call.

"Liam." Brent's smooth as sin voice makes me roll my eyes. "How are you?"

I could tell him that I'm wrestling an alligator in the Nile and he'd just keep talking right over me. The man never hears anything but himself. "I'm fine," I say, regretting answering the phone.

"Listen. Here's the deal. You need to come to the end of this little temper tantrum of yours and get your ass back to Los Angeles."

"Temper tantrum?" I try to keep my voice low but fail.

"Your fans are actually mourning you. Holding

candlelight vigils and shit like that. Some chick literally tried to kill herself because she was so devastated to think she'd never get to see your face again. Some asshole leaked the story that you've been disfigured and we can't get the fans to calm down. You need to come home so we can get on this."

"Disfigured." I run my finger down the scar on my face. It's a long way from healed, but under Bailey's careful ministrations, it's a lot better than it used to be. She massages vitamin E oil into the skin every day and swears the scarring will be minimal.

"I booked you a flight for this afternoon. It's not too late to get in with one of the plastic surgeons. We can save your face, man. Salvage your career."

I'm pacing while rage wings through my body, tightening muscles and quickening my breath. No one cares about *me*. They only care about my face. My body. My image. The fans? Those girls who swear they love me? They don't give two shits about who I really am. How I really feel.

And Brent? My mom? My whole *team* back in LA? They look at me and see dollar signs. They don't see how empty I am. They don't see the nights I lay in bed in some hotel and wish for it all to end. Scratch that. They see it. They just don't care. They know how dark I am in the inside but their main concern is how to spin it for the press. Nothing about this has anything to do with the real Liam McGuire.

I am so tired of all the hollow relationships. So

tired of every single move I make being scrutinized by the entire world. Of the responsibility of living up to my fans' expectations.

"Is she okay?" I ask, pinching the bridge of my nose.

"Who?" Brent sounds irritated.

"The girl. The one who tried to kill herself." I keep my voice low, hushed out of respect for something so heavy and dark.

"Does it matter? Besides, it's fantastic publicity. If you come back now, you can make an appearance, maybe use her name or something. You'll look like a hero."

I refuse to use that poor girl as a way to make myself look better. "You know what, Brent? Go fuck yourself."

Brent laughs darkly. "Fuck me? The way I see it, you're the one fucking yourself," he says before hanging up on me.

Emotions churn beneath my skin. It's too much. It's all too much and I don't want to carry any of it around anymore. Guilt gives way to resentment and I slam the phone into the ground. The screen shatters, but it does nothing to satisfy the rage boiling inside of me. "Damn it!" I scream as I throw a punch right into a concrete wall.

The pain? Now that's satisfying. The bloody cuts on my knuckles? Totally worth it.

Bailey scurries to my side. "Liam! What's wrong?"

She takes my hand in hers and turns it over to inspect the damage.

I yank it from her. "I'm fine." People are staring. Clerks poke their head around corners while customers wheel their carts over to come and stare at the sweating lunatic with the bloody hand and broken phone.

"You're not fine," says Bailey.

If I look at her and see pity, I might just lose my mind, so I look everywhere but her. "I am. Let's go. People are staring." Without waiting for a response, I stomp out to her stupid truck and climb inside, slamming the door so hard the whole thing rocks with the force.

Bailey climbs into the driver's seat but doesn't start the engine. "Liam, what happened?"

I look at my knuckles. "I just split the skin. It's nothing."

"I'm not talking about your hand, dumbass. I'm asking about you."

I finally look at her and the look in her eyes blasts straight through my rage and I'm dumbfounded. She's not looking at me with pity. She's concerned. About me.

"It's stupid," I say, holding her gaze instead of looking away. "You'd think, after all these years, I'd be used to being thought of as a commodity instead of a person."

Bailey shrugs and brings the engine to life. "I don't

know. Seems to me that's not something a person should ever have to get used to."

She's silent on the way home. Doesn't ask me questions. Just lets me think. Once, she reaches over to squeeze my hand and I stare down at her slender fingers holding onto mine. The simple gesture, just a reminder that she's here with me, it means more to me than anything I can remember in a long time.

Chapter 11

BAILEY

We ride in silence for a while, Liam staring out the window while I run through a million possible scenarios as to why he would go off like a psychotic animal in the middle of a hardware store.

"So," I say when I can't stand it any longer. "You wanna tell me what that was about?"

Liam glares at me. "Not really."

"The way I see it, you owe me an explanation."

"I don't owe you anything." Liam pulls his hat down even lower, hiding in the shadows the bill casts on his face.

"Ahh. See, that's where you're wrong." I reach my hand out the window, letting it dip and dive through the rush of air. "You owe me big. Remember?"

He laughs bitterly. "It's just a bunch of silly nonsense you won't understand."

"It didn't look like silly nonsense to me." I shrug. "It looked like something that got deep under your skin. And sometimes talking about that kind of stuff can go a long way to relieve the pressure that's building up inside, you know?"

Liam meets my gaze and then swallows. "My manager just knows exactly what to say to make me feel like I'm not a real person. It's hard to explain."

"I'm listening."

"So, this girl tried to kill herself because of me." His words cut through my sense of calm and slice right into the part of my heart I save for Tyler.

"Shit," I say because I can't think over the rush of memories.

"Right? And here's the thing..." Liam trails off, looking for words. "I feel awful for her. I really do. But she doesn't know me. And I don't want the responsibility of her doing something that drastic, you know? That sounds super shitty and selfish but I'm so tired of people wanting to use me. Like, her doing that puts all the weight of her decision on my shoulders." He runs a hand over his mouth. "And Brent wants to try to use it to make me look like some kind of a hero and I don't want to be a hero. I just want to be me. And I want people to be okay with that."

I bob my head. "I get that."

"I know it makes me sound like a douche."

"It really doesn't." I pull my hand back in the window as I slow for a turn. "And Liam?"

"Yeah?"

"I'm totally okay with you just being you."

He studies me, trying to make sense of what I said, quite obviously looking for the catch. I can't even begin to understand what it's like to live his life. It's so outside of my normal he might as well be from a different planet. But from what I gather, everyone who has connected themself to him sees him as a tool more than a person. Something to use to further their own motives, instead of someone with thoughts and feelings of his own.

"So," I say after a bit. "I feel like we need to get on the same page about this patio."

"What do you mean?"

"You know how there are parts of your life that don't make a lot of sense to me? The fans and the obligations? All the stuff about being true to a brand instead of who you are?"

Liam draws his eyebrows together. "Yeah?"

"Well, I think it's safe to say there are parts of my life that you don't understand."

"Like what?"

"Like how much money counts as a lot."

Liam rolls his eyes. "I understand the concept of money."

I laugh. I can't help it. "I'm sorry," I say, trying to get myself under control. "But I saw the price tags on the materials you were looking at. There's no way you understand the concept of money in relation to my life."

"Alright then." Liam takes off his ball cap and runs a hand through his hair. "Enlighten me."

"I don't have that much." I lock my eyes on the stretch of road in front of me. "Feeling enlightened yet?"

"Not really."

I glance at him, self-conscious. "So, when my parents passed and left me the house, it was paid off. But there was still property tax and stuff like that. I was only eighteen and had a job at McDonald's making barely enough money to support my brother and me. Then you add in student loans and bad decisions with credit cards." I sigh. "Things are getting better. I make enough to get by and have started building up a little savings. But there's not enough in there to even make a dent in what I think you have planned."

Liam eyes me thoughtfully. "Then let me pay for it."

"There is no way that's happening." I flip on a turn signal and pull into my driveway.

"Why not?"

"Same reason I'm not opening a credit card to charge the materials. I don't want to be in debt anymore."

"Okay then," Liam blows a long breath out of his nose. "How much?"

"What do you mean?" I ask, even though I know

exactly what he means. I'm just not sure I'm ready to be this open with him.

"How much do you have?"

I pull up in front of the house and kill the engine, barely able to look his way. This whole conversation has made me feel completely naked. Like he's going to judge me for the tiny little bit of disposable income that I'm actually quite proud of.

"Come on, Bailey. First you make a big deal about me building this thing, now you're making a big deal about doing it on your budget. You need to open up to me if you want it done your way." He undoes his seatbelt and twists in his seat. "Besides. I told you about my silly nonsense. I showed you mine. Now show me yours."

I roll my eyes. "I have fifteen hundred dollars and I'd prefer you don't spend it all." The admission brings warmth flaring up my chest and across my cheeks. I'm both ferociously proud of that number and terrified he's going to laugh in my face.

Liam's lips part, surprise and pity playing across his face before he skillfully schools his features into a very sweet smile. "Okay then. Now I know." He swings open the truck door and steps outside.

I scurry out after him. "That's it?" I ask.

"What do you mean, that's it?"

"You're not going to laugh. Or tell me you make more than that in one hour? Or, I don't know, congratulate me?"

Liam walks around to the front of the truck and leans on the hood. "Why would I do any of those things?"

"I don't know." I shrug. "Because it's not a lot of money."

"The way I see it, that fifteen hundred dollars is the culmination of a lot of hard work and sacrifice on your part," he says, taking my hands in his and pulling me close.

"It is," I whisper.

"Then why in the world would I laugh at you?" He rubs a thumb over one of my knuckles. "I'm proud of you. At the end of the day, a number is just a number. If you worked your butt off to earn it, it's worth celebrating."

I stare up at him. "You're nothing like I thought you were."

Liam throws his head back and laughs. "Well thank goodness for that," he says, smiling down at me. "Because you sure hated my guts when we first met."

"Can you blame me?"

"No. I guess I can't." He drops a wink and starts towards the house, my hand still wrapped in his. "But I sure am glad you're changing your mind."

Chapter 12

BAILEY

"Have you kissed him again?" Lexi asks over the clangs and bangs that are part of her everyday life as a mom. "Gabe!" she calls out. "Come finish cleaning your room, baby." There's a brush of static on the line, probably her hand uncovering the phone. "Sorry," she says to me.

"No worries." I take a seat at the piano and run my fingers along the keys. "And no. I haven't kissed him again."

"Damn, Bay. You are literally zero fun. If you're going to have the world's sexiest man living in your house, you might as well go ahead and sleep with him. Especially if the chemistry between you is as hot as it sounds."

I rise off the bench and twist open the blinds to let in some light. "There will be zero sleeping with anyone around here, thank you very much." Movement through the window catches my attention, Liam pacing off the space he wants to use for the patio. "Although I'm not going to lie," I say, watching him. "The thought has crossed my mind once or twice. Okay, at least twice. I mean, really, probably more than that."

Lexi gasps. "I knew it," she says, a smile in her voice.

"But that, dear friend, is exactly why I won't do it. The last few days have been..." I sit back down on the bench and stare at the ceiling, looking for the right words. "It's just a million tiny moments, you know? And each and every one of them feels special. I can't do anything, say anything, hell, I can barely move without Liam laughing at me for it."

"And he's still alive?" Lexi sounds genuinely shocked.

"Yes." I widen my eyes as I say the word. "He's still alive."

"Because, you know, I've seen you rip into someone just because he kinda almost sort of a little bit looked like he might be laughing at you..." Lexi chuckles. "I'm just saying..."

"I know." Liam catches my attention again and I bite my thumbnail before continuing. "It's different with him."

"Right." Lexi draws out the word. "Sure it is."

"No, really. He's not laughing to make fun; he's laughing because it *is* fun."

But it goes beyond even that. The very sound of his laughter, it's multi-layered and complex. The rich twining of velvet and whiskey. Of chocolate and amber. It's beautiful and it reaches down deep inside me and makes me feel ... what?

Alive.

Real.

Warm.

None of those words work. It's a feeling I can't remember ever experiencing before. Like a piece of the puzzle that makes up who I am has been slipped into place and everything makes more sense. Except, with gibberish like that running through my head all the time, nothing really makes much sense at all.

"Bailey Schultz." Lexi uses her mom voice. "Are you..." She pauses for dramatic effect. "Experiencing *feelings* for him?"

"Nope. Zero room for feelings of any kind."

"How many times have you thought about kissing him?"

"Oh, come on now." I switch ears with the phone. "There's no harm in me appreciating the kiss. I haven't exactly had many kisses in the last few years."

"How many times, Bay?"

"What? How many times have I been kissed?" I laugh. "Do you really expect me to keep a running tally?"

"You know what I mean. Stop stalling. How many

times have you thought about making out with Liam McGuire?"

"Not that many," I say, even though it's a total cop-out. That kiss is the first thought I have before falling asleep each night. It follows me through my day. One minute, I'm working, the next I'm staring off into space all starry-eyed with the strangest flip-flopping nerves sparkling in my stomach.

"Sure. We'll just go with that." Lexi pauses to answer a question from Gabe.

"So," I say when she's done. "He showed me his ideas for the patio last night."

"No way! He's really going to do it?"

"Well, not if he doesn't get a good grasp on reality." Outside, Liam takes his shirt off and wipes it across his forehead before tucking one end into his back pocket. I shift on the piano bench so I can get a better view of him.

"What's that supposed to mean?"

"We had a very real conversation about my finances yesterday." Liam shifts and the muscles in his back and arms twitch and flex. I wet my lips, my gaze traveling along the tattoos twisting around his body. I wonder if they mean anything.

"Bay?"

"Yeah?"

"Where'd you go?"

"Huh?"

"Liam's in the room isn't he?" Lexi laughs like she's got everything all figured out.

"He is not." I tear my eyes off him and start picking my nails. "He's outside."

"Uh-huh. And you can't see him at all."

My eyes bounce to the window and I drag them back down to my fingers. "I can see him," I admit. "Do his tattoos have any meanings?"

"No. Way. He's got his shirt off and you're sitting in the house on the phone with me?"

"Priorities," I say with a smile even as my gaze wanders out the window again. Outside, Liam shakes his head and runs his hand through his hair before turning towards the door to let himself back in the house.

"Oh shit, Lex. He's coming back in. I've got to go."

My best friend laughs. "Priorities. Gotcha." She says a quick goodbye and ends the call.

I sit back so he doesn't catch me staring, put my phone on the bench beside me, and begin playing a melody.

Liam closes the back door behind him and I hear him pull open the fridge. A few seconds later, he appears in the doorway holding a bottle of stupidly expensive water. "That's really pretty," he says, gesturing towards the piano. "What song is that? I don't recognize it."

He takes a swig and I pull my hands off the keys and put them in my lap. "It doesn't have a name."

The truth is, I've never played it for anyone. Not Michael. Not Lexi. No one. The melody came to me the winter after Tyler and my parents died, and I've spent the last eight years refining it, adding to it. Up until today, it's been for me, and me alone.

Liam's eyes widen. "Oh, shit. Did you write that?"

"Yeah." I offer a weak smile. "It's just something I play for myself."

"That's just tragic because that song deserves to be heard. It's really beautiful. Like, I've heard a lot of music in my life and that song is one of the best I've heard." He gestures at me to scoot over and takes a seat next to me.

The smell of summer and sunshine came in on his skin and all I can think about is putting my lips to his and breathing it in. His proximity and the intimacy of sharing this song with him do a number on my ability to communicate. So, I nod and stare at my hands before clearing my throat and meeting his eyes.

Liam puts the lid on his water bottle and sets it on the floor next to the bench. "Play the melody." He furrows his brow and waits for me to move.

"I can't. I mean, I can. It's just..." I roll my eyes at my own embarrassment. "I've never played it for anyone else."

And it's got all my sorrow and hope and fear, and so many little pieces of me wrapped up in it that I might shatter if he so much as chuckles.

"That's silly, Bailey. Play."

And, because I agree with him, I do.

I close my eyes and put my fingers on the keys, the familiar melody pouring out of me. It's my story and this is the best way for me to share it with him. The pain of losing Tyler, of knowing how long he suffered and that I never noticed how depressed he'd become. The knife twisting in my gut, knowing that my parents are dead because of me. The terror of children's services coming to take Michael and the desperation of proving I was ready to become his guardian. And the guilt, oh the guilt, to see what he's become.

It's all there for him, moving through the melody, right there for him to see and understand. If only he spoke the language.

He sways beside me, his shoulder bumping mine from time to time, and then he joins in. Tentatively at first, just a few notes here and there to augment my song, but then he adds a secondary melody coiling through mine. It's sad and it's sweet and it reaches into my soul and touches something I thought had died a long time ago.

I couldn't open my eyes if I tried. The music is too beautiful. Too honest. Goose bumps shiver across my skin, and my past and future fall away and it's just the two of us here in the moment. An eternity spent between each note, each breath, each beat of our hearts.

And then Liam begins to sing. First, he just hums, but then he finds words, beautiful words that express my sorrow. My eyes fly open. Maybe we speak the same language after all. Tears surprise me and I blink them away. I take my hands off the keys and stare.

"I didn't know you could really sing."

Liam shakes his head. "Wow. And just what do you think I do for a living?"

"I mean, I've heard your music. It's just so poppy. What you did just now had so much more soul."

"I'm more than just a dancing monkey, you know." Liam smiles, but the look in his eyes is raw and open. Whatever just happened between us, it was powerful stuff indeed. "I write a lot of songs they won't let me play."

"Why not?"

"Because my brand is *just so poppy*." He widens his eyes at me as he parrots back what I just said to him. "And the songs I write really aren't."

"Play one."

Liam holds my gaze, his eyes flickering across my face. For a split second, I think he's going to tell me no, but then he puts his hands to the keys and starts to play. A new set of goose bumps rush across my skin and I sigh, closing my eyes and letting the music move through me. When he sings, I smile, tears burning in my eyes once again. Music does that to me. Well, the right kind of music does that to me. It renders me immobile, roots me in place, makes me feel so much, so deeply, that all I can do is smile and shiver and cry.

I never thought Liam McGuire, master of pop and

tabloid headlines, would ever have the right kind of music in him.

I know I shouldn't, but I can't help it. My hands find their way to the keyboard without my permission and before I really know what's happening, I start vamping on his song. He sings and it's gut-wrenching, a song of despair and pain and hope, and I recognize every single piece of it. I hum along, letting my voice, one that has no place being heard next to his, duck in and around his music. The effect is chilling. So hauntingly beautiful that it surprises us both.

We stop playing and stare at each other. The memory of the music fills the room while a flock of birds takes off from the ground outside the window.

My gaze drops to his mouth. I want to kiss him but am afraid to move. Afraid that my heart and soul are too close to the surface. That a kiss would fill me and open me and make me admit that Liam is working his way into my life and I like him being here. That I look forward to coming home to him, stretching out on the sofa together, laughing and talking late into the night.

And then he takes the choice away from me.

He runs a hand along my cheek, threads his fingers into my hair, and presses his lips to mine. This is no polite kiss. There's nothing tentative or mannered about it. He devours me, a starving man at a banquet. A soldier preparing for war.

And I kiss him right back. I pull him in close to me, desperate to fill the holes in my aching heart with all the things that he is. He fists his hand in my hair, pulls back so I'm staring at the ceiling, kisses down my jaw, along my throat and collarbone.

My eyes roll closed and I steady myself with a hand on the piano, two fingers striking discordant keys. The moment he releases his grip, I search out his mouth with mine. As good as it feels to have his lips on my skin, I want to participate, to reciprocate.

I bring my hands to his back and revel in the way the corded muscles bunch underneath my palm. He groans as I dig my fingers into his skin, grabs my thigh, guides me onto his lap so that I'm straddling him, my back to the piano. He grabs my waist and pulls me down onto the hard bulge of his cock. I rock my hips, tilting my head back as his mouth travels down my throat and his hands come to my breasts.

I make a sound I don't understand—raw, unadulterated. Uncensored. It should unnerve me but it lights me on fire instead. I should stop this. I should get off his lap and walk away because nothing good can come of this. Not when he's this temporary. Not when he makes me feel this alive.

But I'm way past caring about shoulds and coulds. I fell in over my head the last time he kissed me and have been treading water ever since, just waiting for this moment. I want this. I need this. He is fire and I've been cold all of my life.

His hands slip under my shirt, slide along my ribcage, scorching my skin. I moan again and Liam rocks his hips up into mine. "Yes," I whisper. "I want it. God, I want it."

He pulls my shirt over my head and unhooks my bra, worships my breasts with his teeth and tongue, while I reach between us and struggle with the button on his shorts. Without a word, Liam slides his hand under my ass, lifts me up and sits me on the piano, a dissonant chord filling the room. I brace my feet on the bench and lift my hips while he slides off my shorts and panties. Another jarring set of notes clang from the piano when I lower myself again.

"Are you sure?" Liam pauses, his hands on his zipper.

I nod, chest heaving. "I need you."

A few seconds of fumbling with clothing and he's inside me, so deep it hurts. I wrap my legs around him and pull him in even further. I cry out at the peak of each of his thrusts, my voice keeping time with random notes from the piano. I cling to him, wrap my arms around him, and bury my face in his shoulder. I breathe in the sunshine that still clings to his skin and nip and suck at his earlobe and neck.

He moves with confidence, driving into me, chasing after whatever it is we discovered in each other today, and I spiral further and further from myself. He fucks me against my piano, a warrior, a Viking, and I come harder than I ever knew was possible, screaming his name, my head falling back so that my hair tickles the skin at my waist. As I clench around him, unaware of anything but him and me and our music filling this old house, he growls and grits his teeth, lifting my face so I can meet his gaze when he comes with a shudder and a groan.

I'll never forget the look in his eyes. Whatever happens between us from this point forward, whether he stays or goes, whether he builds me a patio or that just fades into a funny story about my past, this moment will be with me for the rest of my life. We're connected now, the two of us. Maybe we always have been, twin souls living separate lives, just waiting to finally come together. The look in his eyes is changing me. Unlocking some part of me that's been lost.

I don't know whether I should laugh or cry.

I choose both.

Chapter 13

LIAM

Bailey smiles at me, tears brimming in her eyes. "Well, that happened."

I want to kiss away the tears but I don't. It seems too personal.

"It sure did." I'm still buried inside her, one knee on the piano bench, one foot on the floor. This would normally be my cue to gather my clothes and make a hasty exit, but not only do I not have anywhere to go, I don't exactly feel like leaving either.

"Come on," she says after I help her off the piano. "Let's go get cleaned up."

She leads me into the bathroom and the weight of what we've just done hits me. "Uhh. We didn't use a condom." I always use a condom. Always. The fact that I didn't think of it until just now should scare me to death, but it doesn't. Instead of worrying about pregnancy and disease, I'm turned on as fuck realizing that I just came inside her. Somehow, that makes her feel like mine.

Bailey looks up at me through her eyelashes as she flips on the bathroom light. "I'm on the pill. And I'm clean." She seems just as unsure how to process what just happened as I am.

"I am, too. Clean. Not on the pill." I wink at her and she giggles.

"You know what?" Her eyes wander down my chest and settle on my growing dick.

"What?"

"I think I need a shower." She looks up at me, her bottom lip caught between her teeth. "And I think I want you to join me."

The water runs cold before we're done and we finally emerge from the shower, limp and lazy and totally satisfied with each other. While she takes a few minutes to dry her hair, the haphazard melody her poor, tortured piano sang for us while I fucked her against the keys plays through my mind. The ugly notes change shape until they're beautiful and I hum along, pruning the melody while I get dressed, shaping it into something worthy of whatever it was that just happened between us.

Bailey's still messing around in the bathroom. So, still humming the blossoming little tune, I step outside to study the space that should be one hell of a patio instead of a bare expanse of brittle grass. I totally understand why she wants to pay for the thing herself, even if I do wish she would let me put some of my own money into it. But the very fact that she won't let me proves how different she is from everyone else in my life. Bailey doesn't want me for the things I can do for her. She just wants me for me. I'd be one hell of a hypocrite if I started getting mad at her for the one thing that makes her so unique. No one stands up to me. No one except Bailey Schultz, the little nurse with the big attitude.

"You know staring at it isn't going to make a patio magically appear, right?"

She's leaning on the house, her arms crossed over her chest, looking so fucking beautiful out here in the setting sun that I don't know what to say right away.

"Look at you," she says, laughing a little. "Are you tongue-tied, Liam McGuire? Is that even possible?"

"I didn't think it was. And then I saw you standing there, looking like that, and I didn't have a word to describe how perfect you are."

Her face goes slack and she blinks a couple times before a funny look comes over her face. Was that too much? Too sappy, too fast? I don't know how to handle myself. I never stick around for post-sex conversation, and I certainly don't ever have thoughts like that flitting around my head. It never occurred to me *not* to say it.

Bailey pushes off the wall and puts her hands on her hips, a faint breeze blowing a wisp of hair into her face. "But seriously. Maybe if you told me what you're thinking about out here, I could help."

I shrug. "Just trying to figure out how to do this on your budget without it being a boring slab of pavers or something."

The way her backyard is framed by all these trees, I could see her coming out here after a long day at work, kicking her feet up and having a glass of wine, and just, I don't know, taking a long breath or whatever it is that people do when they have time to unwind.

Bailey laughs. "A boring slab of pavers sounds pretty good to me. Especially compared to the nothing that's out here now."

"Yeah, but I still think I can figure out how to make it better."

"You know what?" Bailey comes to stand next to me. "My brother, Michael? He's pretty good at this kind of stuff. Building things on a budget. He's an ass, but I bet he'd meet us up at the bar. Buy him a drink and he'll be yours forever." She smiles at me, but there's pain in her eyes.

I don't know if I should pull her close and ask her

what's wrong or if I should ignore it. And the fact that I don't know how to handle myself right now just proves to me that I'm in way over my head.

I settle on keeping the tone light. "You mean, actually leave the house and socialize with other people?"

"You'll have to wear long sleeves and a hat. And keep the scruff." She rubs a hand along my jawline, her gaze flickering to my mouth. "It suits you." Bailey takes a long breath and then removes her hand, staring past me towards the trees.

"Am I being too touchy-feely?" she asks. "I don't know how to handle myself right now. Sorry if I'm making it awkward."

Of all the responses rolling around in my head, I settle on sarcasm. "What? Awkward? I didn't even notice."

"Don't be a jerk," she says and slaps my arm. I capture her wrist and draw her close.

"Then don't make this weird."

I kiss her. She resists at first and then softens. Runs her hands up my back and down my arms. "So," I say, resting my forehead on hers.

"So," she breathes.

"Are you really going to take me out or are you just being a dirty little tease? Because believe you me, no one likes a tease, Nurse Schultz. I don't care how much they say they do."

Bailey pulls back and stares at me. Really takes my

measure. Her brows furrow and she tilts her head to the side as if she's asking a question, before nodding her head once, as if to answer it.

"Let me call Michael," she says. "You go get changed."

Chapter 14

LIAM

It's not a long drive to Smitty's, her favorite bar, and we fill it by turning on the radio and singing loudly to whatever song comes on. Her voice is pretty, a little rough around the edges, but honest, kind of like her. When we get to the bar, she puts the truck in park, turns off the engine, and turns to me.

"Are you ready for this?" She grimaces.

"You say that like there's something I need to know about this place."

"It's a far cry from LA. And Michael ... Well, he's Michael. He means well." She shrugs. "But he doesn't always come off like it."

"Believe me." I pause and take a long breath. "I understand family members who mean well but manage to push every single one of your buttons anyway. I could write a book about my mom and her totally conditional love."

Bailey lets out a low whistle. "God, I'm sorry to hear that. I'd love to talk about it, but maybe it's a conversation for when we're not sitting in a parking lot behind a bar?"

"If it's a conversation we should have at all."

Bailey shakes her head. "Oh, we'll have the conversation. I want to know everything about you. But I want to do it when we've got time to do it right." She pushes open the door and it groans as it swings open. We climb out of the truck and she leads me to Smitty's unassuming front door.

She pauses. "Just don't say I didn't warn you," she says with a wry smile.

The clink and clack of a good break at the pool table welcomes us as we walk inside. The bar is dirty. And it smells. And has terrible lighting. But people are laughing and the music is good, and I'm sure the beer tastes just like it's supposed to. Bailey leads me to a table where a big man with dark eyes sits hunched over a bottle of Budweiser.

"Ho-lee *shit*. If it isn't my darling big sister and her mystery man."

"Michael, I'd like you to meet Liam." Bailey doesn't offer my last name and scowls at her brother while he scrunches up his nose at me.

"Liam?" Michael studies me and then smiles,

looking more like Bailey by the minute. "No shit," he says as recognition dawns across his face.

Bailey pulls out a chair and sits down, leans in and puts a finger to her brother's lips. "You say nothing, you understand. Not one word."

I take a seat next to Bailey. "What's up, man?"

"I can't even believe this. Liam fucking Mcguire." Michael takes a long drag of his beer, never taking his eyes off me, and then lowers his voice when Bailey shushes him. "Is that the scar that has all the girlies on the news going stupid?"

I shrug and tilt my chin so the light can cut through the shadows the brim of my ball cap casts down my face. "Yep."

Michael shakes his head. "Man, chicks can be so dumb. It's barely visible. No wonder you're hiding out here."

The chair beside me scoots back and I look up, surprised, to see a tall blonde with cherry red lips staring angrily at Bailey. "Well, look who actually exists outside of the hospital." A sweet little brunette beside the blonde smiles shyly and twiddles her fingers in one of those girly waves.

Bailey's eyes light up. "Lexi! What are you doing here?"

Lexi sits next to me, barely glancing in my direction. "Since you've all but abandoned me, I made poor Michelle start taking me out for some serious one-on-

one adult time." She frowns. "That came out wrong, didn't it?"

The little brunette widens her eyes, looking uncomfortable. "Maybe a little wrong." She turns to us. "We're not lovers or anything."

"Ain't that a shame," Michael mutters into his beer and Bailey slaps his arm.

"Michelle and I met at a single mom's support group and it was clear right away that she's pretty damn awesome. You guys are going to love her."

Michelle takes a seat. "I'm right here," she says to Lexi. "Way to make it weird."

"Oh, don't worry about that." Bailey grins. "Lexi always makes it weird."

Lexi sticks out her tongue at Bailey before she turns to me and really notices me for the first time. "Wow," she says. "Now that's a transformation."

"You like? Or do you miss the old me?" I turn my chin from side to side, letting her get the view from all possible angles.

Lexi taps a finger against her chin and gives me the once over. "I think this is an improvement, don't you?" she says, turning to Bailey.

Bailey blushes and Lexi's eyes go wide with understanding—how do girls do that? Communicate so much with so few words?—just as a waitress interrupts to take our drink orders. I'm careful to keep my chin down and my voice low, just in case I'm not as incognito as Lexi would have me believe.

"So, my best friend's banging a pop star and I didn't even know about it." Lexi shakes her head and looks forlorn.

"Oh, Lexi," Michael sits back and grimaces. "Too much information."

Bailey shakes her head. "For real. Time and place, my friend."

The friendship and camaraderie between the three of them is apparent. I like both her brother and her friend, but more than anything, I like watching Bailey smile. She's easy with them, natural. And there's absolutely no difference between how she's behaving now and how she is when it's just the two of us. It's a strange realization, knowing that's she's actually herself with me. So many people wear masks around the great Liam McGuire. Bailey just *is.*

"Hey man," Michael says, flagging the waitress for another beer. "You play?" He gestures toward the pool tables in the back.

"Do I play? Hell fucking yes, I play."

"Why don't you and I let these three chickadees get some time alone so Bailey can tell Lexi all about you, and Lexi can tell Bailey how much she wants me, and poor Michelle can sit there wondering how she got roped into all this."

Lexi rolls her eyes. "As if."

Bailey smiles and laughs, her eyes flashing towards mine, and it does funny things to me. I want to give her a million reasons to never stop smiling, and at the same time I want to take her out back and fuck her against the wall behind the bar. On a whim, I lean down and kiss her, cupping her cheek with my hand. When I pull back, her eyes are wide and beautiful as she stares up at me. I waggle my eyebrows at her and saunter away, Lexi's squeal of excitement bringing a smile to my lips.

I like this. Being out with Bailey and her friends. They're not busy trying to be anyone but who they are and it's really fucking refreshing. I can see myself here. Living this simple life, loving these honest people. The thought keeps me smiling through most of my first game of pool with Michael. Bailey's right. He's rough around the edges, drinking too much and shaping his stories around their shock value, but he has some great ideas on how to get the patio done without going too far over her budget.

"Why are you so determined to build a patio there, anyway?" he asks me as he sizes up a shot. "She hates that place." Michael bounces the cue ball off the wall, sending it around a few stripes to land a solid in the corner pocket.

"She hates it?"

"Yeah. I swear she's only there to do penance or something."

"Penance?" What in the hell would someone like Bailey ever have to pay penance for? And how could it come in the shape of a house?

"Yeah." Michael's face darkens. "For Tyler and our parents."

Needing a distraction, I roll up my sleeves and stalk around the table in search of a shot.

"She didn't tell you about that, did she?"

I lean over and sight down my cue. "Is it a story I should know?" I glance up at Michael.

He tips back his beer and finishes the thing, downing half the bottle in a few swallows. "That's for her to tell you, not me." His tone is light but his eyes are hard and he wipes the back of his hand across his mouth before he gestures towards the waitress, avoiding my eyes.

A million thoughts scatter through my mind, keeping time with the pool balls I send crashing around the table. What in the world would Bailey need to pay penance for? And who the fuck is Tyler?

Michael takes his fifth beer from the waitress and sets up his shot without even the faintest hint of a wobble in his step. The balls go spinning right where he sends them and he looks up, satisfied, before his eyes settle on something behind me. He gestures with his chin before starting forward.

"I said *no thank you*!" Bailey's voice is raised, angry. I spin and find some guy bending over her, his face too close to hers. She pushes at his hands, which he keeps putting all over her.

Lexi pushes out of her chair. "Let go of her, Derrick!"

I'm in motion before I decide just how far I'm willing to take this, dropping my cue on the table and striding across the bar. I grab the guy by his shoulders and pull him into a standing position.

"I think she'd prefer you not to be so close."

Derrick scoffs. "Says you."

"She seemed pretty clear about it herself." I stare the asshole down, pulling myself up to my full height and squaring my shoulders.

Derrick clenches his hands into fists and then quite pointedly leans back over and gets in Bailey's face, opening his dead-fish lips to spew some nonsense in her direction. As soon as he gets close enough, she lands a slap across his cheek and I grab him, spin him, and punch him right in the face. His eyes go wide and stupid and he staggers back before stepping forward again.

Dude's tougher than he looks.

I spin my hat around, getting the bill out of my line of sight, and bring up my fists. Michael appears at my side, looking just as ready to fight as I feel, and the girls are up out of their chairs, trying to get in between us, desperate to make sure no one gets hurt.

Derrick lunges, but I'm ready for him. Stupid fucker doesn't realize that a good portion of my gym time is spent working with a speed bag. My fist connects with his cheekbone and his legs get wobbly, dropping him to his knees. Bailey screams and the bar goes silent. I have one second to enjoy my victory, and then:

"Oh, my GOD! You're Liam McGuire!" It's a female voice, slurring with liquor and excitement.

Derrick looks up at me, squinting, one hand covering his already swelling face. Bailey stares, her eyes wide and her mouth open and I realize what I've done. With my sleeves rolled up to reveal my tattoos and my hat on backwards to show off my face, I drew attention to myself by dropping a man to his knees in a bar filled with people.

Panic strums through my body as I watch the color drain out of Bailey's face. I've got two options, deny it and look like an ass because there's no way I'm convincing anyone I'm not me, or roll with it and see if I can charm these people into keeping my secret.

I choose option two.

Holding up my hands, I smile in the direction of the voice. "Guilty as charged," I say before helping Derrick to his feet and clapping him on the back like we're old friends. "Can anyone bring this guy some ice?" I catch the attention of the bartender and wave him over.

People swarm me, cameras out, voices raised, questions coming at me from every direction. I slide my sleeves back down and spin my hat around. "Put your cameras away." I unleash a winning smile. "I hate to say it, but I have to. My lawyers will be furious if they find out you guys spotted me. If any pictures of me here tonight hit the Internet, we'll *all* be dealing with them." I shrug and wink at a girl who looks barely old enough to drink, smiling up at me like she's finally found Jesus.

It doesn't take long and I've got them in the palm of my hands, answering questions and flirting with everyone. Men. Women. If it has a pulse, I'm smiling and winking and doing my damndest to get them to fall under my spell. It'll be enough to get us out of here without making a scene, but we're still royally screwed. Just because they're promising secrecy right now doesn't mean they won't make a big fucking deal of what happened as soon as they sober up. And that Derrick guy? He's going to take one look at that black eye and swollen cheek and see a money making opportunity. I bet he's got his lawyer yapping at my lawyers before the sun rises.

There's no way around it. I have to call Brent. The PR team needs to know what happened so they can put out this fire because I refuse to let Bailey wake up to the paparazzi skulking around her yard, digging through her trash, peeking through her windows. She's not prepared for that kind of life. Fuck. I'm not prepared to go back to that kind of life.

"Alright," I say to the crowd, careful not to look Bailey's way. The less they have to connect me to her, the better it'll be. "You guys promise to keep my visit here a secret and maybe I'll figure out a way to come back."

They promise to keep my secret—but they're lying—and I walk out the front door like everything's going to be okay—but it's not.

Chapter 15

BAILEY

I FOLLOW Liam outside and find him waiting for me near the truck, leaning on the thing with his arms crossed over his chest.

"I can't believe that was real life right now." I widen my eyes as adrenaline rockets through my bloodstream. "How are you so calm?"

"That was nothing, hot lips." He licks his lips and runs a hand over the back of his neck. "That was a handful of people with stars in their eyes and phones in their hands. It's the people with press passes you have to worry about."

"Yeah, but..." I trail off as we climb into the truck and close the doors behind us. "Fans and paparazzi aside, you hit Derrick. In the face. Hard. How are you not more upset than this?"

Liam flexes his hand. "For one, he totally deserved it."

"I feel like I'm supposed to disagree with you. Out

of some moral code or something." I bring the truck to life and wrestle her into reverse, laughing a little too loud. "But you're right. He totally deserved it. Maybe not off the basis of tonight alone, but off the culmination of sooooo many nights of him acting just like that."

"Well," Liam says before he takes my hand and gives it a squeeze. "That should give any and all future douchebags a reason to stop and think twice before coming up to hit on you."

"Yeah. It'll also give the whole town another interesting chapter in the long-term drama that is my life." Normally, that thought would sober me. Tonight? I'm too high on excitement to care too much.

I wait for Liam to ask what I'm talking about, not sure yet if I'm ready to explain when he does. He looks at me long and hard, and I watch him try to decide how to respond to my statement. Is this where I tell him about my curse? Right here in my dad's truck, in the parking lot of a bar? As I steel myself to explain my past, he finally smiles, gives my hand another squeeze and changes the subject.

"I liked hanging out with you guys tonight. Right up until I hit a man in the face and outed myself as Liam McGuire." He clears his throat and swallows hard. "You mind if I roll down the windows? It's hot in here."

"Go right ahead." As he works on the passenger window, I roll down the driver's window and the wind whips my hair into a frenzy around my face. "And be honest," I say, holding my hair out of my eyes. "You just liked getting out of the house. There's no way that hanging out with me and my friends at a bar like Smitty's came even remotely close to the kind of nights you're used to." I reach for one of the hair ties I keep wrapped around the gearshift and wrangle my hair into a ponytail.

"It's different, that's for sure. But in a good way. It's ... I don't know. Simple." Liam runs a hand through his hair and stares out at the road in front of us. "And I like Michael. You're right, he's rough around the edges, but he's a good man."

I bob my head and smile, at once pleased at the compliment and saddened at the thought of what kind of man he could have been if I'd done a better job when he was younger. "I liked Michelle," I say around the thick swell of regret tightening my throat. "She seems sweet."

"Yep. And Lexi's pretty awesome, too. Now that she's not looking at me like a piece of meat."

"You haven't even scratched the surface of all the reasons that woman's awesome yet. She's been there for me through thick and thin."

"See, that's what I'm talking about. You guys are all so..." Liam rubs his hand across his mouth and then turns to me, his eyes searching my face. "Real," he finishes and laughs a little. "That's the only word I've got. It's not right, but it works. I like it. You've known each other for years and treat each other like people, accept each other's flaws..."

"Hey!" I point a finger at him. "I don't have any flaws. I am quite perfect, thank you very much."

Liam laughs in earnest, a big sound. Strong enough to fight the wind. "You're right. Totally flawless." He settles back in his seat and looks at me strangely. "And utterly perfect."

I blink, turning my focus back to the road, uncertain how to handle the intensity hiding behind his words. Time to change the subject again.

"So," I say after a few seconds of watching the long series of white lines on the road strobe through the headlights. "What kind of problems can we expect after tonight? Is this a big deal or a little deal?"

Liam crosses his arms and runs a hand over his mouth again. "It's a pretty big fucking deal." He sighs and shakes his head. "I need to call Brent and get his advice. See about getting the PR team on it. Maybe come up with a good excuse for why I'm here and an even better explanation for why I had to move on."

Ignoring the little burst of nerves exploding in my stomach at the thought of Liam moving on, I study his face in the low light. "You don't think your little speech in there had any effect? Seems to me they all might just keep your secret for you."

Liam laughs bitterly. "Hell no. They might sit on it for a few days, but in the end, what's the use of having a secret if you can't share it with anyone?"

My stomach sinks. "And small towns love gossip..."

God knows I've learned that first hand.

Liam nods his agreement. "Which means I need to call Brent. I refuse to let me being here affect your life more than it already has. If word gets out and the paparazzi end up at your front door..." Liam pinches the bridge of his nose. "I'm not putting you through that."

I pull into my driveway, the familiar warmth of the porch light welcoming me home as it has for years. What would it look like to the paparazzi? To Liam's legions of devoted fans? This tiny little house nestled up against the woods, with its peeling paint and broken gutters?

"I don't want you to call Brent."

"You and me both, hot lips."

"What if you did something special? Give them a reason to want to keep your secret?" I turn off the engine and spin in my seat to face him. The call of the crickets makes its way through the open windows.

"Like what?"

I wrack my brain for an idea, settling on the first one that comes into my head. "Like what if you performed some of the songs you've been writing that they won't let you record? At Smitty's?" I can tell by Liam's face that he's about to tear the suggestion to shreds.

"That won't work for so many reasons..."

"Like what?"

Liam flares his hands. "Well for one, do you really think people would keep something like that secret?" He shakes his head. "Word would spread like wildfire and we'd be worse off than we are now."

Even though I'm not sure it's the best idea, the mere fact that he's opposing me makes me dig my heels in and fight for it. "You could make it one of the stipulations of the concert. The moment anyone mentions it anywhere, the whole deal's off."

Liam laughs derisively. "No one wants to hear the songs I write. The only thing anyone's interested in is the Liam McGuire who sings the songs you can't stand."

"I'm someone. And I want to hear them."

Liam smiles. "You got me there. You are very much someone."

"It might be a terrible idea." I roll up the window and open the door. "Or it might be a way to get the town on your side and keep Brent from getting involved. We could even tell them that these are songs you're not allowed to play..."

"That's a no go," Liam says as we climb out of the truck and head to the house, the gravel crunching under our feet. "I don't want anyone's pity."

"And that's not at all what I'm suggesting. But," I say, sliding the key into the lock. "I think if people knew the truth about what you go through, they might be more inclined to keep your secret. Join Team Liam or something. Plus, who doesn't love exclusive content?"

"You have no idea what it's like to have fans." His tone is light, but that's because he's forcing it to be. "They don't give two shits about who I am. All that matters is that I put out the right kind of music and look sexy while I sing it." He closes the door behind us. "You hungry? I think I'm hungry."

As much as I want to keep pushing for the concert—because while I started out thinking it was a dumb idea, I've totally talked myself into thinking it's a brilliant idea—I drop the issue. For now, anyway. Liam needs some time to mull it over. If I push too hard, too fast, he'll dig his heels in just as hard as I have and we'll get nowhere.

"I could go for some food," I say. "You cooking?"

Liam grabs my wrist and pulls me into him, presses his lips to mine. Snakes his hands under my shirt, his palms warm against my lower back. I press into him. Breathe him in. The kiss lasts only a moment before Liam pulls back, resting his forehead against mine.

"I've wanted to do that all night," he says.

Me too, I think but don't say.

Instead, I laugh and lead him towards the kitchen. "You can wrap it all up in pretty words, but I'm no idiot. You just wanted to distract me so I'd end up being the one cooking."

"You think so?" Liam grabs my waist and spins me around, pulling me close.

"I know so." I keep walking backwards, Liam's hands on my waist, his steps matching mine, until I bump up against the counter.

"You think you know so much." Liam leans forward, his gaze flickering from my mouth to my eyes.

"I—"

Liam silences me with a kiss, and where before he was tender, now he's insistent. Protective and possessive. With little preamble, he lifts my shirt over my head and then worships me with his mouth, trailing kisses down my neck and breasts, nipping at my nipples through the lace of my bra.

"I thought you were hungry," I say as I crane my head back to give him more room to work his magic.

"I am." He kisses my throat. My jaw. The corner of my mouth.

"For what?" I struggle out of his grasp and reach for a cabinet. "I think I've got some chips up here..."

"For you, Bailey. I'm hungry for you."

Liam takes off his shirt and drops it on the floor. Tugs at the button of my shorts and lets them fall to my feet. In a matter of seconds, we're undressed, lips and tongues and teeth traveling over each other's bodies. With two firm hands on my waist, he spins me around. Bends me over the counter. Presses himself against my opening.

I wait for him to sheathe himself in me. Need him to fill me up. Even push back a little when he refuses to move, but he keeps me firmly in place with two strong hands on my hips.

Confused, I turn to look at him over my shoulder. He meets my eyes with a smile and then slowly, so fucking slowly I might just scream from the deliberateness of it all, he slides into me, holding eye contact the entire time. When his hips meet mine, I gasp, my lips parting.

"Do you like that?" he asks, rolling his hips, thrusting into me.

"You feel so good." I don't recognize my own voice, taut with desire, made molten by his heat. "Please don't stop."

Liam pulls out almost as slowly as he pushed into me and I moan. My eyes roll closed and I melt into the counter as he thrusts forward. His name falls from my lips, a whispered admission of something I don't want to name, something I hope he doesn't hear. He gains speed, moving faster and faster, his fingers digging into the flesh at my hips.

Yes.

My hands scuttle out along the counter, knocking against the jars of flour and utensils.

Don't stop.

Liam lets loose a low growl. "Fuck. Bailey." His voice is low and primal.

Like that.

I come undone, clenching around him as I cry out, his voice joining with mine as he finishes with me. My knees go weak and I sag into the counter, his hands holding me up as he leans over to kiss my neck and shoulders.

"I needed that," he says, kissing that spot just behind my ear that makes me shiver every damn time.

I want to tell him I needed it, too, but that seems too private, too personal. An admission of something deeper and more meaningful than a quick fuck in the kitchen. Instead, I straighten and lean back against the counter, smiling up at him. "Oh yeah? Is your appetite sated?"

Liam rakes his eyes across my body. "Fuck, no. Not even close. But it's a start." He bends to gather my clothes, stepping into his boxer briefs while I go clean up in the bathroom.

When I come back into the kitchen, I find a still shirtless Liam setting a multitude of snack items on plates. "That looks delicious," I say, leaning against the doorframe.

"Yeah?" He steps back and surveys his handiwork, looking pleased.

"I wasn't talking about the food." When he meets my gaze, I give him a little lift of the eyebrows and purposefully ogle his bare chest.

Liam puts his hands on his hips and lifts his chin before striking a series of ever more seductive poses. "This is my underwear model look." He lets his eyes burn into mine. "You like?"

Laughing, I nod my head. "I want to make some

kind of witty remark, but I just can't. Not with you looking like that. You're really hot, you know that?"

Liam pulls out a chair for me. "Oh, I know."

"And modest."

Liam nods sagely and sits across from me. "Indubitably."

"And you've got one hell of a vocabulary." I reach for a plate of cheese and grapes.

"Now you're just flattering me."

When we're done snacking, we share the bathroom as we brush our teeth, laughing as we try to make out what the other is saying around a mouthful of toothpaste. He slaps my ass as I wash my face and I throw water at him as revenge. And then comes the awkward part as we get to the end of the hall and I pause in front of my bedroom door. As much as I want to invite him inside, to bring him into my bed and sleep curled up against him, I can't.

I'm already more invested in this man than I need to be and nothing about him is definite. Any day now, for any number of reasons, he could pack up his things and head back to LA, leaving me here to pick up the pieces of my life and try to put them back together in a way that makes sense. The last thing I need is to let him all the way in, to get used to having his warmth and strength next to me in bed. It's going to be hard enough, getting used to being cold again once he leaves. Getting used to everything feeling smaller, less meaningful. I need to keep at least one part of my life separate from him.

"Good night, Liam," I say as I push through the door.

"Good night, Bay," he says as I close it behind me.

Chapter 16

LIAM

"Fucking hell, it's hot out here." I grab my shirt off the back of the lawn chair beside me and wipe it across my forehead.

Michael grabs his beer and takes a long swig, bobbing his head in agreement. "And just think, it's not even noon yet."

"Isn't it supposed to be fall soon? Isn't September all about things cooling down out here in Nowhere, USA?"

Michael flips me the bird. "Just wait. That'll come before you know it. One day it'll be ninety degrees, the next day it'll be fifty, and the day after that, you'll be sick." Michael takes another drink of his beer and sits it down next to his empties on the step leading into Bailey's house. "The magic of fall out here in the middle of nowhere." He exaggerates a thick country accent.

"Great." I crouch and slide a paver into place, the sound of stone grating against stone startling a tree full of birds. "Looking forward to it." I say as they take flight.

"Sure. I bet." Michael crouches beside me, level in hand, ready to tell me everything I did wrong setting this piece of the patio in place. "Not bad," he says as he runs the tool across the stone. "Just a little high in this corner."

"I had another conversation with Brent last night," I say as I stand.

Michael squints up at me. "How'd that go."

"About as well as it can go when you're dealing with an asshole like that." I wipe my hands on my jeans. "Actually, I'm really surprised. He wants to wait and see if anything else happens before we make any serious moves."

"What do you mean, *anything else*? Has stuff already been happening?"

"Yeah." I run a hand across my mouth. "There was an article on a local website that talked about me being seen at Smitty's. Brent managed to get that pulled and has been scouring the Internet for other stuff to pop up. Plus, I think someone's been going through the trash here."

"Oh, shit." Michael widens his eyes. "Does Bailey know?"

I shake my head. "Not yet."

"You sure that's smart?" Michael stands and wipes his forehead with the hem of his shirt. "I mean, you do know we're talking about my sister here, right? She's not a big fan of being kept in the dark about stuff."

"She definitely likes to be in control of a situation," I say, shaking my head. "I don't know, man." I shrug and then let a long breath out through my mouth. "Brent swears he's got it under control and who knows? Maybe he actually does. I just don't want to freak Bailey out if there's not a good reason."

Michael runs a hand through his hair. "Whatever you say. You're the one who has to deal with her. Not me." He crouches again, picking up the level. "You just let me know when you're ready to stop being a lazy ass so we can get back to work."

I shake my head. "Whatever, man."

It's been hard work, turning the pile of stone and sand Michael and I bought into a patio. Harder than I anticipated. Especially since we only get to make progress on Saturday and Sunday when Michael's off work. But the longer we're out here and the more the hole we dug in Bailey's backyard looks like a patio, the better I feel about it. We finish each day with my hands rubbed raw from sliding the rough stones into place, my back aching from all the lifting and squatting, my body drenched in sweat, but I feel magnificent. Better than I ever have stepping off any stage in any country.

In fact, while the high of performing is pretty

fucking amazing, there's always a low that follows it. Always. I can have the best show of my life, only to end up sitting alone in my apartment later that night, downing whiskey and feeling damn near worthless. Building this patio has been the exact opposite of that. Not only am I learning new things along the way—Michael really knows what he's doing and while he's kind of an ass about it, he's a great teacher—but at the end of the day, we have something real and permanent to show for our hard work. The roar of the audience, that goes away as soon as the lights go down. But the satisfaction I feel building this patio? All I need to do is step outside and see what I've accomplished to feel it again.

"Bailey wants me to do a show at Smitty's," I say, careful to avoid Michael's eyes.

"What?" He sits back on his heels and waits for me to look at him.

I explain her idea and wait for him to give me all the reasons it's bound to fail.

"Huh." He pulls the corners of his lips down and tilts his head to the side before giving a little nod. "That might actually work."

"You're full of shit." I sit down, my knees already screaming at me from all the crouching.

"I mean, it might backfire in a very real way, but this town loves its secrets and you know who loves feeling special? Everyone. That's who. And what better way to feel special than by getting a secret concert from a man who's been mostly naked on billboards all across the country?" He shrugs. "It's something to consider, anyway. Especially if you do it in your tighty-whities."

"Really?" I roll my eyes and ignore his underwear comment. "I just think it'll draw more attention to me. I mean, people are already talking about it. The moment I left the bar, the secret was out. And sure, Brent says he's on it, but that Derrick guy? He's already contacted my lawyers. I feel like I'm living on borrowed time here and a concert will only make it worse."

"It'll definitely draw more attention to you. Especially if you do it in your underwear." Michael reaches for his beer, takes a drink, and then holds up the empty bottle. "Of course, I'm on my way to drunk, so take everything I say with a grain of salt."

Trying not to make it obvious, I count the empties he's got lined up on the step. Five beers before noon and he's just now on his way to drunk. I've done my fair share of day-drinking, but Michael takes it to a whole new level. At first, I ignored it. Then, as I got to know him, I tried to tease him about it. And now, I get this sinking feeling in my stomach watching him get behind the wheel of his truck at the end of each day. I've tried to get him to stay for dinner, get some food and coffee into him before he takes off, but he's adamant about leaving before Bailey gets home.

Today, he's drinking even more than usual. As the

hours stretch on and the line of bottles on the step grows, dread takes a firm hold of my insides. There's no way I can let him get behind the wheel today. No fucking way.

"Hey. You wanna get some pizza tonight?" I ask. "My treat."

Michael lets his gaze drift off towards the line of trees in the back. "Nah. I'll probably be going soon." His words are slurred, just ever so slightly, but that's enough for me. I don't know how I'm going to pull it off yet because he's got the same stubborn streak I fight in Bailey all the time, but Michael is not getting behind the wheel of a car tonight.

"Come on, man. We'll get shitfaced and play cards or something." I grab the shovel from where it's leaning against the house and scoop some leveling sand out of the wheelbarrow.

Michael shakes his head and runs a hand over the back of his neck but doesn't say anything.

"Is that a yes?"

He holds up a finger. "That's a maybe."

"Aww. Come on. You know that's a yes." I stand, propping myself up with the handle of the shovel. "I can get Bailey to ask Lexi and that Michelle girl to come over. Maybe we can get them drunk enough to start up a game of strip poker."

Michael screws up his face. "Dude. That's my sister."

"Right." I bob my head. "So maybe just regular poker."

Michael hesitates.

"How can you even consider turning that down? Do you know how many people would actually pay to eat pizza and play cards with me?" I run a hand through my hair and laugh. "Shit. For that matter, do you know how many people have paid to eat pizza and play cards with me?" I give him a look to let him know I'm trying to be funny.

He turns to me, his eyes distant. "I don't really like being here. And Bailey..." He trails off, frowning. "There's just a lot of history here."

I know better than to ask for more details, but fuck, am I ever tired of the Schultz siblings dropping hints about their troubled past that they then expect me to ignore. "But you'll stay." I nod as if it's a done deal.

"Dude. You're stubborn enough to be a Schultz."

"Nah. But you Schultz's are almost stubborn enough to be a McGuire."

I shoot a text to Bailey, explaining what's going on and asking her to see if the girls want to come over tonight. Her response is almost instant.

Bailey: You got him to stay?

Me: Yep. He was no match to my battle-hardened charm.

Bailey: Get over yourself, McGuire. You're not that charming.

Me: You can pretend to fight it all you want, but you know I'm charming as hell. I smile at my phone, imagining the way she's bound to be shaking her head and smiling at my not-so-humble self right now.

Bailey: So … pizza, poker, more beer, and then get him to sleep it off on the couch?

I smile, pleased that she knew exactly what was in my head without me having to say anything.

Me: That's the plan.

There's a long pause and I assume she got called away by a patient or doctor needing her to assist in the many medical miracles that make up her every day. Just as I slide my phone into my back pocket, it buzzes again and I pull it out without hesitation.

Bailey: Thank you. I worry about him.

Me: I know. Now you get back to work saving lives and I'll go back to being my amazing self over here with your brother.

By the time Bailey gets home, Michael and I are showered, shaved, and looking good. I tried to get him to slow down on the beer and succeeded enough to ensure that he's still on his feet and holding coherent conversations. I'll take it as a win even though I would have preferred he switch to water a few hours ago. I know why people drink as much as he does. He's hiding from something that hurts. Bad. When Bailey's truck rumbles up the driveway, gravel popping and crunching under the tires, Michael frowns.

"Wow. It's like time stands still in this place." He sighs, drawing his dark eyebrows together. "Do you know how many years I've heard that same truck coming up that same driveway sounding exactly like that?" Michael shudders and shakes his head.

Bailey fumbles with the door and pushes through, the rustle of plastic bags and rattling keys coming right in with her. "Oh, goodness no," she says, struggling with the door. "Don't you two bother yourselves to get up. I got this."

I leap up off the couch and take the pizza out of her hands while Michael settles into the couch, crossing his legs. "Dude," he says, looking at me like I'm the jerk. "She said she had it."

The urge to take her into my arms and kiss her until she can't breathe is so strong I can't think through it, but since we both have our hands full and her brother is here, I settle for blowing her a kiss when he's not looking.

"Sure," I say to Michael on my way to the kitchen. "But that doesn't mean I can't be a decent human being and help out anyway."

"You just like making me look bad," grumbles Michael.

"Of course I do," I say over my shoulder. "But you don't have to make it so easy for me."

As soon as we're out of the living room, I drop the pizza on the counter and pull Bailey in for a kiss. "I missed you," I whisper when I'm done.

Her features soften and she smiles but she looks away from me, trying to hide whatever it is she's really feeling. "I bet you did," she says, finally meeting my eyes.

"I hear you in there," Michael calls from the living room. "You guys are terrible at keeping this thing a secret."

I swoop Bailey into my arms and carry her out of the kitchen while she squeals and laughs. "Who says we want to keep it a secret?" I kiss her deeply, loving the way her body feels in my arms.

"Dude. Whatever." Michael laughs nervously, his smile tense and small until he meets Bailey's eyes. Then his whole face warms. "As long as you're happy, I don't care what you do, I guess. Although maybe it was better when you were doing it in the kitchen."

Lexi shows up with Michelle and the night disappears in a series of too many drinks and lots of laughter. I swear there's something in the way Michael looks at Lexi, the way his eyes linger on her face when he thinks she's not looking.

"Do you see that?" I ask Bailey while I'm helping her refill everyone's drinks.

"See what?" Bailey leans into me, a little too drunk to be pouring herself another.

"The way Michael looks at Lexi."

She glances up, surprise dancing across her face. "You see it too? I thought I was imagining it. Wishful thinking and all that." She lowers her voice to a loud whisper. "Could you imagine if they got together? Every weekend could be like this. All of us hanging out here, bringing life back to this old house. Lexi could be so good for him." She sighs, her eyes unfocused and filled with daydreams. "Thank you for getting him to stay," she says after a bit.

"I couldn't let him leave. He had a lot to drink today," I say, hoping she doesn't see the way her words affected me. Every weekend? If Brent can't get things under control, I might not have many weekends here left. But she looks so happy, I can't bring any of that up now.

Bailey waves her hand and shakes her head, dismissing the reason I asked Michael to stay. "Whatever your motive, thank you. He's here. He's safe." She shrugs. "I know it's only one night, but I feel like I'm on the way to getting my brother back. It means a lot."

Laughter explodes from the living room. "You guys can stop making out in the kitchen and bring us our drinks already," calls Lexi.

"Damn it, McGuire!" Michael laughs while Michelle giggles. "Keep your damn hands off my sister!"

Bailey smiles at me, looking happier than she has in the month I've been here, and gathers the drinks onto a tray. "Thank you," she mouths.

I slap her on the ass as she heads to the living room. "I'm sure you'll think of some way to repay me," I say, dropping her a wink as she bites her lip and smiles over her shoulder.

Chapter 17

BAILEY

"I can't believe you talked me into this." My hands shake as I try to apply another coat of mascara.

"Talked *you* into this?" Liam takes the applicator from my hand. "I feel like I was adamantly against the whole idea. Hell, I might still be adamantly against the whole idea. Remind me again how we decided a concert in front of the whole town is supposed to create *less* exposure for me?"

I don't have the ability to fight him on this right now. Never, ever in my whole life have I been this nervous. "I've never sung in front of people before. This whole audience deal? It's bad news." I try not to blink as Liam expertly applies the last coat of mascara for me. "Do I even want to know how you know how to do that?" I ask, waving towards the brush.

"Show business, hot lips," he says as if that explains

everything and then screws the applicator back into the tube. "Here's the thing, your body reacts to anxiety and excitement the exact same way. Instead of focusing on the fear, the negative stuff, focus on how exciting it's going to be to sing with me." He puts a hand on my back. I'm sure it's supposed to be reassuring, but he's so warm and I'm already sweating. It feels like he's scorching his handprint onto my skin.

"There's nothing exciting about this." I look up at him, eyes wide. "You're right. It's all a terrible idea. We should cancel and you should call Brent and make all of this go away."

Liam laughs and studies his face in the mirror they set up especially for us in the cramped manager's office at Smitty's. "You want to know what's worse than trying to talk fans into keeping a secret? Trying to keep fans from getting really mad when you promise them a secret concert of exclusive songs and then pull a no-show."

I suck in my lips. "I really don't think I can do this." My dinner is tap dancing in my stomach right now. "I have to pee again. What if I pee my pants while we're singing?"

"You can try to go again if you want, but if you already went you can chalk that feeling up to nerves. I promise you aren't going to pee while we're singing."

"But how can you know that?"

"Trust me, Bailey. I might not know much about building a patio, but when it comes to pre-performance jitters, some might consider me an expert." Liam straightens and pulls me into his arms. "You can do this. I have total faith in you."

"What if it's a bad idea? What if I was totally wrong and instead of calming everyone down about you being in Brookside, it just revs everyone up? What if it turns into paparazzi central out here like it did when you were in the hospital?" My voice rises in pitch while I speak until it's practically inaudible.

"We're a little late to be worrying about that now." He brushes my hair back off my face. "Besides. As much as I fought the idea at first, I really think you're right. Something personal like this, something so different from what people are used to from me..." He nods. "This will help make me more real. Less of a personality, a cardboard cutout, and more of a person. It could go a long way towards making people more accepting of me staying here in Brookside."

"Normally, I'd have a slew of questions about the whole 'you staying in Brookside' deal, but I can't think straight enough to ask them right now." I bite my bottom lip and stare at the door, wondering how many people are on the other side.

Liam puts a finger to my chin and pulls my lip out from between my teeth. "You'll ruin your lipstick," he says. "Now, look at me. Right into my eyes and don't look away." He waits for me to do as he said. "You've so got this. Not just in a little way, but in a great big, no doubt about it kind of way. You're more than capable of standing out there and singing with me."

"Not like this—"

Liam puts a finger to my lips, careful not to touch my lipstick, and shushes me. "Yes. Like this. It's just the one song. And it's your song. You wrote it. I just embellished it. Five minutes, max. And then you're done. All you have to do is stand up there and look me in the eyes. It's me and you and that's it."

"And all the rest of Brookside." My gaze darts to the door again. "Listening to a song I never intended anyone to hear."

"Just me and you. No one else." Liam kisses me on the forehead just as applause breaks out on the other side of the door. "That's our cue, hot lips."

Without waiting for me to say anything, Liam leads me out into the bar while people clap and scream his name. Amidst the ruckus, I catch sight of my brother sitting next to Lexi and Michelle. He cups his hands around his mouth and bellows my name loud enough to overwhelm the rest of the voices screaming and calling out. The people around him turn and stare and he gives them his best shit-eating grin.

"I'm so glad you guys could join us tonight." Liam smiles out over the crowd and somewhere in the back, a woman shrieks his name. He laughs, totally at ease, and lifts a hand. "The music you're gonna hear tonight is all brand new stuff. Stuff I wrote. Stuff you're probably not used to hearing from me but I hope you'll like it all the same."

He takes a seat behind the piano Smitty's brought in just for this occasion and gestures for me to join him. The audience goes quiet and my hands shake as I hold them over the keys. Liam leans into me, bumping his shoulder against mine, and then plays the first notes.

I close my eyes, trying to find the music inside me. My poor, shaking fingers miss a few chords. The ugly notes rake across my skin and set my nerves on fire. Liam leans into me again and I open my eyes, look up at him, and the rest of the world fades away. He sings, his words just for me, a smile lighting his face. Chills run across my spine, goose bumps traveling out across my skin, an earthquake of emotion racing through my body, and shifting the bits and pieces that make me who I am.

My voice joins his, tentative at first, and then when his eyes soften and fill with love, I find the strength to let go and really sing. My body sways with the music, my heart and soul pouring out through the sound and filling the room with all my triumphs and all my sorrows. It's an admission of all that I am, all that I've been through, and all that I'll ever be.

Tears prick at my eyes and I don't know why, other than the fact that I am happy. Alive for the first time. I've found a part of myself I didn't know existed, sitting at this piano, with this man, baring my soul for a room filled with strangers. I brush my fingers against his and he melts into me, our bodies swaying together, our voices sweeping through the bar, twining into something so beautiful and harmonious that I can't imagine being the person I was before this moment ever again.

It's now, sitting at a piano, singing and playing and fighting tears, that I realize I'm falling in love with Liam. That I never want him to leave. That I'm better when I'm with him. That after all these years of struggling, I feel whole again.

The song ends and I sit in stunned silence, listening to the nothing that fills the bar. No applause. No cheers. Just me staring at Liam and Liam staring at me, and a bar full of people staring at us in turn. I swallow, afraid to turn and find them all sneering and laughing.

And then the applause starts.

"Bay. Look at them," Liam whispers.

I shake my head. "I can't."

"You have to."

And so I do.

The entire bar is on their feet, cheering and clapping, some wiping tears from their eyes with balled up napkins pulled from under their drinks. Liam helps me stand and I take an awkward bow before stumbling off the makeshift stage and collapsing in a breathless heap in a chair next to Lexi.

"I didn't know you could do that," she says to me, eyes wide and filled with wonder.

"Neither did I. Now excuse me a minute while I pass out."

Michael leans around Lexi and smiles, his face awestruck and filled with so much pride that I might burst. "That was fucking amazing, Bay." He puts a hand on my knee and gives it a squeeze.

I smile too, feeling it take root somewhere deep inside me and then grow and swell and fill me up with something that can only be joy. "Thanks." I swallow hard. "Now, I'm going to go get a drink before my heart explodes. It's pounding so hard I'm surprised you guys can't hear it."

The rest of the night passes with Liam holding the audience in the palm of his hand. The songs he sings are nothing at all like the ones on the radio. Where those are hollow, empty things designed to showcase his sex appeal, these are filled with all the million little things that make him who he is. And in that honesty, that reality, he's a thousand times more appealing than he ever has been. When I look around at the faces staring up at him, rapt, I see tiny echoes of all the things I feel. Tonight, these people get a peek at the real Liam McGuire, just a tiny little preview of the man behind the name, and they love him as much as I do. If ever he wondered what might happen if he dropped the pop star act and wanted to pursue his music without all the trappings of his stylists and PR teams, the answer is apparent in the people here tonight.

Liam can be anything he wants and these people will support him. His appeal isn't the image a team of stylists and publicists have built for him. *He* is the appeal. His talent. The light that shines in his eyes as he sings. The way he draws out the notes until you feel them resonating deep within your soul.

When he's done playing, people swarm him. He catches my eyes, his gaze piercing through the crowd and finding me as if I'm the only person in the room. He stands, smiling and holding up his hands in apology, as he pushes past the people around him and rushes to me. Sweeps me up in his arms. Kisses me while the crowd murmurs around us.

"You were magnificent," he says. "I'm so proud of you."

I stare up at that handsome face, lost in more emotion than I know what to do with. "You're amazing," I say when I want to say *I love you. I need you. I want you.*

Liam shrugs. "Pretty much." And then he drops me a wink, wraps his arm around my waist, pulls me close, and turns me towards the crowd.

"I can't believe people actually wanted my autograph." I sweep into my living room and drop onto the couch, rubbing the muscles in my jaw. "I smiled so much my cheeks hurt."

Liam sits next to me, beaming. "Ready for your next performance?"

"God, no." I run a hand through my hair. "That is just too much for me," I say as I lean into the arm of the couch and put my feet in his lap.

He pulls off my socks, using his strong thumbs to massage my arches. "You sure?" he asks as I moan and drop my head back. "You didn't seem to mind the attention while it was happening."

"I can't be sure of anything with you doing that," I say, letting my eyes slide closed.

"Oh yeah? What about this?" Liam leans forward and kisses my ankle.

"That feels surprisingly good."

"And what about this?" He kisses his way up my calf and stops at my knee.

"I don't know, it's hard to tell. My pants are definitely in the way." I lift my head off the back of the couch and meet his eyes.

"Well that won't do, now will it?" And with that, he undoes the button at my waist, slides down the zipper, and helps me wiggle out of my jeans. When I'm naked and stretched out on the couch in front of him, he kisses up along my inner thigh.

"What about that," he asks as I moan.

"That's good."

"And this?" He spreads my legs and draws his tongue across my clit.

"That's..." I lose the word as he lowers his mouth to me again. And then, after he's naked and hard and moving inside me, I lose myself completely.

Chapter 18

LIAM

"You staying for dinner tonight?" I wipe sweat off my forehead with my forearm as a cool breeze rustles through the trees behind the house. Fall has officially descended on Brookside and I'd go so far as to call it downright chilly. When it's not blazing hot. Michael was right. The weather here might be as drunk as he is.

"Probably." Michael stares at the dark clouds churning in gray skies. "You think we can get these last few pavers down before the rain comes?"

"We've only got one row left. I'll work in the rain if I have to."

"I don't know, man." Michael slides his hands into his pockets. "This looks like it'll be a pretty wicked storm."

"Then why don't you stop slacking off and get a move on? Lazy ass."

Michael shakes his head. "Imagine that. Liam McGuire calling me an ass." He smiles and puts his work gloves back on. "You think Lexi is gonna be here tonight?"

"It's a Saturday, isn't it?" I grunt as I slide a paver into place. "She and Michelle will both be here."

Michael doesn't respond, his face carefully expressionless. He can try and hide it all he wants, but he's got it bad for Lexi. So bad he's even been cutting back on the drinking on the nights he knows she's coming over. I teased him about it once but he got so defensive it wasn't worth it. I dropped that topic like a hot rock. Whatever's going on there, it's his business and he'll share when he's ready.

We slide the last paver in place just as the first fat raindrop drops out of the sky, leaving a big wet splotch on the stone at my feet. "We did it," I say, beaming.

"Almost. We still need to seal them in place, but the hard part's done."

The sky opens up on us, dropping a tsunami's worth of rain on Bailey's brand new, almost finished patio. I'm drenched before I can make it the few steps to the door.

"You're soaked!" Bailey looks up from a big pot of chili she's got simmering on the stove.

"But it's done." I shake water out of my hair.

"Like done, done?"

Michael wipes his hands. "Not completely. There's still one more step..."

"Whatever," I say, interrupting him. "You know how your brother likes to point out all the negative stuff. It's done enough that it looks like a patio." I grab Bailey's hand and pull her to the window, twisting open the blinds just in time for a streak of lightning to light up the sky.

"I can't believe you actually did it." Bailey looks up at me and I could eat up the adoration in her eyes. I'd build a thousand patios just to see her look at me like that again.

Michael clears his throat and pulls open the fridge. "Yeah. Sure. I'm totally glad to have helped."

Laughing, Bailey crosses the room and pulls her brother into a hug. He stiffens at first, but then softens, a smile pulling at the corners of his lips as the refrigerator door swings shut.

"Thanks, little brother." Her voice is barely a whisper, as if she's afraid speaking too loud will ruin the moment.

"It's all good, sis."

I turn my attention back to the window, watching the rain run between the pavers. There's more to the moment than just a patio. Whatever was broken between them has started to heal. I've watched it happen over the last several weeks, but this might be the first time I've seen them acknowledge it.

Or, I'm feeling sappy because the project will be finished tomorrow and I'm seeing hearts and rainbows everywhere.

"Lexi coming?" Michael asks Bailey.

"It's Saturday, isn't it?" She rolls her eyes and goes to check on the chili.

"Could you two be any more alike?" Michael shakes his head. "I'm gonna go get cleaned up."

"What was that all about?" Bailey asks as he leaves the kitchen.

"I gave him the exact same answer when he asked me if she was coming while we were outside."

Bailey lifts the spoon from the chili and blows on it. "He's got it bad, doesn't he?" She lowers her lips for a taste and then bobs her head, humming in approval before offering me a bite.

"Oh, damn woman. That's good." I take the spoon from her and help myself to another taste. "And Michael? He had it bad a month ago. Now he's just plain whooped."

"Can you just imagine if they got together? My brother and my best friend?" Baily grins.

"They'd be trouble together."

"That's for sure. But I think they'd be good together, too." Bailey's phone vibrates from its place on the counter and she reaches for it while I steal another spoonful of chili.

"Everything okay?" I ask.

Bailey reads the text. "Looks like Lexi and Michelle have to bring their kids. Flakey babysitter issues." She grimaces. "Think that'll ruin the night? Should we cancel?"

"For me? Hell no. I love little people. I always thought I'd make a great crazy uncle someday."

Bailey makes a face. "Just the idea of having kids freaks me out. Those few years when it was just me and Michael were enough of a preview that I'm not in any hurry to get that show on the road."

I nod, trying not to look overly interested. She never talks about the time after her parents died. Hell, after all this time, I still don't know how they died, only that it was sudden, tragic, and really did a number on her and her brother. It's funny. I'm falling hard for this woman. Fast. And I know so little about her past I wouldn't be able to pick out her story from a stranger's. Shouldn't I know all the things that make her who she is? Not just the little ones, but the big ones, too? And really, of the two, aren't the big ones the most important?

"What about for Michael?" she asks, interrupting my thoughts. "Think it'll be weird for him?"

"If he's the least bit interested in dating a single mom, he better get right about being around kids."

"Who's interested in dating a single mom?" Michael asks as he comes around the corner, all showered and shaved.

"Gee, I don't know," I reply, wrapping my arms around Bailey's waist and pulling her towards me, her back pressed against my front. "Who do I know who has it bad for a single mom?" I rest my chin on Bailey's head and grin at her brother, even as my mind keeps chewing on the realization that Bailey's still keeping herself separate from me.

Bailey twists out of my arms. "You're all wet from the rain, Liam. And look at that," she says, pointing at her brother. "Is that a blush I see happening right now?

I head down the hall to get cleaned up as Bailey and Michael laugh in the kitchen. I stop in my room—well, Michael's room really—and grab some clothes, pausing in front of Bailey's closed bedroom door. If we're falling for each other as hard as we seem, shouldn't I be allowed to go in her room? Maybe spend one night curled up against her? Wrapping my arms around her and breathing her in before we fall asleep? Isn't that part of being in love? Letting people into all the places that not everyone gets to see?

I shower and shave, the tattoos on my arms a reminder of who I used to be. Or who I really am, I'm not sure. Am I really done with that part of my life, or is this time here in Brookside with Bailey and her friends just a tiny blip of happiness in my otherwise miserable existence?

The fact that I don't readily know the answer to that question sends my stomach swirling down the drain with the water. If what we have is real, I need Bailey to open up to me. I need her to show me the parts of herself that she keeps hidden. And, for that matter, she needs to learn all the things I don't want people to know about me as well.

I'd rather she offer up the information without me

having to ask, but there really isn't any harm in asking. And really, maybe that's all she's been waiting for. For me to be interested enough to ask. Just as I make up my mind to bring up our pasts, thunder rattles the windows and someone shrieks in the kitchen. I laugh as I flip off the light in the bedroom. If I believed in signs, that one would be an ominous one indeed.

Chapter 19

BAILEY

"You're so lucky you weren't at work today." I maneuver my beast of a truck onto the road, inwardly cursing the lack of power steering.

"Yeah?" Lexi sounds distracted. "How come?"

"It was one of those days that makes you proud to be a nurse in the same instant that you regret it with every last ounce of your soul."

"Oh, no. What happened?"

"A school bus collided with a tractor."

"Oh God. Enough said." There's some noise on the other end of the line, some bumps and rustles. "How are you?"

"Tired. Ready to drop. But happy to know I helped save some lives." I flick on a turn signal and throw my weight into the steering wheel. "What are you doing?"

"Getting ready." Lexi sniffs. "Are you going to be okay? I know how those kinds of days stick with you."

"Yeah. I'll be fine." I shiver and burrow deeper into my sweater. I don't know if it's because of the chill in the air or the memory of the day. "What are you getting ready for? It's seven o'clock on a Friday and Gabe doesn't have play dates this late."

"About that..."

My eyebrows meet my hairline. "Something tells me I'm either going to love or hate what you're about to tell me."

Lexi clears her throat, a sure sign she's nervous. "I'm going out with Michael tonight."

"Michael, as in my brother Michael?"

"Yep." Lexi pops the *p* at the end of the word.

"I knew it! I told Liam just the other day that you guys would be dating before the first snowfall."

"You're not mad?" Lexi couldn't sound more relieved if I told her I won the lottery and would pay for every last thing Gabe needed for the rest of his life.

"Why in the world would I be mad? My best friend and my brother? I'm thrilled!"

"I just know how rocky things have been between you and Michael. I'd hate to get in the way now that you guys are on the way to fixing whatever was broken between you."

"How could you get in the way? Lex! It's like..." I pause and chew on my bottom lip. "I'm almost afraid to say it out loud. In case I jinx it."

"I get it." A smile warms Lexi's voice. "With things between you and Liam going so well and with Michael being at the house almost every weekend..."

"It's like the curse is broken." I say it all in one long rush, desperate to have the thought out of my head and terrified that saying something will mess things up.

Lexi laughs. "There is no such thing as curses, Bay."

"Says the woman who's never had to live with one." Water droplets fall from the still wet trees and I turn on my windshield wipers to wipe them away. "I'll let you go so you can get ready in peace."

We say our goodbyes and I drop my phone in the seat beside me, finishing the drive home feeling lighter than I have in a long time. Lexi will be good for Michael. Maybe help him cut down on the drinking. It's been hard, the last few years, watching him drown his hurt in alcohol. There have been so many times I've wanted to say something, but pain is pain, and Michael is Michael, and who am I to judge how he deals with it? Especially when he's made it so obvious he blames me for everything.

When I pull into my driveway, all the windows on the front of the house are dark and it sets my nerves on edge. I've gotten used to coming home and having to remind Liam that the lights do come equipped with off switches and that electricity costs us peasants money. Where could he be? Obviously, he's not out with Michael, and the only other people he knows around here are Lexi and Michelle. I hope he's not sick.

Disappointment and worry churn in my stomach as I climb out of the truck. The wind blows, sending a chill shivering down my spine and catching several pieces of paper that go dancing out across the yard. Looks like the trash bins have been knocked over again, although the wind doesn't seem strong enough to be the culprit. I think a family of raccoons must have moved in nearby. It seems like every other day lately, I'm coming home to find my house looking like a junkyard.

After righting the bins and chasing down the random bits of paper floating around the yard, I slide my key into the lock and push inside the house, surprised to find it not fully dark, but lit with a faint, warm light instead. Every surface has at least four candles on it, the flames flickering in the breeze coming through the open door. My stomach growls as I smell food, and damn if the table isn't set for two, with several unopened Styrofoam containers covering the counter behind it. Music comes from the den. Liam at the piano. The song is achingly familiar even though I don't recognize the melody.

I close the door behind me and drop my purse on the floor as Liam begins to sing. I follow the sound, a sailor caught in the siren's song, and wander into the den. I cross the room and lean on the piano, staring down at Liam's fingers dancing around the keys.

It's not until I hear my name, followed by a few dissonant chords chased away by a melody so soulful that it takes my breath away that I understand what I'm hearing. This is a song he wrote for me, inspired by the first time we had sex. My ass on the piano, the keys crying out with each thrust of his hips. My jaw drops as I meet his gaze, his eyes twinkling with wicked humor. The song is beautiful and raw, just the way we are when we're together.

"I think I'll die if I ever hear that on the radio," I say when he's done.

"Nothing to fear there. The powers that be won't let this anywhere near my brand."

I furrow my brow. "Maybe you should stop worrying about your brand and just be who you are."

Liam locks his gaze on mine. "Sounds easy enough, except I'm starting to realize I don't even know who I am."

"I think I do." I pull him up from the bench, thread my fingers into his hair, and pull him in for a kiss. "And I think I like you." I kiss him again. "Actually, I know I like you." Another kiss. "Yep. I definitely like you."

Liam presses his forehead to mine. "Good. I definitely like you, too."

"Liam?"

"Yeah?" He slides his hands up under my shirt, dragging his fingernails across my skin.

"I'm hungry."

He leans down, kissing along my jaw, nuzzling into my neck. "Me too," he whispers.

"For food." I press my hands into his chest and look up at his startled face. "Well, for you too," I admit. "But food first."

Laughing, Liam leads me into the kitchen and proudly points to all the food on the counter. "I know better than to think I can cook anything worth a damn, but I wanted you to come home to a warm meal."

I survey the spread as my mouth waters. "How am I ever going to choose?" I ask as I open each container in turn. "These are all my favorites!"

"I know. Michael helped me decide what to order." Liam takes a plate out of the cabinet and starts scooping large spoonfuls of everything onto it.

"I like thinking of you two hanging out all day." I wonder if Liam knows Michael and Lexi are going out.

"He's a good guy, your brother. But I think it hurts him to be here." His gaze flickers my way and I search his face for any sign that he might know why Michael doesn't like being at this house.

Relieved to see nothing but a question, I take my plate and sigh. "It does." I sit and pick up my fork. "For the same reason it hurts me."

Liam lowers his fork. "And why's that?"

I stab at the piles of delicious food, suddenly certain it'll all taste like sawdust and utterly regretting my brief moment of honesty. "I don't know."

Liam eyes me as I pick at my food and then reaches

over to squeeze my hand. "It's okay," he says. "You don't have to talk about it." He swallows hard. "But I'd like it if you would."

"I want to talk about it. You deserve to know." I suck in my lips and close my eyes. "It's just hard."

"I understand. I'm here and I can't imagine one thing you could possibly say that would change how I feel about you." He squeezes my hand again and doesn't let go until I open my eyes.

"My boyfriend killed himself the summer after we graduated high school." I blurt the sentence out before I have a chance to change my mind. "I was coming over to surprise him with an invitation to a party and heard the gunshot. Like an idiot, I ran towards it. Into his house. Found him slumped over the note he wrote to his parents. Blood was everywhere."

"My God," says Liam, his eyes roving my face.

"I never even knew he was depressed." I shake my head, the grief and blame settling easily into place. "We were together for almost two years and I didn't have a single clue that he was struggling with depression."

Liam looks like he wants to say something, but I hurry forward, the weight of the story bearing down on me.

"I was devastated. So what did I do? Instead of going home, I ran away. Like an idiot, I went to the party in Grayson alone and drank myself into oblivion. I called my parents and told them I was too drunk to drive. I remember my mom sobbing into the phone, just glad to know I was okay." I poke at the food on my plate and glance at Liam. "Tyler's mom had called with the news and no one knew where I was. Obviously, everyone had spent the day scared to death. Mom made me promise not to go anywhere and she and Dad hopped in her car to come get me at three in the morning. A truck full of drunk teenagers coming home from the very same party I was at swerved over the line and hit them head on. My mom died instantly, but my dad held on." My voice cracks under the weight of it all. "He made me promise to take care of Michael. To keep the house up so he had a home to finish growing up in. To take care of his truck. I don't know why he cared so much about that thing..." I trail off, my voice trembling.

"No wonder the whole town finds your life fascinating." Liam looks so solemn that I let out a sound that's starts as laughter but opens the floodgates to my sorrow.

He stands and pulls me to my feet, draws me in close and wraps his arms around me. I dissolve into tears while he rocks and shushes me, running his hand through my hair. I wait for him to tell me it's not my fault, but he never does. He just lets me cry until I'm done and then pulls me into his lap, cradling me like a child. The tears are bitter. They burn my eyes and cheeks, pulled out of the darkest part of my soul, coated with the fire and ice of guilt and sorrow.

"Did you know I tried to kill myself once?" Liam's words are thick, coated in the same pain as my tears.

I twist in his arms to meet his eyes.

"Of course you don't," he says. "Brent and his team of PR magicians made sure the story never hit the news."

"But why?" I ask, devastated to know he ever harbored so much sorrow that he couldn't see another way through it.

His expression darkens. "Can you imagine what would happen if that kind of stuff got out to the public?"

"That's not what I mean. I don't give two shits about Brent and that stupid PR team. Why did you try to kill yourself?"

Liam blinks slowly but holds my gaze. "Because for all the people who know my name, my face... Hell, for all the people who can even recognize me by tattoos alone, no one—not one single person—has a clue as to who I really am."

"I do." I wipe my eyes and take his face in my hands.

Liam nods once. "You do." He runs a thumb along my cheek, a secret smile playing across his mouth. "But here's the thing, hot lips. No one knew I'd been thinking about it for weeks. I spend my days surrounded by people and no one knew." He raises his eyebrows and peers into my eyes. "Not because they weren't paying attention, but because I didn't want them to."

I shake my head. "Yeah, but it's different. Tyler and I were close. I should have seen the signs..." I trail off. Liam can try to make me feel better all he wants, but that's not going to change the fact that I know all of this is my fault. If I'd only been paying attention, my entire life would look different.

"And I guarantee that he did everything in his power to hide those signs from you. If he truly wanted to die, there wasn't much you could have done to stop him."

I bury my face in his shoulder. There's nothing he can say to make me think this mess isn't my fault. Lexi and I have been on the same merry-go-round for years.

"You lost all three of them on the same day?" Liam asks.

"August fourth." I swallow and sniff. "Well, my dad held on until the next day. But we knew he was lost the moment he came out of surgery."

He nods his understanding, no doubt remembering the night I came home and woke him up playing the piano.

"And I lost Michael shortly after." For as much as the memories hurt me, it feels good to talk about it, like some of the pressure building up inside has been released.

Liam runs a hand through my hair, smoothing it back off my forehead. "He doesn't look too lost to me."

"You should have seen the kid he used to be. He's lost and it's my fault. I'm cursed or something," I say, admitting my deepest fear. "I bring tragedy to the people who love me." The words are raw and rake across my throat.

Liam puts a finger to my chin and lifts my gaze to his. "I'm going to call bullshit on that right now. You're not cursed."

"How do you know?"

"Because I love you and you've been nothing but a blessing to me."

As if my emotions weren't already trying to run off with my sanity. "What did you say?" I whisper the words, frozen in place.

"I love you, Bailey. I don't know when it happened. Hell, I certainly didn't mean for it to happen, but it did. Somewhere between you hating my guts and telling me my music sucked and me hitting some guy in the face for looking at you wrong, I fell in love with you. No one has ever been as real with me as you are. No one has ever made me laugh like you do, challenged me like you do. I mean, you've got me thinking really weird things, things I don't know what to do with. Like wondering how I could protect you. Provide for you. The fact that you didn't let me put money into the patio infuriates me because I want to give you everything you've ever wanted. And that's how I know you're not cursed. Because I love you that much, and every day I spend with you is better than the last."

Every thought I could possibly have is flying around inside me, bumping into more emotion than I have the capacity to understand. His words fill me up, lift me towards the sky like a daydream on a cloud as fear clamps its steely talons around my ankles and pulls me down towards the mud. I stare into his eyes, a smile pulling at my lips as tears roll down my cheeks. "And that scares me more than anything," I say as my soul cries out the words I wish I could say:

I love you.

I want him to hear it, to know it, to smile down at me and kiss the words from my lips. But my throat grows tight and my teeth clamp down, my lips pressed into a thin line.

"I know you're afraid to say it," he says. "I know you're afraid that if you tell me how you feel that you're going to pull me into this curse you think you have hanging over you. But I'm going to prove to you that you're not cursed just like I had to prove to myself that I could build you that patio..." His eyes go wide. "Oh! Come see!"

Liam helps me to my feet, takes me by the hand, and leads me to the back door.

"You finished!" I step outside and turn to look at him as he leans in the doorway. "I have a patio!"

Liam scrunches up his face. "You have a flat square of pavers that I refuse to call a patio. But we finished just inside your budget, so you should be really proud of me."

I rush into his arms. "I am," I say. "It looks so great. I love it." I pause, looking up into his eyes. "I love you."

The words are hushed, barely more than a whisper. Something I've known for a while but hadn't admitted, a truth that terrifies me.

"Did you just say you love me?" Liam wraps his arms around my waist. "Is that what I think I just heard?"

I nod. "Maybe."

"Say it again." He peppers my face with kisses.

"You first." I can barely get the words out past my laughter.

Liam scoops me up into his arms, carries me inside and, while I shriek and squeal and kick my legs, he makes a beeline straight for my bedroom. He pauses at the closed door, having never been invited inside.

"In here?" he asks, as if he understands the gravity I've attached to something as silly as letting him in my room.

"In here."

He pushes through the door and spreads me out on my bed, pinning my wrists to the mattress and kissing me deeply. "I love you," he whispers as he trails kisses down my jaw.

"I love you," he whispers as he pulls my shirt over my head.

"I love you," he whispers when he slides himself inside me.

He moves and my world shifts to make room for

him, the cracks in my heart filled by his voice, his strength, his passion. My back arches and I grip the sheets, balling them up tightly in my fists.

"Look at me, Bailey," he says, his words barely more than a growl.

I don't just meet his eyes, I fall into them. Tumbling over the edge, erasing the line that delineates me from him, blurring it until there's simply us.

Chapter 20

LIAM

"You know what this place needs?" I sit back in my chair at the kitchen table, my coffee gripped between both hands, and study the worn cabinets and dated appliances.

Bailey sighs. "For you to find something to do during the day so you stop coming up with home improvement projects I can't afford?" She leans forward and gives me a sad smile.

"I could completely redo this kitchen for you. It can't be that hard, can it?" I drum my fingers along the side of the ceramic mug. "And I bet Michael knows how to do it cheaply."

"Liam." Bailey sets her coffee down heavily. "Every last dollar I had to spend is sitting out there in that patio. I have zero disposable income right now. Literally zero."

"I know." I offer her my most winning smile because she's not going to like what I say next. "But"—I hold up a finger and raise my eyebrows—"I could pay for this next project."

Bailey shakes her head. "I don't want your money. I just want you. And your..." She blushes and points to my crotch, biting her lip and looking adorable.

"You can say the word *cock*, you know. You are officially an adult. And a nurse, no less. The human anatomy shouldn't make you blush."

"I know. Maybe I just like hearing you say dirty words."

I widen my legs, giving her a better view...

Damn it.

I know exactly what she's doing.

"You know you can't distract me with sex every time I start talking about things you don't want to discuss," I say as I cross my legs primly.

"You sure?" Bailey giggles. "It's been working pretty well so far."

"I'm not trying to buy your love, you know," I say after a long drink of coffee.

A devilish smile quirks the corners of her lips. "Good. It's not for sale."

Bailey gets up from the table and comes around to me. I open my arms and she slides into my lap, resting her head on my chest. It's a habit she started after the night I finished the patio. Every day before she leaves for work, she curls up in my arms and closes her eyes.

Neither of us says a word, but I run a hand over her back and can feel her soften into me, her body melting into mine. Today, I kiss the top of her head, breathing in the scent of her shampoo.

"Promise you'll be here when I come home?" she murmurs before pressing herself up to meet my eyes.

"I can't think of anywhere else I want to be more."

When Bailey leaves for work, the wind that blows through the open door is downright cold. It's been a long time since I've lived through a real fall, with the leaves changing colors and the chill sneaking into the air. I've loved every second of it and now that the leaves are falling from the trees and the days are ending earlier and earlier, I'm curious to find out how I'll handle the cold of winter.

There's a part of me, a tiny voice in my head, that wonders if I'll even get a chance to handle it at all. Now that the patio is done, there's no real purpose for me to be here. I can't stop worrying that Bailey is going to kick me out. There isn't one reason for me to think that. She hasn't given me any indication that she wants me to be anywhere but right here with her. But knowing something is true doesn't always make it easy to believe in that truth. As much as I remind myself that Bailey isn't like most people, that she wants me for me and not what I can do for her, I keep ending up right back here, looking for ways to make myself useful so she doesn't lose interest in me.

Needing a distraction, I grab my phone out of the

living room and call Michael.

"What's up?" He bites off his greeting, hungover and grumpy on his way to work.

"Just wanted to chat."

"Dude. You need a job. You're getting hella needy."

"That's what I'm calling about. I want to redo Bailey's kitchen."

Michael sighs and I hear the click of his turn signal through the phone. "There's no way she can afford that, man."

I lean on the counter and wrap an arm around my stomach. "Believe me. I'm very aware of her financial situation. She won't let me forget it."

"Bailey's been doing stuff on her own for a long time. It's like her personal badge of honor or something. She's not going to let you pay for a new kitchen as long as the old one is still in working order."

"What if she doesn't have a choice?" I suck in my lips and stare at the pock-marked linoleum floor.

"Dude. Bailey always has a choice. Just ask her."

"What if I go ahead and do it for her?" I grimace, picturing Bailey's eyes flashing in anger. Those hands, balled up into tight fists and pushed into her hips as she shifts her weight back on her heels to really let me have it.

Michael laughs. "Do you even know my sister at all?"

"I mean, sure, she'll be mad at first, but she'll get

over it. Right?" Even I can hear the uncertainty in my voice.

"I'm just saying. If it were me, I'd wait until she asked for help before I did anything."

I run my hand along the back of my neck. "Why is she so damn stubborn?"

There's a long pause before Michael speaks again. "Probably the only way she got this far." He clears his throat. "Look, man. I'm in dire need of coffee. I'm gonna say goodbye so I can run into this gas station."

We say our goodbyes and I hang up with a sigh, sliding the phone into my back pocket. And just like that, the anxiety-riddled thoughts creep right back in. Now that Bailey has no use for me, what with the patio being done and all, why keep me around? Sure, she loves me, but our relationship is brand new. Living together is kind of pushing it. Besides, how long can she love me if I'm not doing anything for her?

Lately, I've made sure the dishes are done before she gets home from work so she doesn't have those waiting for her. I've been dusting and cleaning and straightening everything up so much that I don't think the house has been this clean since long before her parents passed away. I even make sure she has warm meals waiting for her every night when she gets home. Hell, one evening I tried cooking dinner myself.

I won't be doing that again.

She ate it all with a smile on her face. Even asked for seconds. But that's because she's sweet and more concerned about my feelings than her taste buds. The meal was awful, equal parts underdone and burned.

When I first got here, I loved sitting still for extended periods of time, but that didn't last long. Not at all. There hasn't been a time since my mom started aiming me towards stardom that I haven't been insanely busy. And it's not even that I crave the work it's just that I crave the ... what? What is it I'm missing?

Being needed?

Being wanted?

Being useful?

My stomach drops to my feet and I push off the counter to clean up the dishes from breakfast. That's it right there. The answer to what's bothering me.

Now that I'm not useful, why would Bailey want me? The thought joins forces with the black coffee churning in my stomach and I feel a little queasy. With a groan, I run my hands over my face and puff out my cheeks. All this introspection proves that I really do spend too much time alone and I need something to occupy my time.

I know she's told me time and time again not to use my money on her house and I still don't understand why. Now that she has me, she doesn't have to do things alone anymore. I wish she would lean into me a little bit, let me hold her up when her days get hard. Shit, at this point, it would feel like a privilege if she admitted she didn't have everything she wanted and let me take care of her.

I slap my hands on the table and scoot my chair back. It scrapes across the tile and the harsh noise sounds like a decision. Bailey might think she doesn't want me to spend my money on her, but that's only because she hasn't lived that life yet. She doesn't know what it means to let me spoil her the way I want to. The way she deserves.

Like it or not, I'm going to renovate the hell out of her kitchen. That woman—*my woman*—has no idea what's in store for her. She'll come home one day to marble countertops and gleaming appliances. To new plates and silverware and glasses. She'll have plenty of space to work and bake and cook. And when I'm done with the kitchen, I'll get to work on the bathroom. Shit! I'll even get a second one added on. When I'm done with this house, there will be so little of her parents left here, she won't have a reason to be sad anymore.

I grab my iPad and start pacing the kitchen, Googling ideas and trying to figure out where in the hell I need to start. It would be easier to call a contractor and let the professionals do everything, but I want to do this myself. I want to prove to her that I have worth. That there's more to me than a pretty face. More than a brand. That I'm more than a name. That the person buried deep under years of PR and branding is worth a damn.

This stupid kitchen is too dark. Is there room for a skylight up there? As I twist to look at the ceiling, movement catches my eye in the backyard. My jaw tenses. My iPad hits the counter with a clatter as I put both hands on the laminate and lean in towards the window, twisting open the blinds just a little more to get a better view of who's out there.

It's a woman. Or a girl, really. Someone right on the line between childhood and adulthood. She's got her cell phone out, ready to take a picture at a moment's notice as she creeps forward on tiny, catlike steps towards the window in the den.

She hasn't seen me yet. Her focus is split between the window and her phone. She stops every few steps to tap out a text, giggling at the screen. With a sigh, I crank the blinds closed and take a seat at the kitchen table. I can't believe she's out here in the daylight. The upended trash cans were one thing. Suspecting that people were out there in the dark somehow felt less threatening, less real. No matter how much I assumed people were snooping around, there was always a part of me that wondered if maybe it was a family of raccoons. But now? Seeing that girl out in the middle of the day? There's no running away from reality with her right in front of my face.

There's only one reason she's here and that reason is me. And that sucks because enough time has passed between our little performance at Smitty's and now that I had actually begun to believe my fans would leave us alone. That as idiotic and counter-intuitive as the idea had sounded, it had worked. I should have known better, but every time I called Brent, he kept telling me not to worry. I guess I just wanted everything to work out so badly that I let myself believe it had.

But people being here? That's just not okay. The last thing Bailey needs is to have her life upended by crazy fans snooping around her house and digging through her trash. She doesn't need the paparazzi crowding her as she leaves for work, snapping pictures when she least expects it. I've got to put a stop to this before it becomes a real problem.

I shift in my seat to pull my phone out of my pocket, my hands moving on muscle memory as I pull up Brent's information and initiate the call. My stomach churns just seeing his name, let alone his contact picture with his sleek hair and oily smile.

"Liam! Baby! How are you? You were on my list of people to call today, you beautiful bastard." He sounds like he's ecstatic to hear from me. Which he probably is. I can hear the dollar signs cha-chinging through his mind from here.

"We've got a problem." I stand, careful to keep the chair quiet against the tile, and head back towards Bailey's bedroom, filling him in on the concert at Smitty's and reminding him about everything that's been happening around here. "And now," I say as I perch on the edge of Bailey's bed. "Now there's a girl stalking around outside the house. Phone out. Snooping around. Get PR on the phone. Handle this. Now."

When Brent speaks, the disdain in his voice is

evident. "I'm sorry, man. But there's no amount of PR that can fix this. Are you insane? You sang for them? Gathered them all up into a shitty bar and sang for them? Why didn't you tell me this sooner?"

"Because you seemed so sure that you had everything handled." I close my eyes. "Because I wanted to believe I could stay here."

Brent laughs. "You don't get to lead anything resembling a normal life. You need to get a handle on whatever existential crisis you think you're having and face the facts. You, my friend, are fucking *royalty*. And royalty doesn't get to hang out with the peasants because it's always just a matter of time before the *fucking* peasants go *fucking* crazy."

I can just see the spittle flying out of his mouth as he yells into the phone.

"I'm not coming back to LA," I say, dropping onto the bed and picking a picture of Bailey's parents up off the bedside table.

"So, what are you going to do? Just sit there and let the whole town work themselves into a Liam McGuire-fueled frenzy? Let that bitchy nurse handle the crowds gathering at her doorstep? She might have enough attitude to make them think twice about swarming past her to get to you, but how long until she gets tired of dealing with it? How long before she kicks your pampered ass right out? And then what? It's time for a reality check, my friend. You'll be coming back here sooner or later. Might as well skip all the drama and just come home."

I stare at the strangers in the picture I'm holding, a man with Bailey's eyes and a woman with her smile. "You're not my friend," I say.

"Fine. I'm not your friend. But that doesn't mean I don't have your best interest at heart. Someone needs to look after you, especially if you won't do it yourself. And apparently, that someone is me."

I don't have anything to say. My thoughts swirl around in my head, a swarm of angry bees and hornets and snakes and whatever other vile things gather in disgusting places. Is he right? Is it only a matter of time before Bailey gets tired of what my life is and kicks me out? Is this just the beginning of the end? Would it be better to leave now before what we have gets ruined by the shit-storm that's about to come crashing down on our heads?

I can't bring myself to believe that. What Bailey and I have runs deep. I can feel it rooted in the most basic parts of who I am, bits and pieces of her anchored to my soul.

"Look, man." Brent's voice is hard and harsh, the whitewash of his congeniality crumbling as we speak. "I'm not saying you have to like it," he continues. "I'm just saying that in the end, your only course of action is to come back to LA. Bring the girl with you if you have to. Get her out of that shit town and show her what the real world looks like." He sighs and I can just imagine him staring out of the wall of floor-to-ceiling windows in his office, one hand pinching the bridge of his nose, the other pressing his phone to his ear. "You just need to get real honest, real fast. You and I both know that you staying where you are is nothing but bad news. It's only going to get worse. Come home."

I bite back my response before it comes out of my mouth:

I am home.

"I'll think about it," I say instead.

"Don't think too long. It's only a matter of time before things explode. I'll do what I can here to make it look like you're anywhere but where you are. But your smile is witchcraft, man, and your fans are under your spell. They will keep coming until they get what they want, regardless of what I say and do."

I hang up the phone without saying goodbye. Brent might be an asshole, but he's right. There's absolutely no way to keep me being here in Brookside a secret, especially after what we did at Smitty's. If they've discovered I'm staying at Bailey's house, then, as much as I hate to admit it, I'm blown. The dream is falling to pieces at my feet, trampled by a million fans screaming my name.

I stand and pace, thread my hands into my hair, grab a fistful, and pull. My jaw pulses. My stomach boils with anxiety.

I don't want to bring Bailey to LA. People treat me with a certain deference there. Like Brent said, I might as well be royalty. I don't want Bailey to see that and think I'm anyone other than who I've been here with her. Besides, she loathes the person I used to be, the person they all think I still am. I don't want to be there with her, my past and my present colliding in the worst possible circumstances.

The frame around the picture of Bailey's parents digs into my hands and its only then that I realize I've been clenching it between my fists. I set it back in its place and stare at the smiling couple.

"I'm stuck between a rock and a hard place," I say to the woman in the picture, Bailey's mom with Bailey's smile. "I can't stay here and I don't want to take her there."

I take a breath and stare around the empty room.

"And, I'm sitting alone, talking to pictures of strangers." I stand and then gesture towards the smiling couple in the frame on the table. "No disrespect intended, of course."

Or, and this thought is so uncomfortable, I can't quite wrap my mind around it, maybe I *should* take Bailey to LA. I could sit down with the PR team, my asshole manager, and my bitch of a mother and get them to understand that I don't want to do this anymore. That I'm tired of being a dancing monkey, selling soulless songs to people who dig my brand. I want to write music that shakes my foundation.

And hell, maybe I don't care if I never sell another song. Maybe I don't care if all I ever do is play for

Bailey and her family because I'm tired of selling out just to hear the crowd scream. Tired of having people look through me instead of at me. I want to be loved for who I really am and not who I've been molded into.

Something powerful rises from the pit of my stomach, something certain and bold.

This is the way it needs to work.

I'll take Bailey to LA; we'll hang out there while I forge a plan with the powers that be. And if they tell me that they won't support the change and the Super Pop Sensation Liam McGuire will have to disappear, so be it.

The more I think about the idea the more I love it. Bailey works her ass off. The trip to LA would be a vacation for her. A chance to unwind. A chance for us to get to know each other even better, to figure out how we fell so far in love in so short a time. I want to know all of her and this will give me a chance to do just that.

I'll take her out to LA and show her my house and buy her some clothes and take her to fancy restaurants. We'll take long walks on the beach and I'll let my stylists play with her hair. I'll treat her like a queen because she fucking deserves it.

Feeling more and more excited about the trip, I slink into the kitchen, grab my iPad, and start planning our time in LA.

Time for us.

Just Bailey and me.

Chapter 21

BAILEY

I can't wait to get home and see Liam. The minute I walk in the door, I'm going to drag his ass into the shower with me, take my time worshipping his naked body, then beg him to fuck me until I scream. If only this old truck could go faster. My phone vibrates with an incoming call from Lexi, interrupting my fantasies of Liam's glistening wet body covered in suds, water streaming over his chest and shoulders.

"Hey! Miss me already?" I cradle the phone between my ear and shoulder so I can use both hands to turn this brute of a truck.

"Already? I've *been* missing you. I never get to see you anymore," Lexi says, pouting.

Great. I steel myself against the incoming guilt trip. "I just spent the whole day with you. We see each other almost all week, silly."

Lexi sighs. "At work. And work Bailey doesn't get drunk and sing karaoke with me."

"Maybe she should," I say, laughing a little. "Might help the patients decide to hurry up and get better in order to keep their poor ears from bleeding."

"Whatever. You've got a beautiful voice." Gabe's tiny voice chimes up in the background, but I can't make out what he says. "You've got a beautiful voice, too," my friend says to her son, pausing patiently for his response.

It warms my heart. "I love the way you love him."

"There's no way around it. Motherhood is something else." Lexi sounds tired. I listen as Gabe climbs into her lap and starts jabbering away about something. "So," Lexi says after shushing him. "As I said before, I miss you. You wanna come hang out with me? Mom said she'd watch Gabe for the night."

My heart sinks because the last thing I want to do is disappoint my best friend. "Oh, damn. I was going to take Liam out for drinks." I pause, biting my lip. "You want to come?"

"Ugh. And be the third wheel?"

"I could call Michael and invite him out, too?" The thought of a double date makes me smile.

"Uh, and be the one in charge of getting him home when he's too drunk to drive?" Lexi answers one of Gabe's rambling questions, sounding more and more dejected by the moment.

"Uh-oh. Are things not working out between you

two?" I try not to sound heartbroken, but I am. The idea of my brother and my best friend falling in love was too delectable for me to resist.

"Oh, no. Things are fine. Believe me, they're fine. He's just in a mood today."

"Ugh. Enough said." I yank the wheel to turn into my driveway. I swear this truck gets harder to drive with each passing year. "Can I get a raincheck? We can schedule a girl's night for just the two of us."

"I need that more than you can ever understand."

"Next Friday? Just you, me, and the karaoke machine at Smitty's?"

"It's a date."

I smile. "Good."

"And Bailey?"

"Yeah?"

"If you cancel on me, I'll show up at your house, walk right into your bedroom, and drag you out naked. I don't care how much Liam begs me to join you."

I laugh as I kill the engine. "I wouldn't cancel. Not on you. You're the most important girl in my life."

"You bet your ass I am."

We say our goodbyes as I climb out of the truck. She's right. I've basically disappeared since Liam and I started sleeping together. But, who could blame me? When faced with the option of having mind-blowing, life-altering sex versus going out to the same smelly bar that I've gone to since the moment I was old enough to drink, who wouldn't go with the first option?

I bound up the porch steps and push through the front door. "Oh, Liam!" I call out in a sing-song voice. "Where are you?"

I shrug out of my purse as he stands from the kitchen table where he'd been staring at his iPad.

"You haven't been obsessing about the kitchen all day, have you?" I ask as I wander in to join him.

Liam smiles and the look in his eyes makes my stomach drop. "Can you sit? We need to talk."

"I don't think there's been a conversation in the history of the world that started with 'we need to talk' and ended well."

Liam smiles again, one of those branded ones I hate so much. "It's not a huge deal. I mean, not yet. It will be, though. Which is why we need to talk."

My good mood comes crashing down around me. I never knew this man could ever be nervous. And if he's nervous, then I'm terrified. "What's wrong, Liam?"

"There was a girl out here today. Snooping for pictures," he says, looking so distraught my heart skips a few beats. "Our cover is blown." Another smile, a real one, tainted with sadness and resignation.

"Okay," I say, drawing out the word. "We kind of figured that would happen, right? Do we need to schedule another secret concert or something?"

Liam lets out a long breath and my nerves start drop-kicking my heart. Something bad is coming. I know it.

"I'm taking you to LA." He picks up his tablet and turns on the screen. "I've got it all planned out."

"What?" I stare at the tablet, a picture of some fancy restaurant up on one of the thousand tabs he has open. "Can't you just make a phone call to your people or something?"

"I did." The light in Liam's eyes dies a little. "And we have to go to Los Angeles."

I press my hands into the table. "I can't just leave," I say, shaking my head incredulously. It's been too long of a day to get into something serious like this. I had my hopes set on a much different kind of night.

"I'll buy your tickets, hot lips. In fact, I already have. It's time you start letting me treat you like the princess you are."

I sit back in my chair, still shaking my head. "It's not just the tickets. I mean, that's really sweet of you, but come on, Liam. I have a job. People who depend on me. I can't just up and leave."

Liam puts down the tablet and reaches for my hands. "If by people, you mean Michael, maybe it's time you realize he's a big boy now. And your job? It will be waiting for you when you get back."

"Right. And my patients? And the people who have to scramble to cover my shifts? And then there's the fact that if I don't work, I don't get paid." I shrug and give his hands a squeeze, trying to ignore the little surges of indignation and anger that keep boiling to the surface. "Isn't there something they can do without us flying out there?"

Liam scowls. "Why does it always come down to money with you?"

His tone stings my pride. "Because that's what happens when you don't have a whole lot of it. Every choice comes down to what's in the bank account."

"Yeah, well, if you would just shut up about it once and awhile, maybe you'd realize that I am right here, with more money than I know what to do with, totally willing to share it with you."

"Did you really just tell me to shut up?" I don't know what hurts more, the fact that he's been silently judging me for counting my pennies, or the fact that he actually used those words. *Shut up.*

Liam rolls his eyes. "Fuck. Please don't blow this out of proportion."

"Blow what out of proportion? You telling me to shut up, you getting mad at me for worrying about my job, or you thinking you can decide for me that I'm leaving on a moment's notice and flying halfway across the country? Why am I not surprised that *the* Liam McGuire doesn't see the problem in any of that?"

"Nice." Liam folds his arms over his chest. His eyes flash with anger but he takes a deep breath, visibly calming himself down. "We don't need to fight dirty. Not us. We're better than that."

I roll my eyes. "What does that even mean?"

There's a voice whispering in the back of my mind,

telling me to calm down and take a beat. To stop being mad so I can listen to what he has to say. That voice wants me to apologize for getting upset and to take his hands in mine and tell him I'll go to LA with him, that I'll go anywhere with him. Because it's starting to feel like wherever he is, is home.

But I don't feel like listening to that voice. That voice sounds weak when I need to be strong, and damn it, I promised myself I'd never be anything but strong. When Michael started being difficult, skipping class and drinking, and getting into more and more trouble, I wanted to crumble and cry but I couldn't. I had to be strong to get us through, and I am not going back to the girl I was. It sucks to be weak and afraid.

"I'm just trying to protect you, Bailey." Liam's nostrils flare as he leans forward. "You have no idea what kind of bullshit is about to erupt in your backyard. My fans are—"

I hold up my hands, interrupting him. "I don't need anyone to protect me. I'm pretty good at it all by myself, thank you very much."

Liam studies me for a long time. "You know what I see? I see a woman who's so afraid of letting go of her past that she just digs in her heels and refuses to let anything change. A woman who is so afraid of the pain in her heart, she isolates herself and walks away from the people who want to help. You think you're being strong? Bullshit. You're broken and hurting and are too stubborn to admit it. You're stuck in this house, frozen in time, unable to move on because that would mean you'd finally have to man up and face all the shit that happened to you."

My jaw drops. My eyes fill with tears. My heart stutters and my stomach plummets and a tiny voice inside me whispers that he's right.

I stand, the tile squealing in protest as my chair scrapes back. Without a word, I stomp into the bathroom as I tap out a text to Lexi to let her know I'll meet her at Smitty's in an hour before I power down my phone and bury it at the bottom of my purse.

Chapter 22

LIAM

Bailey comes out of the bathroom looking absolutely drop-dead gorgeous. "Where are you going?" I ask.

She doesn't look at me. "Out."

"Out?" There's no way she really wants to leave. Not now. Not when we're in the middle of a fight. I stand, folding my arms over my chest, ready to call her bluff.

"Yes, Liam. Out." Bailey grabs her purse and digs through it.

"Looking like that?"

"Like what?" She glares up at me.

Like an angel. Like a goddess. Like everything. "Like you're about to fuck any random douche with a dick?"

Bailey's jaw drops, pain filling her eyes. "Fuck you," she whispers, her voice quaking.

"Really, Bailey? Do you really need to go there?" I stand as my stomach drops into my feet. "I thought you were better than this."

She stares at me for a long time, her eyes growing hard and distant. "So did I." She leaves, slamming the door so hard the windows rattle, leaving me standing there, seething.

The clock on the microwave says it's just after seven. The flight I reserved for us doesn't leave until after midnight. I laugh at myself, staring after her like an ass in the middle of her kitchen. It sounds cold. And wrong. And out of place.

Kind of like me.

This is not at all how I thought the night would go. I imagined her getting excited about the trip, wrapping her arms around my neck and telling me how romantic it all was. I thought she'd be happy.

Maybe I don't know her as well as I thought I did.

I consider calling a cab and meeting her at the bar. But going to Smitty's now is a terrible idea. We're both still angry and the inevitable confrontation will only draw more attention to the two of us. The last thing she needs is to have more people connect the dots between me and her.

I consider waiting here for her to come home, but that will only make me mad, each hour that ticks by on the clock fueling the fire in my gut.

I consider going to sleep and waiting to talk to her in the morning but there's no chance in hell I'm sleeping tonight. Not with this huge rift between us. Not without her tucked in close to my body, my arm wrapped around her waist, my breath moving in her hair.

That only leaves one answer. I'll be taking that flight myself.

I head back into the guest room and stare at all the stuff hanging in the closet. At first, I'm irritated because I don't have anything to pack it in, but then I realize that none of it is really mine. It's all just part of an elaborate costume I wore for the last couple months, stuff Bailey and Brent picked out for me. I spend a few minutes trying to feel mad and self-righteous about it all, except I like who I've been in these clothes. I think, maybe, living here with Bailey, I've finally found out what kind of man I want to be. I think I'm starting to understand who I really am.

And yet, as much as I want to stay and tell Bailey how much I love her, and fix whatever just happened between us, I have to leave. I have to draw my fans away from her, from this house, from our life. She's not designed to handle the kind of attention that's about to descend on us. Hell, I'm not designed to handle that kind of attention either, I've just gotten used to it.

I pull my phone out of my back pocket and tap out a text to Bailey.

Me: I have to go. I have to take care of this before things get worse. I'll be back as soon as I can. I love you.

There's so much more that needs to be said, but not like this. Not over text. I need to understand what I did that made her so angry and we need to have a real conversation, but that's going to have to wait until I get to LA. Right now, a plan is starting to form. The tiniest little scraps of an idea are blazing into awareness in the back of my head. I don't even think it will take that long to get things taken care of.

And so, when the cab comes crunching up the driveway, I climb into the back carrying nothing but my phone and my tablet. As the driver backs out towards the road, I stare at the front porch and let out a long breath. This is the only place I remember ever being truly happy and I'll be back, damn it. Soon. I nod once, and stare at my phone, waiting for a response from Bailey.

BAILEY

"Alright. Spill it. What happened?" Lexi raises an eyebrow and purses her lips.

"He's a fucking asshole, that's what."

She frowns. "Liam? I thought he was God's way of

making up to you for the last eight years. What with the cooking and cleaning and all the crazy good sex."

"Yeah. Well. Turns out life's a bitch." I tell Lexi what happened, expecting her to look appropriately appalled. Imagine my surprise when she doesn't.

"So, he planned a surprise vacation and you're mad?" She looks genuinely confused.

"No. That's not it. He caught some girl sneaking around the house and has to go back to LA for whatever and he just told me I was going with him. No options. No consideration. He just made a decision without talking to me first."

"Because he couldn't stand the thought of being without you."

"No! Because he's an asshole on a power trip who thinks he can just wave his money around and get his way." I take a sip of my margarita, but it tastes awful.

Lexi shakes her head. "I hate to say it, Bay. But it sounds more like you're being a bitch than anything."

I squint at her, horrified. "Excuse me?"

"Do you have any idea what happens when his fans find him? You don't, do you? It's *insanity*. There's no way you're prepared to have that circus hanging out in your front yard."

"Yeah, but there was only one girl." Wouldn't you know it, one of his songs blares over the speakers at Smitty's. I fight the urge to plug my ears.

Lexi sighs. "You are so out of touch it amazes me. That one girl is only the start. She'll bring three friends who will bring three friends who will bring three *more* friends. And they'll tear down your front door to get to him." She shakes her head, looking incredibly disappointed in me. "He had to leave. And he wanted you to go with him and you told him to fuck off because he wanted to pay for it."

"When you put it that way it sounds awful."

"That's because it is awful. This was not one of your most shining moments."

"What about my job?" I slide my margarita out of the way and lean forward. "I can't just up and leave."

"So, what? You pass up on the opportunity of a lifetime instead? Because of some job?"

"Okay, so tell me. What happens after I go with him, lose my job because of it, and he decides that he's done with me? What then? I'd be screwed, that's what." Liam's voice croons over the speakers and even though I hate this song, it feels like coming home.

"And what if he doesn't?" Lexi purses her cherry-red lips.

"Doesn't what?"

"Doesn't decide he's done, you idiot? What if Liam is your forever? Your one and only?" Lexi takes a sip of her beer and waits for that to sink in.

I shake my head. "It's too soon to know anything like that."

"Is it? Can you even imagine your life without him?"

I sit back and drag my margarita close to me. Pick

at the salt on the rim and chew on the straw. The truth is I can't. Not only do I not want to imagine a life without him, but when I try, he just keeps popping back up with that stupid smile of his all over his face.

Lexi points a finger at me. "Exactly."

"I didn't even say anything!" I can't help but laugh. "You say that like you're some kind of psychic or relationship guru or something."

Lexi wrinkles her nose. "Nah. I'm just the one person in this world who knows you better than you know yourself."

"I really was a bitch, wasn't I?" I drop my head in my hands.

"If you were half as bad as you described, you were pretty awful."

The urge to get home is so strong I start to fidget. "Lexi...?"

She waves her hands in a shooing motion. "Go on. Go to him. Apologize. Have maniacal makeup sex. Just promise to name one of your babies after me."

"Right. Because I totally see babies in our future." I stand, hug my friend, and practically run to the truck, suddenly desperate to get home so I can tell Liam just how sorry I am.

BAILEY

The house is empty when I get home. Liam's gone. His clothes are still in the closet, but his iPad is missing. There's no note, and as much as I want to think that his clothes hanging neatly in Michael's old room are a sign that he'll be back any minute, something tells me he's gone for good. I dig my phone out of the bottom of my purse and power it back on. Of course, there's a text from Liam. That's the whole reason I turned my phone off in the first place. I didn't want to deal with him while I was out with Lexi.

I drop onto his bed as I read his text.

Liam: I have to go. I have to take care of this before things get worse. I'll be back as soon as I can. I love you.

He left? I press a hand to my belly, my fingers and lips tingling, and read his text over and over, trying to find more information, desperate to understand how we got here. He says he'll be back soon, but what does that mean? And for how long? Just when he was starting to feel like the most stable thing in my life, he does this. Upending everything, leaving on a moment's notice. Changing everything before I even have a chance to get used to the idea.

I start to text him, and when none of the words come out right, I give up and call him. The longer it takes for him to answer, the deeper the sense of dread pulls me down. By the time I get sent to voicemail, anxiety churns through me, skitters across my skin like electricity over sheet metal.

"Liam." I say his name like a prayer. "I'm so sorry. I was a total bitch. Please come home." I pause, wondering what else I can say when there aren't enough words to express what I'm feeling. "I love you," I finish lamely. "Call me."

And then I hang up. Change my clothes. Go through all the rituals that lead up to sleep. And lay down to watch my ceiling until the sun comes up. We had one fight that wasn't even really a fight. Was that really a good reason for him to leave without saying goodbye? With no more explanation than three worthless statements? Was I fooling myself into believing there was more between us than there really was? For me, Liam is everything I ever wanted and never knew I needed all wrapped up into a love that feels bigger than anything I've ever experienced. I thought he felt the same. Was I wrong?

I don't hear anything from him until late the next morning when my phone buzzes and I leap out of bed to grab it.

Liam: I'm here in LA. We need to talk, but not now. I love you, B. Home as soon as I can.

We need to talk. My poor exhausted brain zooms in on that one sentence and it echoes through me, beating itself against my bones like a bat trapped in the attic.

Me: When will you be home?

Liam: When I can. Love you.

It's not enough. I need more. I can't live in ambiguity. I need a clear-cut path. But I don't say any of that because I don't want to push him for more when I was the one who pushed him away in the first place.

Me: I love you, too.

I hit send and stare at my phone, hoping for a reply that never comes.

The next three weeks are awful. His texts come less and less frequently until finally, my calls and texts go unanswered and I stop even bothering to reach out. I struggle through long days and longer nights, living in some weird limbo where I constantly half-expect him to walk through the door and swoop me into his arms and kiss me until I can't breathe.

I don't cry.

I don't grieve.

I just wait.

Because I believe in what we have. Liam and I? We're not done. There's no way we're over. There are years stretching out in front of us still. I know he'll be back in the same way I know I love him. It's a truth akin to gravity. The only way to fight it is to leave this world entirely and neither one of us is doing that anytime soon. We might have a lot to work through when he finally comes back to me, because let's face it, each and every minute that goes by without him reaching out just adds to the hurt and anger building up in my heart. But we will get through it. Why? Because I'm stubborn enough to make sure we do.

And then, while checking on a particularly sweet older woman recovering from a broken foot, I see him.

And that's when it all falls apart.

"You see that man up on the TV?" asks the woman, pointing towards the flat screen on the wall, her hand trembling with age.

I glance at the thing and my heart sinks into my stomach. My knees go weak and I clutch at the side rail on her bed to keep from falling over.

"Can you believe he was here in this very hospital?" she asks, incredulous. "He's some kind of singer, I think. My great granddaughter has his posters all over her room."

Without bothering to ask her if she minds, I turn up the volume and watch as Liam flashes that awful *branded* smile of his. He's getting out of a limo, cameras going off like strobe lights, questions flying, all while he smiles and waves like none of it bothers him in the least. Like he didn't spend night after night talking about how much he hated being some other version of himself all the time.

The reporter on screen finally gets his attention, shoving a microphone into Liam's face. "Liam! Where have you been?"

Liam smiles into the camera, tilting his chin so the scar trailing down his cheek is more visible. "I was hiding out, giving this baby time to heal." He runs his finger down his face and drops a wink into the camera.

"And what about the tour? Any chance you'll pick up where you left off?"

Liam shrugs. "All things in good time, you know?" He blows a kiss at someone off-screen and hordes of girls and women hidden behind the cameraman scream and squeal, chanting his name like he's their messiah.

Liam starts walking away, but the reporter keeps pace with him, not ready to end the interview. "And what about the rumors of a mystery woman out in Ohio? Has someone finally stolen Liam McGuire's heart?"

Fear grabs me, its steely fingers a vice grip on my spine. I pop a finger into my mouth and chew on the nail, needing his response in the same way an addict needs her next hit.

"Are you a fan?" the woman behind me asks, her tremulous voice distracting me from Liam's answer.

I turn, pulling my finger from my mouth and lifting my eyebrows. "I'm sorry, what?" The TV tries to steal my attention, but I tune it out. "A fan?" I shake my head. "No. Not at all."

At least not of this version of him.

Onscreen, the interview is over and I give my attention back to the TV just in time to see Liam walking away, turning to wave and smile before he disappears through a door. I finish the day on auto-pilot, focusing on getting through it without breaking down, and drive home without even turning on the radio. The house is dark when I push through the front door, dishes piled in the sink in the kitchen. I dig through the fridge even though I'm not hungry. Turn on the TV even though there's nothing I want to watch.

And then finally, when I've done everything I possibly can to distract myself, I climb into bed, curl up with his pillow, and wait for the tears. Seeing him on TV today, falling into his old life like a bad habit, it made me realize that Liam's not coming back. It's time for me to grieve what I thought we had, pull all the pieces of him out of my heart, and move on.

The pillowcase smells like him and I breathe it in, remembering night after night of him rolling over to smile at me, pulling me close and pressing his lips to mine. It took so long for me to let him into this room. Once I did, I regretted all the weeks we slept apart. The last time I felt as safe as I did with his body wrapped around mine was years ago, when I was still young enough for my mom to sing me to sleep.

When those memories don't bring the tears, I think about the music we made in the den. The way the piano sounded when we made love against it. The song he wrote for me afterwards. The night we sang together at Smitty's, his presence beside me making me stronger than I ever thought I could be. The truths I thought I uncovered about him, the person I found buried underneath the persona, the man I thought was the real Liam McGuire.

And still the tears don't come.

I wander through my memories, deliberately poking the bruise created by his absence, needing the swell of emotion to wash over me, to carry me away so maybe I can finally start to heal. After nearly a month of no contact, it's time to admit we're done. That as much as I loved him, he obviously didn't feel the same way about me. It's time to grieve and move on. Liam doesn't want me anymore.

And still the tears don't come.

I sit up, frustrated, and look at the picture of my mom and dad on the bedside table. After all these years, I've memorized every detail. The adoration in her eyes. The off-center quirk to his smile. The way his arm wraps around her lower back, his hand on her hip pulling her in close, a silent promise that he would protect her and cherish her for the rest of their lives. My parents loved each other desperately. In a world where love takes a backseat to everything else, where it's out of fashion to completely give your time and energy to anyone other than yourself, they had something precious and rare.

I thought I had that with Liam. I thought our love would blossom into one of those great stories our grandchildren would tell their own children when they first started to fall in love.

So why won't I cry? Why can't I mourn him? Why, when I feel so damn hollow and alone, frozen from the inside out, why don't I have tears for him?

Night falls as I wallow in my misery. The shadows in my room lengthen, swallowing up the last slivers of light streaking across my floor. Even though I'm both mentally and physically exhausted, sleep is a pipedream. And so, driven by some masochistic need to feel something, anything, I slide my phone off the table and send Liam a text, something I swore I'd stop doing after the first two days' worth of calls went unanswered.

Me: I miss you.

I hit send before I can think better of it, certain that his continued silence will be the push to topple me over the edge so I can grieve. My phone buzzes in my hand and my breath catches in my chest. Really? Is he really ready to talk to me now? When I'm finally ready to walk away from him?

Liam: I miss you too, hot lips.

I stare at the words in shock, relief spreading a smile across my face, and finally the tears come, gathering in my eyes so that the screen wavers in front of me. My fingers hover over the keyboard, waiting for some direction. I want to reply, but what should I say? Do I apologize? Try to explain myself? Ask him how he's doing? Lay into him for three weeks of silence? Minutes tick by as I worry through all the possible responses.

These are the times I wish for my mom. The times when I know there's a right answer but I can't for the life of me see what it is. How many times over the last eight years have I been here? So confused, utterly unsure how to move forward, and desperate for someone to put me on the right path. Each and every pivotal moment of my life since their death has been terrifying. Just me, staring at a million possible outcomes, wishing someone would give me a nudge in the right direction with a hug and a promise it will all be okay.

Instead, I have spent my life blindly picking a path and pushing my way forward, dealing with the repercussions of it all while trying to keep a brave face for Michael. I was too young to handle everything that landed in my lap after their death. Too young to be catapulted into adulthood, struggling through things like mortgages and property taxes and what to do when a little brother starts making bad decisions. And now? After so many mistakes and missteps, I can't for the life of me see the right way to handle this moment with Liam.

I feel like I'm supposed to be angry. Hell, I *am* angry. But the relief I feel at seeing his name on my phone is monumental. My heart reaches out for him, begging to return to the safety of his arms while my head keeps wondering if it's better to leave well enough alone.

Abandoning the phone on my bed, I swoop up the picture of my parents and run my finger along their smiling faces. "I've needed you so much." A sob swallows the end of my sentence. "I've been so lost and so scared and I've messed it all up, and I'm so sorry."

I clasp the picture to my chest. "I'm so sorry." I whisper the words over and over and something inside me loosens. Tears fall down my face and sobs wrack my body. "I don't know how to do all of this alone and I've ruined everything."

I clutch their picture and cry until my head hurts and my body aches. I cry for them. For Michael. For eight years of me making my way through life, a steady stream of one foot in front of the other when I haven't had a clue as to how to get where I was going. When the tears finally subside, I know exactly what I need to say to Liam. The answer is so clear to me I don't think twice. I swoop up my phone and tap out a simple text.

Me: Come home.

Before I can hit send, an incoming call from an unknown caller covers up the screen. Confused, I wipe my nose with the back of my hand and wipe the tears from my eyes before answering.

"Hello?"

"Ms. Shultz?" A man's voice. Tentative.

"Yes?"

"This is Sergeant Leighton, Brookside PD."

A giant yawning hole opens up in my world and threatens to swallow me. My hands shake and darkness creeps into my peripheral vision.

"Yes?" I barely recognize my own voice.

"I'm sorry to inform you that there's been an accident..."

I hear the rest of his words through a thick layer of confusion swarming in my skull. Michael's in the hospital in Grayson. He was drunk, and the idiot got behind the wheel anyway. He drove right off the road and straight into a tree.

"Oh my God." The worst form of déjà vu settles over me. "Is he okay?" My voice echoes through my head, mixing with the memories of a similar phone call about my parents.

"I'm sorry, miss. I don't have any information for you. But," he pauses and clears his throat. "You're going to want to get yourself to that hospital."

Chapter 24

BAILEY

Why does this keep happening to me? Why does each and every person I love get ripped out of my life by the roots? My heart is nothing but people-shaped holes, crumbling to dust around the edges. If it doesn't stop soon, if life can't stop using me for a punching bag, I'm not going to have anything left.

I hang up the phone and race through the house, scoop up my keys and my purse, and hop in the truck. It's at least an hour drive into Grayson and all I can do is pray that I make it in time. The first few snowflakes of winter filter down from the sky. They sparkle in the slices of light my headlights cut through the dark, oddly beautiful on this awful night. I forgot my coat. My hands tremble as I fidget with the heater, wondering how long Michael sat on the side of the road before someone found him.

Was he cold?

Was he conscious?

Was he hurting? Crying out for help when no one could hear him?

My throat constricts and I swallow hard against it. I will not cry for him. Not now. Because Michael's going to be fine. There's no need for tears, only anger. How could that dumbass get behind the wheel after he'd been drinking? Especially after what happened to Mom and Dad? How could he be so fucking dumb?

Things were going so well. We were making room for each other in our lives again. He was drinking less. Smiling more. Things were good between him and Lexi.

Oh, God.

Lexi.

I check the time. It's late—edging past midnight—and she and Gabe are sure to be in bed. But she deserves to know and I can't make this drive without her. I dial her number on autopilot.

"Bay?" She sounds groggy and confused. "What's wrong?" Lexi's familiar voice tears through me. Everything about this situation is too familiar, ripping open old wounds that still haven't fully healed.

"It's Michael." I swallow back a sob.

"What's going on?" She's instantly more alert. "Is he okay?" There's movement on her end of the line, the rustle of bed sheets.

"I don't know, Lex. Nothing about anything is

okay." I didn't think I had any tears left. I was wrong. I swipe angrily at my cheeks as they leak from my mutinous eyes. "He's at Grayson Memorial. Ran off the road..." I sniff. "The idiot was drunk, Lex. He drove his stupid ass right into a tree."

Lexi's sharp intake of breath is an icepick to my heart. "But I was with him tonight. We had dinner at Smitty's. But Bailey, I swear, he only had two beers."

"That you saw." Michael could have been drinking all day. He's better at hiding his problem than any of us want to admit.

"That I saw." There's a finality to her voice because she knows as well as I do that we've all been ignoring his problem when we should have taken action. "Oh, shit. I'm so sorry. I should have known..."

"It's not your fault. Or it's all of our fault for not paying more attention." I slap the steering wheel with an open palm. "Damn it. Why didn't I talk to him about his drinking?"

"I'm getting Gabe dressed. I'll meet you at the hospital." There's a pause. "And Bay? This isn't your fault."

I want to tell her not to drag her son out of bed. That this is most definitely my fault because Michael was fine until my parents died and has been anything but fine ever since. I was the one in charge of raising him right, and tonight is finally the concrete proof of how badly I failed him. But I don't say any of that, because right now it's not about me. It's about my brother.

"I don't think I can go through this again, Lexi. He's all I've got left."

"Don't think like that. This is just a hiccup. A wake-up call for all of us. Michael will be fine." Her voice trembles and my chin quakes.

Lexi and I say our goodbyes and I let her last sentence play on repeat in my head, a mantra, a prayer. I say it over and over, blinking back the tears that threaten to overtake me again. I've had my chance to wallow in weakness; I have to be strong now.

What started as a few polite little snowflakes turns into a full-on frenzy. It doesn't take long for a thin layer of white to cover the road and for visibility to drop to almost nothing. I lean forward, my back ramrod straight, and peer through the dense white nothing in front of me.

Out of nowhere, brake lights.

I tap the brakes and the back end of the truck starts sliding out from behind me. I won't stop in time. I'm going to crash right into that car and I'm going way too fast to come out of this okay. For the space of one heartbeat, I sigh in relief and welcome the end.

The truck stops sliding and I skid to a stop inches away from ramming the car in front of me. I droop over the steering wheel, gulping huge breaths of air into my lungs.

"Get a hold of yourself, Bailey." I close my eyes and count my heartbeats as I slow my breathing.

Michael needs me. And this time, I'm going to be there for him. I wasn't old enough to be what he needed when my parents died, but damn it. I've got a world of experience under my belt now. I will not let my little brother down again.

My knuckles are white from gripping the steering wheel so hard, and even though I didn't bring a coat and I'm shivering, I'm sweating too. My nerves are shot by the time I make it to Grayson. The roads are better here. The street crews have been out, throwing down salt.

For as many times as I push away the questions in my head, they just keep coming right on back.

Why did he have to get behind the wheel? Why, after what happened to Mom and Dad, would he ever drink and drive? How many times have I begged him to call me if he's ever too drunk to get home?

It's the curse.

That insidious little thought sneaks into my head and the bottom drops out of my world. Michael was fine when we were estranged, when our lives were separate and he didn't have frequent contact with me. But now? Just weeks after coming back into my life, he's in the hospital. Probably fighting for his life.

And what does that mean for Liam? If I'm cursed, what terrible thing is waiting around the corner for him?

My heart, already made of crepe paper, crumples in on itself, crying out for Liam like a lost child. I need him right now. There's not enough of me left to make it through this. I need him to hold me up, to wrap me in his safety and security and go back to making everything okay again. Why, when I had everything, do I have to go back to doing it all on my own?

"Damn it!" I slap the steering wheel again and the pain brings me out of my head and back to reality. Curse or not, I have a job to do.

I make the turn into the parking lot and pull into a vacant spot. With one last muttered prayer, I slide out of the truck and race through the emergency room doors and rush to the front desk.

"My brother's been admitted here. Michael Schultz?" I don't know the nightshift very well, but I've seen this particular woman enough to know her by name.

"Bailey?" The woman—Tara—looks up at me after she pulls up his information.

"Is he…?" My throat tightens and I swallow hard.

"He's still in surgery." Tara looks at me with so much sympathy it makes me want to retch. How many times have I been where she is, staring at facts on a screen and that may or may not ruin someone's life? "You can have a seat and I'll let them know you're here. Someone will be out to talk to you shortly."

And so, after all that, there's nothing to do but wait and pray.

Chapter 25

BAILEY

I take a seat in the waiting room. Pull out my phone and scroll through my apps, never really paying enough attention to anything to warrant having the thing out. An eternity passes between every tick of the clock. My eyes burn and my nose won't stop running, so after stopping at reception to let Tara know where I'll be, I head into the bathroom to wash my face. The woman staring back at me is a stranger. Mascara rims her vacant eyes and trails black smudges down her cheeks. I do what I can to clean my face, but I really don't care what I look like, not when my worry for Michael takes up all that I am. When I'm done, I check with reception—still no news—and drop back into one of the cheap seats. Every time the doors swing open my heart leaps and falls in the same instant until Lexi arrives at some point, two cups of coffee in hand.

"Gabe's at my mom's." Her hair is pulled back in a low ponytail, still frizzy and fuzzy from sleep. There's not one drop of makeup on her face and I realize it might be the first time in our adult lives that I've ever seen her without her red lipstick.

I take the coffee she offers and sip it. The warm liquid should be soothing, but I think I prefer to be cold right now.

"Any news?" The hope on Lexi's face is more weight on my shoulders.

I shake my head and we take a seat. I'd do anything for my parents to be here right now. My mother on one side of me, my father on the other. Not so they'd have to go through the pain and fear of a wounded child. God, no. But because I need someone to tell me what to do. I need someone to take my hand and help me stand when my knees feel like they're ready to go out from under me. I need someone to tell me what to say when Michael wakes up. How to help him past this. I need someone to explain where things went wrong and show me how to fix it.

I'm so tired of muddling through everything, making mistakes that affect not just my life, but his. My dad made me promise to take care of him. To take care of the house and the truck, and to give my brother a chance at stability. I've failed so miserably. Sure, I stayed in the house, but it's falling down around me. The truck? It's rusting away. And Michael? He's in the same kind of shape, rotting from the inside out.

Hanging on when shit's so broken he should have fallen to pieces long ago. All this time, I knew he was drinking too much. I knew he was reckless. I knew he wasn't okay. But I just kept thinking if I continued to put one foot in front of the other, kept smiling through it and never looked the problems square in the face, that everything would be okay. But you know what? Nothing's okay and it hasn't been for a long time.

The moment Michael is strong enough, he's in for one hell of a reality check. He's gonna get his ass into a recovery program. Face his demons and get his shit straight. We both are. No more of this hiding our pain behind rotting exteriors. This is the year the Schultzes start putting things back together.

"Remember that time Michael fell out of the tree when we were little?" Lexi traces a finger around the pattern on her pajama pants.

"How could I forget?" I laugh, a humorless sound. "I ended up grounded for the rest of my life and he got treated like a prince for a week."

"We were so scared." Lexi leans forward, elbows on knees, and looks at the floor.

"Yeah, we were. I knew I was going to get in so much trouble if we didn't find him."

"Leave it to Michael to sneak out of the house when we weren't paying attention." She glances at me. "You swore he did it just to see you get grounded."

I shake my head, lost in the memory. Lexi and I were all of thirteen, barely old enough to watch a kid as wild as my ten-year-old brother. While we sat at the table and talked about boys, Michael managed to sneak out and find the tallest, oldest, most rotten tree in the woods behind our house and climb to the very top.

"And then," Lexi says, looking me straight in the eye. "When we found him, we thought he was dead."

"He *looked* dead." I shiver at the memory. "He was so pale." I still wake up some nights, sweating, the image of his crumpled body and ghostly white skin fresh in my mind.

Lexi nods, swallowing hard, her face full of determination. "But he wasn't dead, was he?"

"Nope. Just a concussion and a broken leg." I sit back in the cheap plastic chair. "Doctors told my mom he had to be part cat and had just used up at least three of his lives."

"Which leaves him with six, right?" Lexi laughs and sits back. "Okay. It's Michael, so he's probably used up at least one or two more since then, but you know as well as I do that he has at least one left, Bailey." She meets my eyes. "He's gonna be okay."

I lick my lips. "Not after I get my hands on him. Life's about to get really hard on Michael R. Schultz."

We wait for an eternity, but somehow, I feel hopeful. Instead of drowning in worry, I draft a master plan to make my brother better after tonight. He might hate me for a while, but damn it. I'm going to make him okay.

As fear dissipates, I pull out my phone and open

up the text from Liam. I never sent my response. Just as I lean over to ask Lexi's opinion, a tall man enters the waiting room.

"Ms. Schultz?"

I stand, shoving the phone in my back pocket. "That's me."

One look at the doctor's face sends the hospital room spiraling around me. My knees go weak and I clutch at Lexi's arm.

"I'm Dr. Morgan. Your brother's surgeon."

He blinks and I swallow, my breath so shallow I feel dizzy.

"He's resting now, but I want to make sure you're fully aware of the situation. The trauma he suffered was severe."

A buzzing in my ears blocks out most of what he says next.

"...on a respirator..."

My heart thunders in my chest.

"...ruptured spleen..."

A flash of Michael's smiling face, his eyes warm and happy as he throws his head back and laughs.

"...traumatic brain injury..."

Michael's skin so pale. His tiny body crumpled at the base of a tree, his dark hair wet and clinging to his forehead.

"...get ready to say goodbye."

My face crumbles and all the air leaves my lungs in

one long breath. "What?" I dig my nails into Lexi's arm as my legs threaten to drop me to the ground.

"I'm so sorry." Hollow words.

A nurse I went to school with leads me and Lexi through the maze of hallways and rooms that I could walk in my sleep. Faces swim in and out of focus, people I know and work with, sympathy tightening their lips.

Poor thing.

Such a shame.

Saw it coming.

I ignore it all. I'm here for one thing and one thing only, and that's to say goodbye to my little brother. A good kid who took a few wrong turns. A man who's paying for my mistakes with his life.

We stop in front of a room and the nurse steps back. "Take as long as you need," she says, and I recognize the wall she's putting up between us. I'm not Bailey anymore. I'm Grieving Family Member and will be dealt with accordingly.

It takes me a minute, but I enter the room and stop just inside the door, unable to go more than a few steps. My brother is the wrong color, so white his dark hair looks black. One side of his face is covered in bandages. His mouth is hidden by a breathing tube. A tangle of wires snake to his body from the machines near his bed, monitoring his heart, pumping oxygen into his lungs, medicine into his veins.

Lexi appears beside me, her face crumpling as she

covers her mouth with her hands. "Oh, Michael." She rushes to his side, drops to her knees beside his bed and takes his hand in hers, crying and sobbing and pressing his fingers against her cheek. "His skin's so cold," she whispers, her wide eyes seeking mine.

I stand there for longer than I should. After all these years of being strong, smiling through so many tragedies, I might not have it in me to take one more step. Maybe I'll just stand here and watch him slip away. Succumb to my grief and let someone else take care of it all. I've been strong for so long and I'm so damn tired.

Except Michael deserves better than that.

Reaching deep down inside myself, borrowing against tomorrow's strength, I force myself forward until I'm standing at his side. He looks like our father, and yet he looks like he did when he was little, before everything got bad. It's like the two men I mourn the most are stretched out in that bed and I have to say goodbye to them both all over again. My lips wobble and my eyes water, and I drop to my knees, clutching at his clammy hand and pressing it to my cheek.

"I'm so sorry. I failed you." I close my eyes and let out a shuddering breath. "And I miss you already. I did everything I could but it wasn't enough." Sobs wrack my body while my heart wails its sorrow. "Oh Michael, you deserve so much better than this." My tears eat my words and I cry until I'm raw.

I want him to open his eyes one last time, just like my dad did.

To look at me and smile and tell me it's all going to be okay.

To tell me he loves me and that he forgives me. That he will be waiting for me with Mom and Dad.

I need him to give me a task. A job to carry out for him that gives my life meaning after this because without him, what do I have? But Michael doesn't move and I fall asleep to the steady rhythm of the machines keeping him alive.

Sometime during the night, while I hold his hand and beg for forgiveness, my brother lets go and slips away, leaving me to deal with the rest of my life alone.

Chapter 26

LIAM

"The whole world thinks you've lost your mind, you know." My mother sits at my dinner table, her perfectly manicured nails drumming an imperfect rhythm on the lacquered wood. "Chicks dig scars, Li-li. This little accident is an opportunity. You're getting too old for pop, anyway. Maybe it's time to transition into movies." Her smile is sweet and venomous, cyanide whipped in cotton candy.

The woman wields my childhood nickname like a weapon. She stopped feeling things like love and affection for me years ago. I'm nothing more than a business decision to her. She only calls me Li-li when she wants something.

"There's only one chick I care about and she doesn't give two shits about my movie career." I pace my dining room, realizing that Bailey's entire house could fit in here.

"You can quit trying to punish me with this ridiculous charade. You and I both know that you aren't going to throw away your entire life for a two-bit whore in Trash Heap, Ohio."

I stop in my tracks and level a finger at my mother. "You can say whatever you want about me, but you leave Bailey out of this."

"Bailey," she says, as if it pains her to get the word out past her teeth. "What a stupid name. What is she? A cat?" She picks at an invisible piece of lint on her dress.

"Bailey is the only person in this whole world who really knows who I am."

"Oh, please. I brought you into this world and I built you from the ground up." She tosses her hair over her shoulder and settles her gaze on the miles of sky on the other side of the wall of windows. "Although it's painfully obvious I didn't build you strong enough if this tantrum is any indication of anything."

"Tantrum?" I pull out a chair and take a seat across from her. "You mean the one time in my life I've ever made a decision based on what I want?"

"And what about me? Your mother? This decision"—she wrinkles her nose—"is bigger than you realize. It affects more than just you."

"Right." The word is caustic. "Because none of this

has ever been about me. I am the one who has to live this life, you know."

"How can you say that? Look around." She gestures to my monstrous dining room. Cold. Sterile. And lacking anything that makes me feel like I'm home. "You really are as spoiled as they say. I guess if I failed you at all, that's where I went wrong. You act as if having all this is a prison sentence. Do you realize how many people would be thrilled to have a fraction of what you have? Although," she says, rolling her eyes. "That lawsuit you got hit with for punching a fan in the face set us back a pretty penny, didn't it?"

I stare at the woman across from me. She stares right back, not one ounce of warmth in her gaze. There was a time when I used to crawl into her lap and beg her to sing to me. She'd smile and stroke my hair and I'd press my ear to her chest and listen to the way her voice moved within her body, vibrating with an energy all its own. No matter how scary the nightmare, how hard the day, how long the night, I could crawl into her arms, ask her to sing to me, and she'd make me feel safe. Now? She sits across the table, her back straight as steel, and stares at me with so much loathing it steals my breath.

"All I ever wanted to do was make you proud of me."

"And I've never been more disappointed in you in your life." My mother leans forward, her eyes cold. "Don't do this."

"It's done." I sit back in my chair and let out a long breath. "The studio is letting me out of my contract because, unlike you, they're smart enough to admit the scar is a deal breaker and they want out before my career completely crashes and burns."

"Bullshit."

"It's my face that sells my music, Mom. Without it, it's just a slow-motion fall into obscurity. Better to go out on a high note. You're the one who beat it into me year after year. Always leave 'em wanting more, right?"

"So, just like that? You get to decide when it's over?" She sucks in her cheeks, her nostrils flaring. "After all this work, all the time and effort I put into you, and it's all gone because you say so?"

"Pretty much." I push the chair back from the table and stand. "And you know what? I'm happier than I ever thought I could be. I smile for no reason. None at all. I get to go back to Bailey and finally live a real life. Can you even imagine what it feels like to put down the weight of being Liam McGuire and just be me?"

"You're not making any sense. You *are* Liam McGuire." My mother draws her eyebrows together until she remembers that emotions give you wrinkles and purposefully relaxes her face.

"No. That's the thing you don't understand. The man you've built, the one the whole world sees when they look at me, that's not me. Not who I want to be. I just want to be real. I don't want to be a face or a name. I don't want to have to worry about every little thing I say or do, worry about if it's on brand or not. I just want to be a normal person."

"Then why aren't you there with her now?" My mother crosses her thin arms over her chest. "If that woman is everything you've ever wanted in the whole wide world"—she widens her eyes, sarcasm dripping from every word—"why are you here instead of there?"

"Because I didn't want the train wreck that is my life to derail hers."

"So you left her?" My mother shakes her head. "Why are we even having this discussion, then?"

"Yes, I left, but it's not permanent. I'm only here long enough to get my life straight. To protect her." Those words feel so damn good, I smile despite myself. "I love her."

My happiness enrages my mother. "And now, a month later, you're going to show back up on her doorstep and expect her to welcome you with open arms?" She straightens her posture, sitting even taller. "You say you're not the man the world sees, but that sounds pretty damn spoiled and self-centered to me."

Her words hit me in the gut and I slam a fist down on the table. "Get out."

My mother jumps, her lips parting in surprise. "Liam..."

"Get out!" I point at the door, spittle flying from my mouth.

She purses her lips and looks away. "Don't be an ass..."

I lean in, growling at her through clenched teeth. "Get. Out."

My mother stands, smoothing her hands over her dress—bland and black and made by a designer that charges more than Bailey makes in a month—and lifts her chin. "You'll regret this." She gathers her handbag and drapes it over her wrist. "I gave you everything," she says, and leaves without another word.

I stare after her, my teeth grinding together until my jaw aches, my hands balled into fists. I pace, waiting for the guilt to set in—and considering my mother knows how to push each and every single one of my buttons, the guilt should hit anytime now. Imagine my surprise when I don't feel anything at all. I grab my phone and check for a text from Bailey. Nothing. Tension settles into my shoulders and I drum my fingers across the screen. I've been trying to get a hold of her for a few days and it's like she's disappeared.

I didn't think it would take so long to take care of things here. Each time she called, each text she sent, she needed answers, a timeline for when I was coming back. But with Brent tying up every single hour of the day, keeping me busy day and night, trying to get me to forget her and my life back in Brookside, I never had the time to give her the attention she needed. I kept waiting until I could say I was coming back to her. That we wouldn't have to worry about paparazzi and crazy fans stalking around her yard and digging through her trash. I wanted to have the solution to the problem ready before I gave her any details. Proof that I'm capable of taking care of her. Negotiations took longer than I expected, although each and every day brought me closer to where I am now.

Free.

For the last few weeks, I fell asleep each night worried about Bailey. Afraid that she was sitting at home wondering what happened between us, hurt and confused. Or worse, questioning my love for her. The thought of her crying herself to sleep wrecked me. And yet the whole time I consoled myself with the knowledge that the moment I explained why I had to disappear, she would understand. The way I feel for her—that just doesn't go away because of one little fight and a few weeks of separation. And I know she feels the same. I have more faith in our love than in anything I've ever encountered.

The moment Bailey walked into my life I was forever changed. The scar that runs down my face? I should hate it for taking everything away from me.

But I don't.

Because it didn't.

This scar brought me Bailey, which means it brought me everything. My soul is tangled up with hers. We're twined together and there's no undo on this one. She'll be a part of me for as long as I live.

The longer we went without contact, the more I worried that I had it all wrong. That things were taking too long out here and that I needed to reach out and explain what was happening before I knew if it was real or not. But then she texted a couple nights ago—three little words, *I miss* you—and I thought that was my proof that she wasn't mad. That she hasn't been planning nine different ways to rip off my balls and shove them down my throat. She was simply waiting for me to come back to her so we can go on with our life.

Except I haven't heard from her since. The texts I sent went unanswered until I gave up last night and called. She didn't answer so I left a voicemail and when she didn't call back by the time I was ready for bed, I called again. No answer. This morning? Nothing.

I've been talking to Michael almost every single day since I left. He helped me keep a pulse on Bailey. Let me know how she was doing. And he told me that she hadn't burned my stuff in the front yard yet, which was a damn good sign that we'd be okay. But he hasn't been answering his phone for the last couple days either.

After weeks of working on that damn patio with the man, I got used to seeing his stupid face every couple of days. I haven't had a best friend since I was ten years old, but I'll give that title to Michael Schultz without flinching. He's a drunk and an asshole. He hides his broken parts behind a sardonic smile and has a sarcastic streak a mile wide, but he's one hell of a good person. And he promised to call me the moment things with Bailey looked like they were going downhill.

The shit with my mom today, it's such a stark contrast to what I had in Brookside. Life here in Los Angeles is like an old black and white movie while life in Ohio was full, high-definition color. Sitting here in this fancy house way up on the hill like some kind of prince overlooking his subjects, it makes me lonely. And my mom's visit? It just added weight to how empty my life is. When my own mother sees nothing more than dollar signs when she looks at me? Fuck. No wonder I want more.

I check the time. Michael's home from work by now. I dial his number. The phone rings once. Twice. A third time.

A fourth.

And then voicemail.

Frowning, I hang up and call Bailey. Nothing.

A shadow of doubt spreads through me. Something's wrong.

Chapter 27

BAILEY

The mattress sags as Lexi sits down next to me. "Bailey?" Her voice comes at me from so far away. So far. I wonder if I should meet her eyes, but that seems too difficult. Too much. So, I don't.

Her hand on my arm. Too much sensation. She leans down, trying to meet my eyes.

"Bay?"

Her voice is sandpaper. Her touch feels like nettles digging into my skin. She runs a hand over my hair and I flinch.

"I've got soup." The bed bounces as she stands and then kneels in front of me. "Are you hungry?"

No. I'm not hungry. I'm filled with an aching void, frozen and numb. There is no hunger when you're nothing.

"You need to eat, sweetie." Her voice cracks and

it's just one more thing I can't bear. Her grief is too heavy for me when I'm drowning underneath the weight of my own.

She stands. Moves to the window. Leans her arm on the wall and her head on her arm. Her shoulders shake as she cries. If there was more of me, I'd call to her. Tell her it would be okay. But there's nothing left in me and nothing is okay. So, I stay silent.

"I don't know what to do," she says. "God, it all hurts so much. I miss him every day and now I'm losing you, too." She sniffs and I close my eyes.

Too much.

A buzz. My phone.

Lexi crosses the room and plucks it from the night table. "It's Liam again. Want me to answer it?"

I shake my head and the world spins. "No."

She drops to her knees, her face level with mine, the phone buzzing in her hand like a nest of hornets. "He needs to know."

I shake my head and close my eyes.

"You need to talk to him." Desperation in her voice.

The phone stops buzzing but the thoughts in my head don't. So many words I can't hear any of them because they're all jumbled up together. It hurts.

Oh, God.

It hurts.

Lexi sighs and stands. Puts the phone back on the nightstand with a tiny little thump. I expect her to leave but she doesn't. Instead, she throws back the covers and grabs my arms. Hauls me into a sitting position.

"You need to listen to me," she says, even as I curl up into a little ball.

"You're wasting away in here and it's not going to get better if you don't do anything. You need to move forward."

"I can't."

"You have to. Life doesn't stop. It just keeps on trudging by whether we want it to or not." Lexi sniffs.

"What am I supposed to do?" I ask, finally meeting her eyes. "I've cried. I've begged. I've prayed. I don't have anything left."

Tears waver in Lexi's eyes. "You need to get out of this bed. Out of this room. You need to find a path and take it. You always feel better when you take action. Indecision kills you."

She's right. I'm not ready to hear it, but she's right. "I miss him, Lex."

"Oh God, Bailey. Me, too." And as I watch her face crumple, her hands shake as they cover her mouth, I cry. I wrap my arms around my friend, cling to her with every ounce of strength I have left in my body, and cry.

LIAM

My phone vibrates with an incoming call and I smile to see Bailey's name and contact picture fill the screen. Relief floods through me and I let out a long breath I didn't know I'd been holding.

"Hey, hot lips," I say as I put the phone to my ear and step through the French doors onto my balcony.

"Liam?" It's a woman's voice. Not Bailey's. Shaky and uncertain.

"Yeah?" I pull the phone away and check to see if I somehow misread the caller ID.

The woman on the other line sniffs. "It's Lexi..." She trails off, her voice strained.

"Lexi?" Fear twists in my stomach. "What's wrong? Is Bailey okay?"

"Oh, Liam. She really needs you right now." Lexi trails off again, her voice thick with tears. "Michael was in an accident. He was drinking, and he ran off the road and hit a tree." Lexi's crying for real now. I can barely make out the words around her tears. "He's... Liam? Michael's dead."

All the air leaves my lungs as my jaw drops open. A breeze rustles in my hair and the sun breaks through the clouds, warm on my face. I stare off into the sky, unable to process more than that while I listen to Lexi sob through her explanation of what happened.

And then in one strong rush, it hits me.

Grief surges through my body. Like the tide rolling up on the shore and dragging away bits and pieces of sand and debris, it changes the shape of the world every few seconds. Each new breath in my lungs leaves me more and more hollow. My stomach twists and my knees soften. I put a hand on a wall to steady myself.

"When?" I ask, the ache thrumming through my body taking root in my voice.

"Monday." Lexi takes a long breath. "I should have known he wasn't okay to drive. I should have known."

What do I say? How do we exist in the face of something like this? There aren't words that can possibly convey the weight of my grief.

Lexi swallows hard. "You need to be here." Her voice cracks. "Bailey needs you. She's really struggling right now and she needs you."

My throat tightens and I close my eyes. "I'm coming."

I end the call and book a flight, moving through the

world on autopilot, driven by a fierce need to get to Bailey. I don't stop moving until I get on the plane and then, with my hat pulled down low so no one can see, I lean my head against the window and cry.

Chapter 29

BAILEY

This morning, for the first time in I don't know how long, I crawled out of bed and stared at the stranger in the mirror. Lexi is right. I need something to focus on. A job. A task of some sort. And so, after sitting down to eat some of the soup she left in the fridge for me, I head to Michael's apartment to sort through his things. Or maybe I want to be there so I can find some hint of my brother, to wrap myself up in all the things that are his.

I prepare myself on the drive to his place. It's going to hurt. Maybe more than I'm ready for. I prepare myself to cry, to rage. I prepare myself to want to crawl right back into bed and never get out again. But nothing could have prepared me for what I find when I push through the door.

Empty beer bottles cover the coffee table and the end tables. Some have fallen over, rolled off and lay there, forgotten on the floor. Liquor bottles litter the counters. Rancid food clings to plates in the overfilled sink. Pizza boxes and burger wrappers spill out of the trashcan and cover the floor. There's stuff cluttering every possible surface. And the smell. Dear God, the smell.

If a tidy house signifies a tidy mind, what does this place say about Michael? How long did he live like this? Sinking in a quagmire of his own shit? How could I let him live like this?

Guilt and self-loathing settle on my shoulders as I weed through the trash and pick out the bits and pieces of my brother's life that are worth saving. There's not much. I box up his clothes. A tattered copy of *The Lord of the Rings*. A few trophies from his junior high attempt at baseball stardom. The rest? I have no idea what to do about it all. It hurts too much to be here, getting an intimate glimpse of just how off the rails my brother is.

Or was.

Fuck. That hurts.

I take a breath in through my nose, close my eyes and tilt my head up to the ceiling before letting the breath out through my mouth. When the pain subsides, I take one last trip through the small apartment, looking for anything else worth saving. Where my house is a shrine to the past with our family photos still hanging in the same spot they have for decades, Michael's apartment is devoid of anything personal at all. His walls are bare. His shelves covered in dust and empty beer bottles are arranged there like prized possessions. Just when I'm about to take the few boxes I already packed up and leave, I find a small wooden box shoved into the back of his closet, mostly covered by musty old boots he probably forgot he had. I dig the thing out and sit on the edge of his unmade bed and balance it on my knees.

Years of dust have settled into the engravings on the lid and there's a residue left on my fingers just from touching it. I open the thing, my heart pounding in my chest, my breath stuck somewhere in my throat. The lid creaks in protest and I gasp, tears pricking in my eyes. I've spent the whole day looking for Michael in this awful place and he's been in here the whole time. There are pictures of Mom and Dad. Of the four of us on vacation in Florida. I was all of ten, all knees, elbows, and buckteeth, and Michael looked dashing at seven, his arm wrapped around my waist as the ocean licked up around our sunburnt legs. He's got letters I wrote to him right after mom and dad died, my looping handwriting scrawling across the worn pages. The ink is thin and blurry, the creases in the folded paper so frail they're about to fall apart.

How many times did he sit in here and read these words? An outpouring of emotion and apology from me to him? All this time I thought he threw them away. Thought he never knew how desperately I worried about all the things I was getting wrong. And here I find he knew all along. Judging by the delicate condition of the paper—torn from my notebook years ago—Michael read them frequently. I gingerly unfold each one, trace a finger across the words and then place them on the bed beside me.

Underneath the letters are strange things. A worn pocketknife, old and dirty. A pocket watch I vaguely remember belonging to my grandfather. And more pictures of our family than I ever remember being taken. A box filled with bits and pieces of people who have left me to fight through the rest of this life alone.

At the bottom, hiding beneath it all, is one more piece of folded paper. So clean and crisp I struggle to believe it's been looked at since he put in in here. I pull it out, unfold it, and gasp.

My name, scrawled at the top of the page in Michael's unruly print.

Bailey,

I know you blame yourself for all the shit I get myself into. I know you see each mistake I make as proof that you failed me. But I'm not your fault. I think I just came this way. You did your best, stayed with me when I made it damn near impossible, and I'm a better person because of it. Because of you. You ask for forgiveness but there's nothing to forgive.

I love you.

Michael

I stare at the words. Read them over and over and over again until I've got them memorized and hear them in his voice, as if he were standing right next to me and whispering in my ear. Blinking back tears, I press the note to my chest and look up.

"I love you, too," I say.

I place everything back in the box, the discovery of the note tearing through my composure like a chainsaw through rotting wood. I can't be here anymore. I gather the wooden box and lock up Michael's apartment, sweating even as I shiver against the cold. The sun shines down from a clear blue sky. One of those rare bright days in the stream of gray that is winter in Ohio. The world seems made of plastic, too shiny and smooth and unrefined.

I can't keep living like this.

I don't *want* to keep living like this.

"The least you could do is take me with you," I mutter as I climb into the truck where my dad's ghost still lingers. The drive home is short and I spend it with Michael's wooden box on my lap. The crunch of gravel under my tires as I pull into my driveway mocks me. There is no sense of homecoming without the people I love. How can there be home when I am an island, disconnected from everyone? Alone is alone, regardless of where I am.

And wouldn't you know, there's someone on my doorstep. I don't have it in me to put on a brave face for anyone. It's been a steady parade of people stopping by, casseroles in hand and platitudes on their lips. They're not here for me. They're here to be part of the drama.

I put the truck in park and close my eyes. Clench my jaw and look down at the box in my lap. I don't want to leave it in the truck, but I don't want whoever's standing up there to see it, either. They weren't part of Michael's life and they sure as hell won't share this treasure with me.

Squinting into the sun, I stare at the figure on my porch, trying to decide if I should just put the truck in reverse and leave. Whoever it is has his back against the wall, arms crossed over his chest, one leg bent at the knee, the foot resting on the siding. There's auburn hair. A quirk of a smile.

Oh my God.

My lips part.

Tears spring to my eyes.

My heart leaps for joy and races, pumping my blood through my veins so it roars in my ears.

My hand grabs the door handle without permission, my body acting against my will. Drawn to him like mercury rolling across a table. He is my sun and I am Icaraus, flying too close even as my skin burns. I run. He pushes off the wall. Smiles. Holds out his arms to me.

I stop at the first step leading up to my porch. Frozen. My need for him pulsing through me with every beat of my heart while anger surges up from my gut and flashes in my eyes.

"Liam?" I ask, one hand coming to my stomach.

Liam steps forward, the collar of his pea coat pulled up around his neck. "Oh, Bailey, I'm so sorry..."

I hold out my hands and step back. "Stop."

He doesn't. He keeps coming to me. His eyes hold mine and his smile fades. "Lexi told me—"

"No." I hold up one finger, tears welling in my eyes as I fight for my breath. "You don't get to disappear for weeks and then come riding back in like some goddamn knight in shining armor."

"I never disappeared—"

"Never disappeared?" My hands tremble and my breath puffs out into the air, a frozen burst of rage. "You fucking left and never came back. That's disappearing, Liam."

Liam rushes down the steps, reaching out for me, and I know I won't survive his touch.

I back up again. "Don't you dare. You're not the hero of this story."

He stops, his face as broken as my heart, and sinks down onto the step. "I'm sorry."

"I needed you." Tears strangle my words. "I

needed you more than anything and you weren't here." Sobs wrack my body. "My brother died and you weren't here."

I wrap my arms around my center because if feels like my insides are going to fall out. A blast of wind hits the tears on my cheeks, so cold they feel hot. My knees buckle and I crouch, one hand on the ground, the other covering my face. My mouth opens and my eyes close and nothing happens. No sounds. No breath. Just this awful nothingness. And then, a keening sound. High and long and drawn out from the base of the pain anchored inside me.

A strong arm wraps around my shoulder. God. I can smell him. His scent envelops me. I lean into him, no longer able to support the weight of everything sitting on my shoulders. He staggers, drops to a sitting position, and pulls me into his lap, rocking me. Shushing me. Wiping my hair back off my forehead.

"I'm here for you," he whispers.

"But you weren't." I bury my head in his chest. "I needed you and you were gone."

"I was with you the whole time. Not one day passed that I didn't think of you." He pulls me tighter, closer to his warmth. "I love you, Bailey. I'm so sorry I wasn't here when you needed me, but I'll never leave you again."

"Damn you for coming back." I wipe my eyes and nose on my reddened hands and lean into him, rage seeping out of my body as I soften into his arms.

"Don't say that."

"I have nothing left. No strength. No fight. I can't do this."

"That's why I'm here. I'll hold you up. Give you all I have. I've got you, Bailey."

"But you didn't. When I needed you, you weren't here."

"I was..." Liam puts a finger to my chin and leans down to look in my eyes. "I have reasons, excuses for being gone so long, and they made sense to me then, but none of that matters now because..." He swallows hard, tears shining in his eyes. "I fucked up. I left to protect you and utterly failed you. And when Michael needed me ... I failed him, too."

His words light a fire in my heart. "You left to protect me?" Gathering every ounce of strength I have, I pull out of his arms and stand. "Well, I'm leaving to protect you."

"Don't say that."

"I'm cursed, Liam." I fling my arms out to the side and stare up at the sky. "I'm cursed!" My voice echoes through the trees and rakes its way out of my throat, like fingernails digging into my flesh. It's an admission, an accusation, a personal truth I can't escape. I lower my face and point at him, widening my eyes. "Leave me alone." My finger shakes as I fight the urge to take it all back.

"I won't." Liam stands, wiping his hands on the back of his jeans.

"You have to." My throat is so raw, my voice scraping against it as I fight for breath.

"I can't. I won't. You're not cursed, Bailey." Liam stands, holds his hands out to me.

I run my hands up into my hair and pull. "I can't handle losing one more person." The wind gusts, biting my skin. "Especially not you. I love you so fucking much!" I'm screaming because this isn't a conversation for whispers. There's nothing quiet or polite about the storm raging in my heart.

He pulls me back into his arms and I melt into him. "You're not cursed and I can prove it. Lexi? Michelle? They're still here. You love them."

I shake my head against his chest and suck in my lips. My breath comes so fast I'm afraid I might pass out. "I don't love them like I love you," I say as I pull away one more time, turn my back to him, and stagger through a spinning world to get Michael's stuff out of my truck.

Chapter 30

LIAM

Of all the ways I imagined our reunion, I never expected Bailey's rage. Her hatred. I didn't expect her gray skin and greasy hair. I didn't expect the purple circles standing out like bruises under her eyes. The flared nostrils. The gut-wrenching sobs. But that doesn't mean I'm going to leave. She might think it's better if she pushes me away, but she's never needed me like she needs me right now. I meant what I said. I'll never leave her side again. Squaring my shoulders, I follow the love of my life into her house.

If seeing Bailey was a shock, then seeing the inside of her house ruins me. Trash on every surface. Sink overflowing with dishes. Piles of clothes on the floor. The lid on the piano is down, covering the keys, and for some reason, of all the tragedies in this house, that one hits me the hardest.

Bailey has silenced her music.

I was a fool to leave her.

"Bailey?" The house is small, there aren't many places for her to go.

Silence.

It's the silence that scares me the most. I head down the hallway to the bedrooms. Her door is closed, another sign she has shut herself off again. But she's not in there. I know it without looking. I lean on the door-frame to Michael's room, the room I spent some of the best weeks of my life in.

"Bailey?"

She's sitting in the middle of the room, surrounded by piles of clothes. Some of it I recognize as mine, the stuff I wore while I was here. The rest? I can only assume it's Michael's. She looks up at me, pale and empty. Even her skin looks fragile, like it will crumble to dust if I touch her. "I don't know what to do with it all."

Ignoring my need to run to her, to swoop her up and hold her close, I shift my weight against the wall. "We can figure that out later."

She drops her head into her hands. "I'm so tired."

"When was the last time you ate?"

She shakes her head without looking up. Silent.

She needs so many things at the same time, I don't even know where to start. As much as I want to apologize, explain myself, tell her why I was in LA, I know she can't handle any of that right now. Bailey is barely holding on. She needs me to hold her up, not put anything more on her shoulders.

I push off the wall and crouch down in front of her. Without a word, I take her hands. Help her to her feet. Support her weight when her knees buckle. Lead her to the bathroom and draw a bath. When I try to help her out of her shirt, she flinches.

"I can't." She won't look at me, arms crossed over her stomach. "I can't be more bare than I already am."

"Trust me?" I lean down to meet her eyes, but she avoids them. "I don't want anything from you. I just want to help."

The nod is imperceptible, but it's there. I drag the shirt over her head, dismayed at the bones of her chest and ribcage standing out from her pale skin.

"I'm here now." I whisper because I don't believe she can handle anything louder than that. "I've got you. And as much as nothing feels okay right now, I'm going to do everything in my power to make it better." I help her out of her pants. "I'll carry you when you can't carry yourself."

She stands there, looking frail and broken in her bra and underwear and finally looks me in the eyes. "I'm okay."

I smile. "You are now." I pull my shirt over my head and Bailey averts her eyes.

"Liam." She shakes her head, her eyes communicating how she misunderstood my gesture. "I can't..."

"And I don't want you to. I just want to warm you

up because you look so cold." I kick off my shoes and step out of my pants and underwear. Climb into the warm tub and hold out my hand.

I half expect her to walk away from me and judging by the look on her face, she does too. But she doesn't. After a few seconds of hesitation, she unhooks her bra and slides off her panties, takes my hand, and climbs into the tub with me.

Water sloshes up against the sides and she sighs as the warmth works its way into her body. I help her down so she's sitting with her back to my front. I hold her. Run my hands through her hair until it's wet and slicked back from her forehead. She sinks into me, her tiny body melting into mine. Before I know it, I'm humming, the song brought to my lips unbidden. The song my mom used to sing to me when I was a little boy, scared of the monster in my closet and the gremlins under my bed.

She's crying again but I ignore it. The tiny little hitches and hiccups feel less like agony and more like acquiescence. She's giving me her pain, leaning into me, letting me take care of her. I wash her body and her hair, careful strokes of my hands over her fire-eaten body. And through it all, I hum. My mom's song. Our song. A new melody. She turns, leaning her ear into my chest and damn if my heart doesn't crack in half. She's listening to the music in my body the same way I used to when I was a boy.

"I love you Bailey," I whisper.

She doesn't reply. Just closes her eyes and sighs.

The next few days are hard. Between getting the house cleaned up, helping Bailey finalize the funeral arrangements, and putting my beautiful girl back together again, I have my hands full. The day of the funeral is the coldest of the week, dreary and snowy and perfectly appropriate for something this awful. Bailey gets dressed and then watches me as I tie my tie.

"I thought he didn't know." Her voice is stronger today than it has been. "I thought he didn't know how sorry I was. How hard I tried and how much I knew I failed him. But he knew." She smiles weakly.

"Of course he did." I meet her eyes through the mirror.

She averts her eyes. "I wrote him all these letters. It was childish. My way of trying to get him to understand that I didn't know what the hell I was doing. I'd leave them on his bed when he was out all night when he still lived here. And after he moved out, I even went so far as to drive to his apartment and slide them under the door."

She meets my eyes through the mirror and I smile. I can't help it. Even in her grief she's the most beautiful thing I've seen.

"He kept them, Liam. Each and every one." She gives me a tight-lipped smile, her eyes brimming with tears. "I found them in a box in his closet." Bailey swallows. "I know it's stupid, but it gave me peace, seeing them in that box. But," she says and licks her lips. "I found a note from him in there, too. One he never gave me. He told me none of this was my fault. That he knows I did my best and he's a better person because of me." She takes a long shuddering breath. "And he said he loved me. Michael never said that to me." She smiles, a sweet thing.

I turn. Cross the room and take her shoulders in my hands. "Your brother knew you loved him. He didn't show it. At least not in ways that were easy to understand. But each and every stone in that patio is a testament to his love for you." I lean down and kiss her forehead. "And mine. My love's out there, too."

Bailey threads her fingers in mine and stares down at our hands. "As if I didn't love that thing enough already."

The funeral is an exercise in cruelty. The entire town of Brookside filters into the funeral home for the viewing, gawking at me while they offer Bailey sympathy in between snide comments and whispered judgments. She stands tall through it all, her small hand gripping mine as if I am the only thing keeping her tethered to the ground.

"He looks so handsome," says Lexi, a balled-up tissue in her fist. She touches his hand, just a finger on his cold skin, her face crumbling with the devastation of hopes and dreams gone too soon.

"You were beautiful together." Bailey lifts her chin, her voice thick with emotion. "I think the end of his life was the best part, because of you." She turns to me. "And you."

My heart swells with pain and sorrow. "And you," I say, squeezing her hand.

While the viewing overflowed with people, the service at the graveside is small. Just four of us. Lexi, Michelle, Bailey, and me. We cry as the pastor speaks. And when he's done, Bailey takes three flowers from the arrangement on the casket.

"One for me," she says. "And one for each of them." She gestures towards a large headstone with the names Miranda and Samuel Schultz engraved in the marble. She puts a hand on the casket. "I love you, Michael." She looks up towards the gray sky. "Wherever you are, I hope you've finally found peace."

Lexi and Michelle say their goodbyes and pick their way back across the frozen ground to their cars, heads down, hands in pockets. Bailey crouches in front of her parents' headstone. Brushes off a few dried leaves. Lays a rose down in front of each name.

"I don't come here enough." Her voice is raw. She

straightens and takes my hands. "Mom, Dad? I'd like you to meet Liam." She smiles up at me, embarrassed and unsure.

I nod, my throat too tight for words.

"He's my everything," she continues. "The way you guys were each other's everything." The wind blows her hair into her face and she brushes it away. "I'm stronger when he's here. He makes me better than I should be." She looks up at me and smiles weakly before looking down again. "Michael says he doesn't blame me. I hope you guys don't, either." She finishes in the harshest whisper, a child speaking her darkest fear.

And then, out of nowhere, the sun pushes through the clouds. Warmth falls on our faces like the faintest brush of a hand on our cheek. The moment is brief. Just a few heartbeats of light before the clouds swallow the sun again.

Bailey smiles up at me, blinking away tears. "It's like they know."

"Of course they know." I wrap an arm around her shoulders. "You're the only one who ever blamed yourself for any of this. The rest of us," I say, gesturing towards the sky with my chin. "We know how hard you tried to get it all right."

Bailey leans her head on my shoulder. I don't say it out loud, because this is her family and not mine, but I send a thought out to Michael and their parents:

I love her. And I promise to protect her from this

day forward. I want to be in her life for as long as she'll have me, making her happy and keeping her safe each and every day. I'd do it right if I could. Ask you for her hand and all that good stuff. So, I guess this is it, here and now. When the time is right, I want to ask Bailey to marry me. To be my wife. And I will do everything I can to erase the wounds on her heart in the same way she's done her best to erase mine. This is me, asking you for your permission to make your daughter happy for the rest of her life. I know you can't answer, but I'll be listening anyway.

As I help Bailey pick her way through the frozen grass towards her truck the clouds dissipate and the sun shines down on us. Once was a coincidence, but twice? I look up at the sky and smile, imagining Michael shaking his head in dismay as I wrap an arm around his sister's shoulders and pull her tight.

Chapter 31

BAILEY

"When are you leaving?" I heave a box filled with Michael's stuff onto the back of the truck and glare at Liam. "I'm still mad at you for disappearing in the first place, you know. Don't think you're getting out of here without having that particular conversation. Besides, I need to apologize and you have no idea how rare that is." I wipe my hands and fold my arms over my chest to hide how much they're trembling at the thought of having to confront what happened while he was in Los Angeles, and then, after that, figure out how to tell him goodbye.

He slides a box onto the tailgate and purses his eyebrows. "This is a big conversation, Bay."

"Yeah, well, I can't keep sleeping next to you each night when I know it's all coming to an end sooner rather than later."

Liam laughs and it makes me want to kick him in the balls.

"Really? You're going to laugh at me about this?" I shake my head. "Obviously, you have zero idea about how to be a decent human being." I grin at him and purse my lips, eyebrows raised.

"Ouch," he says, still laughing.

"Yeah, well, you deserve it."

"So the whole time I've been here, holding your hand and keeping you upright over the last couple weeks, that's not something a decent human being would do?" Liam sucks in his lips, still looking like he's fighting laughter.

"That's beside the point. I don't need a knight in shining armor. I need..." I hold out my hands and roll my eyes, looking for the right word. "A fortress. I don't want you to save me, I want you to stand by my side while I save myself. And I sure as hell don't want you popping in and out of my life whenever it suits you."

"Bailey..."

"I'm just saying, Liam. It was a douchey move, leaving me after one fight, only to swoop back in when it made you look good." I huff, my breath frosting in front of my face.

"Bay..."

"And you know what? I swear to God, if you don't stop laughing at me, I'm going to end you right here and now."

"Can I talk now?" Liam smiles and it blinds me.

Every ounce of my being reaches out for him while I stand here, as stoic as I can possibly manage. If he's leaving, I need to be careful about how much of myself I give back to him so I can keep on healing once he's gone.

"Sure. By all means." I lift my chin and my eyebrows at the same time.

"I was wrong to leave without a solid explanation and I was even more wrong to go so long without letting you know what I was doing. I apologize for both things, but I do not, under any circumstances, apologize for leaving in the first place." Liam licks his lips, staring at me with so much love in his eyes, I start to wonder what I'm missing. "I had to go. If I had stayed, things you don't even understand would have blown up right here in your front yard. You have no idea what it's like, fighting through a sea of paparazzi and crazed fans just to get through the normal parts of your day. You've already talked about hating how the town pays too much attention to you. There was no part of me that thought you were ready to handle the shit-storm that was brewing."

I shake my head. "I call bullshit on that. You wanted to protect me and the best way to do that was to just leave?"

"Yep." The bastard has the audacity to look smug. "I had to go put out the fire."

"And just what does that mean, exactly?"

"By leaving, I was protecting you—"

"But I wasn't protected at all. You left me alone and my life blew up."

Liam takes me into his arms. "And I'd take all that back in a heartbeat. I really would." He puts his hands on my shoulders and pushes me away so he can look in my eyes. "I spent the last couple weeks in meetings with my agent. My manager. The PR team. The studio. My mother." Liam shudders a little, and I don't think it was for effect. "I needed a solid plan, a bullet-proof exit strategy. One that would let me out of the spotlight, out of the public eye, without all kinds of people going crazy and swarming your house."

"So why didn't you tell me what was going on? Why let me sit here and think I was losing you?"

Liam shoves his hands in his pockets and looks down. "That's where I messed up." He meets my eyes. "It was a good idea..." He shakes his head. "No, an *idealistic* idea, gone bad. That was me making plans that were based on too many movies filled with dramatic moments and not enough common sense."

"Go on."

"I wanted to have all the answers before I called you. I wanted to be able to swoop back in like the damn knight in shining armor you say you don't need with the solution to our problem. I wanted to show you that I really am capable of taking care of you. That I'm worthy of you. That I'm not the spoiled pop star everyone says I am. That I'm a man who can take charge and solve problems."

"Do you have any idea how I suffered?" I step forward. "The biggest wound on my heart is caused by people leaving without me being able to say goodbye, leaving me to live a life that doesn't make sense without them, and you thought the best way to prove that you aren't a spoiled child was to leave me without an explanation? Just so you could swoop back in with everything all solved?"

Liam's face crumbles. "I can see now just how wrong I was."

"You were so wrong it bordered on cruelty." I chew on my bottom lip, watching him watch me. "I waited for you to reach out. To prove that what we had was stronger than one disagreement. I wanted a chance to apologize for blowing up. For being such a bitch. And day after day passed and nothing. You gave me nothing. I..."

Liam steps forward. Takes my hand. "But now I want to give you everything. I'm not a perfect man. Far from it. But with you? I'm as close to it as I'm ever gonna get. I don't ever want to be without you. I never, ever want to leave you ever again. I didn't want to say goodbye because it wasn't an ending." I start to protest and he holds up a hand. "I can see how it seemed like it to you. I really can and I'm sorry. But to me, I was working on our beginning. Our fresh start."

His nose is red from the cold, high points of color stand out on his cheeks, but his eyes are warmer than the brightest summer day. "So what does our fresh start look like?" I ask.

"I severed my contract with the studio." Liam's face is expressionless, waiting for my reaction. "The PR team has already started putting out press releases, spinning the bus accident into something far worse than it was so my fans don't feel like they need to come hunt me down—"

"Won't that make them even more frantic to find you?"

Liam laughs. "Shows how little you understand the power of the right kind of publicity. I've been here for two weeks now. Been out with you in public. How many crazed fans have come up to bother us?"

He has a point. "I just assumed that was out of respect for me and Michael." I flinch. It still hurts to say his name.

Liam shakes his head. "I'd love to be able to give people that much credit, but experience has taught me they don't deserve it. The privacy we got? That's all courtesy of my team in LA." He laughs. "Although they're not really my team now. They're the studio's team, putting out the fire that started the first moment I laid eyes on you." He runs his thumb along my cheek.

"What are you saying, Liam?"

"I'm saying that I'm here to stay. If you'll have me." He drops a wink at me, a very Liam McGuire wink. "And I'm really hoping you'll have me because I don't have anywhere else to go."

I stare up at him, counting my breaths, fighting the urge to lean into his hand. Then I purse my lips and draw my eyebrows together. "And just what's in it for me?" I ask, as if I'm actually weighing my options.

Liam grins. "Me. You get me. An imperfect man who loves you perfectly. And we'll fuck like bunnies and make music and fill that house with so much love and laughter that all the angry ghosts and memories have no choice but to smile."

Damn it. I'm so tired of crying, but here we go again. "I love you, Liam," I whisper.

"I love you, too, hot lips." And then he kisses me and I fall into him and for the first time in a long time, I feel like maybe everything's going to be okay.

Chapter 32

BAILEY

"And these are the countertops he wants to put in." I slide my new iPad across the table to show Lexi and Michelle the pictures.

"Holy shit. Those are gorgeous." Lexi smiles, but it doesn't reach her eyes even though she tries like hell to force the happiness into them.

"They're really very pretty." Michelle uses her fingers to zoom in on the image.

I sip my beer. "You can swipe through if you want. That whole album is ideas he has for this place."

Lexi flips through the pictures, shaking her head. "This house isn't even going to look the same when he's done," she says, and then pauses. "Is this a recording studio?" She looks at me with wide eyes.

"It is." I smile and nod. "He's thinking about producing his own album with all the stuff he wrote. I keep telling him to do it because I think those are songs people need to hear."

Michelle sighs, her eyes faraway and dreamy. "Please tell me you'll sing with him. Especially that song you sang that night at Smitty's. It's so very beautiful."

I blush. Even the thought of people hearing me sing in a recording makes me uncomfortable. "I don't know. Maybe."

Lexi rolls her eyes. "Oh, please. You weren't satisfied with your fifteen minutes of fame being due to the fact that you were Liam McGuire's nurse. Are you telling me you're going to pass up your chance at real fame?"

Michelle gives me a confused look while I laugh. "You've got the memory of an elephant," I say to Lexi before explaining to Michelle about the things Lexi said to me when Liam and I first met.

Several hideous notes come clanging out of the piano in the other room followed by the low murmur of Liam's voice, instructing Gabe, and Michelle's daughter, Claire. A few shaky notes begin to form a song.

"There it is! You've got it!" Liam exclaims. The song stops and there's the sound of two high-fives and some very happy children giggling in excitement.

"He's really good with them," says Michelle.

"He tries." I shrug. "I think it's because he's mostly still a child."

Lexi smiles and then runs a hand over her mouth as

if to wipe it away. Michael's death still sits heavily on her shoulders. Who am I kidding? It sits heavily on all of us.

"You know," I say to my friend. "I've almost gotten used to seeing you without your cherry red lipstick."

Lexi laughs and captures her bottom lip between her teeth. For a moment, it looks like she wants to say something, but then she settles on silence.

"How much of this are you going to let him do?" Michelle asks, waving a hand towards the iPad on the table.

"Honestly? I don't really know. On one hand, I love the idea of taking this place and fixing all the broken parts. There's something really beautiful about the idea, you know? On the other, I can't afford any of it. And I still don't know if I'm cool with him spending his money on me like that."

Lexi leans forward, crossing her arms on my kitchen table. "Bay. He's got plans for a recording studio." She taps the picture on the iPad. "I don't think he's spending anything on you alone. It looks to me like he's spending it on *you*." She makes a motion with her hands, like she's smashing something between them. "On both of you. Together."

I look towards the den, listening to Liam tease Gabe and Claire. "Really?" I look back at my friends. "I mean, wow. I guess you're right."

Michelle puts a hand to her mouth and gasps.

"What if he proposes on Christmas? Oh, Bailey! What would you say?"

"That's a silly question," says Lexi, finally sounding like herself for the first time this evening. "Look at her blush."

"He's not going to propose." I stand and grab another beer. There are a couple of Michael's left in the fridge, one of the few things I haven't been able to bring myself to touch. They're too heavy. Too dirty. Too awful.

"Yeah, but what if he does?" asks Michelle, looking dreamy as I swing the fridge door closed.

"Yeah, Bay. What if he does?" Lexi wrinkles her nose. "Good lord, you'll be Mrs. Liam McGuire. You were so smart to hold out on those fifteen minutes."

I shrug and twist the top off the beer, tossing it onto the counter. "First of all, you say his name like it's a thing that's bigger than a person. Liam is a man, perfectly imperfect. He's more than a smiling face on a billboard."

"Exactly, says Lexi while Michelle nods knowingly. "He's also one hell of a hot body, half naked on a billboard."

"Lexi!" Michelle looks appalled.

"Sorry." My best friend holds up her hands. "I know what you mean and you're very right. I'm sorry for objectifying your hot piece of man candy." She smiles widely, and then pain turns it into a grimace, a hideous transformation that all of us understand but none of us want to acknowledge.

"I'd totally say yes," I say after a few awkward heartbeats.

"Of course you would." Michelle offers me an encouraging smile.

"Then let him go to town on this house." Lexi sits back, wrapping one arm around her stomach and taking a tiny sip of her mostly full beer before putting it back on the table and sliding it away from her. "Let him gut it. Rebuild it from the ground up. Let him show you how much he loves you by building you a palace. And when he's done, tell him just how manly he is and how much you love all his grunting and man-sweat and hard work."

I laugh. "You're a little weird, Lex."

"Maybe," she says with a shrug. "But I'm also one-hundred percent right."

Chapter 33

BAILEY

Christmas comes and goes without a proposal. I try not to be hurt but damn it, Lexi and Michelle got my hopes up. Even if there wasn't a diamond ring waiting for me this morning, we still have a lovely day. We exchange our gifts, sit at the piano and sing Christmas carols, and then go to visit my family. Liam waits while I clean off the gravestones. Holds my hand while I talk to them, pouring my heart out and yes, shedding a few more tears.

These tears, though, they cleanse my soul. They are a spring rain on lush grass. Each time I come here—and after years of barely ever visiting, Liam has made sure I come frequently—I cry a little less.

"You'd be amazed at what we're going to do to the house," I say, running a finger along my mother's name. "Liam finally talked me out of being a stubborn ass about him changing the place. You'd love it, Mom. It's basically going to be a shrine to music."

"Would you expect any less?" Liam places a hand on my shoulder.

"And we're going to sell the truck." I suck in my lips. "I know I promised to take care of it, Daddy, but I think I'm going to let Liam take care of me for a little while, you know? I've been standing strong all this time while the water just kept creeping up around my neck. I don't think you'd mind if I ended up with air conditioning and power steering." I cringe, waiting for a lightning bolt to zigzag out of the sky and strike me dead. When it doesn't, I stand and take Liam's hand.

"And the patio is a thing of beauty," I say to Michael. "I think it's the only thing around that place we're not going to change. Whenever I get to missing you too much, I go sit out there and everything starts to feel okay again."

I lean into Liam.

"I love you guys," I say to them. "Merry Christmas."

"You ready?" Liam asks.

I nod. "Yeah. Thanks for coming here with me."

He offers me his elbow as we start toward the truck. "Of course, silly. There's no reason to thank me. I'm here for you. Always."

"No more leaving?" I glance up at him.

"I never left. My heart and soul were with you the entire time I was in LA."

"Yeah, well. I'm in the market for all of you. No more bits and pieces."

Liam stops and pulls me to him. "I thought you liked my bits and pieces."

I roll my eyes. "I like all of you. Every single bit and piece. And I claim each and every one of them as mine."

"You sure you don't want to go out?" Liam asks from his place on the couch. "It's New Year's Eve."

I drop down next to him and kick my feet up on the coffee table, leaning my head on his shoulder. "Nah. Do you? Have you been cooped up too much?"

"Honestly, after all that time touring in front of thousands of screaming fans, I'm all about a quiet night at home."

A smile pulls at the corners of my lips as I stare down at my hands clasped in my lap. Liam shifts so he can see my face.

"What?" He furrows his brow and looks so damn adorable I want to kiss him. So I do. I take his face in my hands and press my mouth to his, parting my lips, letting him in. His hands snake up into my hair, cupping my face before he runs them down my back. Goose bumps flare out across my skin and I smile without breaking the kiss.

"What did I do to deserve that?" he asks, pressing his forehead to mine.

"I like that you called this place home." I look up at him through my eyelashes. "I've lived here my whole life, but it hasn't felt like a home in a really long time."

"As long as you're here, it feels like home to me."

"You always know just what to say to make me smile." I drop my gaze to his mouth, wanting to kiss him again.

"You say that like my words are calculated." Liam pulls back and looks me square in the eye. "Nothing about me is pretense with you. That's part of what's so beautiful. I'm just me, living my life, being happy with you, and you love me anyway."

We laugh our way through the evening, and when we're not laughing, we're kissing. And when we're not kissing, we're holding hands, his thumb running across my knuckle. For as long as I can remember, this house had ghosts hanging in the corners, judging my each and every move and finding them all lacking. Over the last couple weeks, those ghosts have dissipated, the shadows giving way to light. When Liam came into my life, I thought he was the one with the wounds that needed caring for, but it turns out I needed to heal as much as he did.

As the clock edges towards midnight, Liam stands, pulling me to my feet. His eyes sparkle as he looks down at me.

"I love you so much, Bailey Schultz. I can't think of

a better way to start the New Year than with you in my arms."

I bite my lip. "You're making me blush." I reach for him but he steps back.

"Actually," he says, digging into his pocket. "I *can* think of a better way to start this year."

He holds out his hands and I look down to find a diamond ring gleaming in a black box.

"I don't just want you in my arms. I want you in my life. I want you forever, a lifetime of New Years, each filled with more laughter than the last. I came to you a broken man and you saw through all the bullshit and found the real me. You healed me inside and out and I am forever yours because of it. I'm no prince. Not a knight in shining armor. No fortress to keep your safe. You are my queen and I am your slave. Totally and completely at your mercy. You move and my whole world shifts to move with you."

Tears gather in my eyes and my bottom lip quivers. "Dammit. All I ever do is cry anymore."

Liam plucks the ring out of the box and holds it out. "Then let me be the one to wipe away your tears. Say yes, Bailey."

I nod, frantically, swallowing hard. "Yes." I swipe at my eyes. "But I'll wipe away my own tears, thank you very much."

Liam slides the ring on my finger and draws me in, so close I forget where he ends I begin. "I love you, Bailey," he whispers. "Forever." He kisses my nose.

"And ever." He kisses a cheek. "And ever." He kisses my forehead. "And ever."

I grab his face and kiss his lips, my tongue seeking entrance to his mouth. "And ever," I say when we're done.

Liam swoops me up and throws me over his shoulder, slapping my ass so hard I squeal. "And ever," he says, carrying me back to the bedroom while I laugh and laugh.

The end

Want a sneak peak at Michelle's story, the next book in the Brookside Romance series? Turn the page!

INEVITABLY YOU SNEAK PEEK

Prologue

MICHELLE

I never thought I'd be the girl with a gun in her face. Someone like me isn't supposed to understand the way fear boils in your gut when you stare at the business end of a deadly weapon.

But here we are. I guess bad guys don't understand that bad things shouldn't happen to good girls.

He thumbs the hammer and fear sears through my veins like fire down a fuse. The tiny click might as well be a lightning strike. Chills race across my skin and I forget what it means to breathe.

"Is this what you want?" My husband steps towards me, the gun trembling in his hands as spittle flies from his lips. "Or is it this?" He presses the thing against his temple and I run from the room, chased by the demons in his head.

I grab my daughter, her wrist fragile in my fist. "Why is he doing this, Mommy?"

I press a hand to my chest, begging my heart to slow while I hold in the bits and pieces that crack off and crumble inside me. I pull my daughter down the hallway, her little feet stumbling behind me as her father lumbers out of our bedroom.

"Damn it, Michelle! Get your ass back here!" His voice eats through my resolve like acid through metal.

I grab my phone before I lose my nerve. Dial 911 as I race out of our home, praying the neighbors open the door in time.

"Why, Mommy? Why is he doing this?" Claire's wide eyes stand out like little moons in the dark.

"Because," I say as I run across the yard, grass clippings sticking to my bare feet. "I told him he couldn't anymore."

MICHELLE

A bead of sweat drips down my back as a light breeze plays in the tendrils of hair falling free from my ponytail. April in Ohio shouldn't be this hot. In a typical year, daffodils would just now be poking through the rain-drenched soil and people would be praying that an overnight frost wouldn't kill the delicate buds. Claire and I should be tucked into our jackets, her too-short sleeves exposing the skin at her wrists because she grows so fast nothing lasts more than a season. Instead, we're decked out in shorts and tank tops as we make our way home from the grocery store, while she points out all the flowers in full bloom along the way.

"My feet are so tired, Mommy." Claire stops in the middle of the sidewalk and slumps her shoulders, blowing a puff of air past her lips. "And the sun is as hot as fire."

"I know, Bear." I adjust my grip on the bags of groceries in my hands, trying to relieve pressure where the plastic handles have dug into my skin. "But the good news is we're almost home."

"I wish gas didn't cost any money at all." My daughter puts her hands on her hips and blows a long breath of air past her lips. "It should be free. The stuff people need shouldn't cost money." She nods with all the finality her five-year-old self can muster.

I wrestle with the bags and wipe a drop of sweat from my face. "But we don't really need it, do we? Not while we have legs that work." I smile as guilt hollows out my stomach. She shouldn't have to accept this much sacrifice as a normal part of life.

Claire sighs. "But that's just it. I don't think my legs will work anymore."

"Come on, Bear." I readjust my grip on the bags. "You're stronger than that. You'll be surprised what you can do if you keep pushing yourself."

She's tired and it kills me that I have to make her walk to and from the grocery store, but we only have a half mile left. Mom's late on my paycheck again and this is the best way to save on gas. I always thought running a dance studio with my mom would be a dream come true. The reality has been more like a nightmare.

It turns out trying to support two households off a small business based in a small town isn't as easy as we thought. People are always paying late or quitting in the middle of the season, or the bathrooms in the small, underground facility we rent flood, and we have to spend a bunch of money to fix the plumbing because the landlord can't be trusted to do it herself. Long story short, even as a co-owner my paycheck isn't guaranteed.

Which only makes things harder. Ever since the divorce, money is tight for me when my paychecks come on time. When they're late? Especially when they're late several weeks in a row like they have been the last two months? Things go from tight to non-existent and I fall further and further behind on everything. I might as well be scrambling up a sandy hill, doing my best to make progress, but all I do is slide backwards, earning myself a mouthful of sand.

The thought of money makes me panic, which brings tears to my eyes, but I blink them away. I can't waste energy on any of that nonsense right now. I'm doing the best I can and so is Mom. All we need is to have a couple solid weeks at work and things will improve. They have to, because I can't afford for them to keep going the way they are. In the meantime, I'll keep putting one foot in front of the other, keep figuring out how to smile through it as best I can, keep cutting corners here and there, and better days will come to me.

My sweet, sweet girl doesn't complain again for the rest of the trip home. She keeps her chin up, chattering away about every little thing she sees along the way—a steady stream of happy sounds that make me smile despite my weary heart. My arms and hands ache as we make our way up the short driveway to our small house. The weight of a few days' worth of groceries surprises me. Even the few essentials I bought ended up weighing me down. The plastic bags rustle as I drop them at my feet and stretch the tendons in my hands and wrists.

Claire hops from one foot to the other. "Oh hurry, Mommy. I have to pee!"

"Well don't do it out here." I give my girl a silly look and fumble with my keys.

"Eww." Claire rolls her eyes. "That's gross."

"Which is the whole reason you shouldn't do it." The key slides into the lock and I shimmy it open with a few practiced wrist twitches.

As soon as the door swings open, Claire bolts past me and sprints down the short hallway to the bathroom. I gather the bags and deposit them in the kitchen before taking a few minutes to open all the windows and let in some fresh air. I hate keeping the house closed up while we're gone, but I can't leave with the doors and windows open, either. We'll be uncomfortable for about an hour, but once the air starts circulating, we'll cool off. I could always turn on the air conditioner, but I can't bring myself do it this early in the season. That's a luxury I'll figure out how to afford later in the summer.

"Mommy?" Claire's voice comes sing-songing down the hallway. "The toilet won't flush!"

"Okay, babe," I call back to her. "I'll be right there."

Dread settles in my gut, heavy and toxic, while I try to remember how late I am on the water bill. I cut it close this month—the shut-off notice came the other week—but Mom swore she'd be able to pay me my full paycheck, plus everything she owed me. I was certain I'd have enough money to pay the bill on time. But despite her promises, she's late paying me, so I'm late paying them. Again. This is how we live now. I always have more month than money and I'm constantly behind on my bills. Without bothering to unpack them, I shove the grocery bags into the mostly empty fridge and turn on the faucet at the kitchen sink.

Nothing.

I grip the counter and close my eyes, shoulders tense, jaw tight. How many more decades of this do I have stretching out in front of me? How many long years of never having enough am I going to have to live through? There are tiny moments in my life where I wish I could just stop.

Not that I want to kill myself. Nothing like that. But there are times when the desire to fade away, to put my head down and close my eyes until I don't have any of this sitting on my shoulders anymore overwhelms me. If I could simply stop existing, that would be so much easier. Of course, those moments don't last long.

My daughter is always the very next thought I have. I think of her needing me and I wipe all the weakness and self-pity right out of my head. I'm not allowed to throw a pity-party for myself because life is harder than they taught me in school. Not when she needs me.

"Mom?" Claire calls from the bathroom. "What do I do about the toilet?"

I shake my head and open my eyes, pushing away the guilt that's crowding my heart. Claire needs me. I refuse to do anything but my absolute best to take care of her and make her life as beautiful as I can, despite all the struggles I face.

"Did you wipe?" I call as I push off the counter and head down the hallway.

"Yep!"

"Then you've done all you need to do." I peek into the bathroom. "The rest is up to me."

Claire buttons her shorts and reaches up on her tiptoes to wash her hands in the sink.

"I have a bottle of sanitizer on the kitchen counter," I say before she can discover that we don't have water anywhere. "Use that, okay?"

She gives me a funny look but doesn't ask any questions and skips out of the bathroom, her blond pigtails bouncing behind her. I fish my cellphone out of my pocket and flip it open. I swear I'm the last adult in the free world who hasn't gotten a smart phone, and I only have this thing because my stepdad put me on his family plan. I can't afford one of these things on my own. I dial Mom's number and lean against the sink, one arm wrapping around my stomach.

"Misha! How are you?" The smile in my mom's voice is yet another weight on my shoulders. She doesn't have any money to pay me, but she'll figure out a way to give me the money I need, even if she ends up going without something she needs.

"Hey, Mom." I clear my throat. "Hey, listen. Is there a chance you've got any money to pay me? It doesn't even have to be my whole paycheck..." Part of me wants to tell her that it very much does need to be my whole paycheck. That I'm tired of not having enough money to pay my bills and making my daughter go without some very basic things. But I don't listen to that part. My mom is doing the best she can in the same way I'm doing the best I can. Me adding pressure to her isn't going to change anything for the better, and might alienate the one person who is always on my side.

Mom sighs and that's all the answer I need. "I'm sorry, but I don't. I've got four families who owe me for this entire season. As soon as they catch up, I'll be able to catch up, too. It shouldn't be too much longer." The weight in her voice stirs fear in my heart.

"Here's the thing." I close my eyes, searching for the strength to drag words past my lips. "They've turned off my water and I only need enough to catch up on the bill so..." I trail off, unable to say the words out loud. I need money to turn my water back on because I am so close to bankrupt I can't keep the necessities my daughter and I need to survive.

"Oh, Mish." Mom sighs again, her guilt piling on top of my guilt and doing the tango in my stomach. "I'm so sorry," she continues. "Yeah, I'll figure out how to get you something. Can you stop by? Will a hundred do? I can give you that, I think." She sounds so uncertain and the shame in her voice breaks my heart.

"Yeah. A hundred will be great." I lick my lips. "Thanks, Mom. Is it okay if we stop by now? I'd like to make it down there before they close for the weekend."

"Or course, love. I'll be here."

I hang up the phone and head out of the bathroom to find Claire playing with her dolls in her room. "Come on, Bear. We've gotta go."

She looks up, crushed. "More walking?"

"Not this time. We have to take the car."

Claire's eyes light up. "Yes," she cries as she leaps to her feet. "Where we going?"

"Couple places." The animal shelter is right next to the sanitary engineering department. I'll take her to visit the animals after I pay the bill, and maybe she'll never understand what happened today.

We hop in the car and roll down the windows. The gas gauge hovers just below the halfway point, which means I'll have enough to make it to the studio tomorrow even after this unplanned trip. Maybe someone will pay Mom before I leave for the day and she'll be able to pay me. If so, I can fill up on the way home. I make the short drive to Mom's and she's waiting for us outside her apartment when I pull up out front.

"There's my Bear," she says, a huge smile stretching across her pretty face as she passes by my window in favor of her granddaughter. "Look how tall you are! You can see right out of the car, no problem." She leans her elbows on the open window.

Claire giggles. "I'm not that big. I'm in my booster seat, silly."

"Of course." Mom shakes her head. "What was I thinking?" She straightens as I swing open the door and stand. "You have time to stay?" She sounds hopeful.

"I don't. They close in forty-five minutes." A kid on a skateboard rolls past us, the wheels whirring across the pavement as his T-shirt ripples in the wind. If only I could be so free.

Mom hands me an envelope, pausing for minute to grip my hand. "I couldn't find a hundred, but I got close. I promise you'll get the rest as soon as I do."

"I trust you, Mom." Not one part of me thinks she has any more than she gave me because if she did, I'd have it right now.

"Have you thought about asking your dad for a loan?" My mother picks at the hem of her shirt, avoiding eye contact.

"No." A lifetime's worth of things left unsaid hang in the air between us.

She nods, sucking in her lips. "I understand. I wouldn't want to call him either."

I give her a quick hug and wait while she leans in to kiss Claire on the cheek. A breeze whispers past my hairline, cooling the thin layer of sweat at my temple as I pull onto the road, pausing to wave before turning down the street.

The Greene County Sanitary Engineering Department is fifteen minutes away and Claire and I fill the time by playing I Spy, laughing when neither of us can hear the other over the wind rushing through the windows and dancing in our hair. I pay the bill, fighting the urge to apologize to the woman behind the counter. I want her to understand that I'm a good person. That I'd pay on time if I could. That I didn't mean to end up where I am. That I didn't intend to fight my way through life as a single mom, overcoming the mountain of debt my ex-husband left on my shoulders.

Claire studies the pamphlets in the rack and I wonder if she comprehends where we are and what we're doing. Does she realize how hard our life is? Or is this all just normal to her? Of all the awful experiences in her short life, maybe this past year hasn't been that bad in comparison. That thought does nothing to alleviate my guilt, because that in and of itself is a tragedy.

"Wanna go look at the kitties?" I ask as we step outside, nodding towards the animal shelter on the other side of the parking lot.

"That's a silly question." Her eyes light up and a smile stretches wide across her face. I can't help but smile in return. "I always want to play with the kitties."

"You know we can't adopt one..."

"I know," she says, nodding sagely. "Just for looks."

We cross the parking lot, her small hand folded in mine, and push through the door to the animal shelter. We come here a lot. She likes to play with the kittens and the people who work here don't seem to care when we hang around for hours and never take an animal home. Typically, we're the only ones here, but today a man crouches in front of one set of cages, making the already small room seem crowded. He looks up when we come in—his eyes warm and his smile easy—before giving his attention back to the cats in front of him.

"These are all the last-chance cats?" He directs the question to a tired looking woman leaning against the wall and fidgeting with a hole in her wrinkled T-shirt.

She nods once. "Yep. Today is their last day."

"Last chance?" Claire looks up at me, concerned and confused.

How am I supposed to explain to my five-year-old that if these kitties don't find a home today, they'll be euthanized? I try on a few different explanations in my head before I divert her attention to a big fat cat in a cage on the other side of the room.

The man stands, shoving his hands in his back pockets as he stares down at the cats in the cage. I appraise his profile—high cheekbones, strong jaw, dark eyebrows and lashes—and then he turns and catches me staring. He smiles, showing a row of straight white teeth and a glimmer in his eyes that warms my poor, tired soul. I drop my attention to the three cats living their last day in a cage too small to fit them all.

"I'm gonna take all three home," the man says to the woman leaning against the wall.

"All three?" the woman asks, the surprise in her voice capturing Claire's attention.

"Yep." The man nods. "They'll all be fat and happy out in the barn, catching mice and living the high life before the end of the week."

The woman pushes off the wall and makes a face. "Whatever floats your boat. You need a box?" She gestures towards the cage. "To carry 'em in?"

"I've got two carriers in the car, but if you've got a box for the third, that'd be great. Give them a little breathing room." The man wastes a smile on the employee. "You mind if I take them out?" he asks as she trudges out of the room.

"Whatever you wanna do." The poor thing sounds so tired, it makes me wonder what kind of struggles she's fighting through. Life can be so cruel.

Claire edges closer as the man kneels and works the lock on the cage door. As he reaches inside, she drops to her knees beside him.

"Claire, honey..." I don't want her to crowd him. He doesn't need a little girl encroaching on his personal space.

He looks up, recognizes her curiosity, and smiles again. "She's okay," he says to me. "You wanna see?" he asks my daughter as he pulls a tiny kitten out of the cage.

Claire reaches for the little fur ball and buries her face in its side as she cuddles it close. "She's so soft," she coos. "Oh, Mommy." She looks up at me and I can guess what she's going to say. "Can we please adopt one?"

A fissure opens along the surface of my heart as the attendant comes back in the room, carrying a card-board box. "How much does it cost to adopt a kitten?" I ask, even though she can't give me an answer that means I can afford it.

"Eighty-five." She drops the box on the ground and takes the kitten out of Claire's hands before putting it in the box.

"Dollars?" I squeak, appalled.

The woman looks at me like I'm an idiot. "Right. Dollars."

Claire sighs. "It's okay, Mommy. I know we can't get one. I just got excited."

The man runs a hand through his dark hair, staring down at Claire with a funny look in his eyes.

This day is just one embarrassing moment right after the other. As if it wasn't bad enough that I have to say no to Claire at least three times an hour, but now I have the good fortune to do it in front of strangers, too. Deep down in my soul, a small voice cries out that life must be about more than making sacrifices and playing a never-ending game of catch up with my bills. Surely I have more to look forward to than a steady stream of *no* and *not enough.* And I don't care how many luxuries I have to do without right now, as long as the day comes when I can start saying yes. And damn it, when that day comes, my daughter will have as many kittens as her little heart desires.

DAVID

I can't stop thinking about giving the kitten I just adopted to the little girl in the worn sneakers. The thought is ridiculous on so many levels, but that doesn't stop it from popping back into my head every time I push it away. In what world is it okay for a grown man to give a kitten to a little girl he doesn't know, especially after her mother just finished saying no? In fact, I'm pretty damn sure that would classify me as creepy as hell. So what if the look on the woman's face told me she would rather say yes to her daughter? I have no right to interfere at all, nor do I have any reason to justify the urge to give a kitten to a stranger, even if the little girl does look a little like Maggie.

I ball that thought up and shove it way back where it belongs, a place so deep and dark I won't stumble across it again in the near future. As soon as the attendant finishes putting the kitten in the box, I open it right back up and wave the girl over. "You can hold her some more if you want."

The girl looks to her mother. "Can I?"

The woman wraps her arms around her stomach and narrows her eyes at me. I understand. If I was in her situation, I'd be wondering about my motives, too. "For a minute," she says after some thought and gives me a tentative smile. She should do that more often. Smile, I mean. She's fucking beautiful when she does.

I help the girl with the kitten and then stand, extending my hand to her mother.

"David," I say, "David Carmichael."

She places her small hand in mine. "Michelle." Her eyes—an extraordinary blue framed by dark lashes—meet mine and I lose my train of thought. She reclaims her hand and points at her daughter. "And that monster trying to sneak your kitten out of here without either one of us noticing is Claire."

"Hey! I'm not a monster." Claire pouts and then returns her attention to the creature cuddled in her arms.

"And isn't that exactly what a monster would say?" Michelle crouches beside Claire, her light brown hair falling over her shoulder like a curtain closing her off from me.

I fill out the adoption paperwork with my attention split between the forms and Michelle. She's a stunner, but nothing about the way she holds herself makes me think she has one single idea how beautiful she is. Those blue eyes, that creamy skin. I have a sudden urge to see more of it, all of it, to trail my fingers down her stomach while she arches her back in anticipation of all the pleasure I'm about to give her. Her hair fanned out across my pillow...

"Mr. Carmichael?" The tired woman on the other side of the counter leans in to catch my attention.

I wrench my focus back to the task at hand. "Mmm?"

"Will that be cash or credit?" she asks. "For the cats," she adds when I don't answer right away.

"Sorry. Cash." I smile as I reach into my back pocket for my wallet. "I was thinking about work," I add.

"Sure. Whatever you say." The woman glances at Michelle and Claire, still crouched down and cuddling the kitten I'll be adding to my family of barn cats. I pay her and then approach the women, kneeling beside them.

"So," I say to the little girl, Claire. "I know you can't take one home with you, but if you'd like, you could name this one. That's the next best thing to having your own."

The little girl grins widely. "Do you mean it?"

I nod. "Yep."

"And you promise to take good care of her?"

I nod again. "I take good care of all of my animals."

Claire studies the little ball of fur in her lap. "I

think..." She trails off, peering into the kitten's face. "I think her name is Mouse."

"Mouse, huh?" I ask. "Is that because she's so small?"

"Nope. She's only small now 'cause she's a baby. She'll grow up big and be a great hunter. I can tell. If her name is Mouse, she'll blend in better and they'll never see her coming."

I laugh. "That's a very good point."

Michelle stands and draws her hair over her shoulder. "Why don't you say goodbye to Mouse so Mr. Carmichael can take her home," she says to Claire before turning to me. "That was kind of you. Letting her name her like that." She twiddles the ends of her hair around her fingers.

"It's no skin off my back, you know? And if it makes her happy..." I shrug, losing myself in the prettiest eyes I've ever seen.

"Well, it's nice to be on the receiving end of that kindness." Her eyes lock on mine and her lips part before she blinks, swallows, and turns her focus to Claire. "Isn't it, Bear?"

"Isn't it what?" she asks, rubbing her cheek against Mouse's back.

"Nice to have someone do something nice for us. I don't know many men who would let a strange little monster name his kitten."

Claire rolls her eyes at the nickname and then beams at me. "Oh yeah." She stands, careful not to jostle the kitten. "You promise you'll take good care of her?"

"Cross my heart." I take Mouse back from Claire and put her into her box.

"You need help?" Michelle gestures to the other two cat carriers.

Under normal circumstances, I'd say no and let her go back to whatever it is she's doing here, but the prospect of having a few more minutes with her is more than I can pass up. "Sure." I grin. "I appreciate it."

Michelle carefully lifts one of the carriers, laughing as the poor cat freaks out inside, jostling the weight around and bouncing the carrier against her leg. With Claire carrying the other kitten carrier, we load everyone up in the back seat of my truck without any problems.

"Thanks." I close the door and run a hand through my hair.

"It's the least we could do," says Michelle, placing a hand on Claire's back and leading her across the parking lot. "Have a good one," she calls over her shoulder.

"You, too." I consider calling out to her. Running up and asking for her phone number, because what kind of man would let a woman that beautiful walk away? As Michelle helps Claire into the back seat and then slides into the driver's seat, yanking the door shut behind her, I realize that I'm the kind of man that would let her walk away. Beautiful or not, I don't have time for a woman, her child, and all the things that come along with them. I climb into the truck and watch Michelle's car through the rearview. I think she turns to look my way as she passes, but the way the sun glances off the roof of her car, I can't be sure.

I bring the truck to life and turn on the air conditioning. This April might as well be August, given how hot it is. The whole winter was mild, which might have spelled disaster for me if the temperature had dropped back down to normal after all the plants started popping. It still could, we're not technically out of the woods yet, but each day that passes without a frost warning has me more confident that things are going to be okay at the farm.

One of the cats starts yowling a few minutes after I hit the road and doesn't stop until I pull to a stop in front of the Carmichael family farmhouse. "Come on, then," I say as I lift the carrier out of the back. "Let me show you your new home."

Pogo, my over-zealous—if slightly clumsy—Australian Shepherd comes bounding out of the barn to meet us. One at a time, I bring the cats out and open the carriers in front of the food and water dishes I keep out here for them. Pogo sniffs each one, his little nub of a tail wagging so hard his hips wiggle with the effort. The two adult cats don't give him the time of day but Mouse? She puffs up and hops towards him, her back arched, a teeny-tiny ball of hissing ferocity. Pogo barks and I call him over to me so the kitten can relax and start to settle in.

A lot of farmers swear by having unneutered cats that have to fend for themselves, only filling their bellies off what they can hunt down. They say they're more aggressive and hungry and are therefore better mousers. Me? I'd rather adopt a cat who can't find a home and do my best to give it a great life. I feed them to keep up their strength and love it when they run up to greet me, bumping and nuzzling their little heads against my legs.

"Did you find some good ones?" My brother Colton strides into the barn, his hands shoved in his back pockets and his hat pulled down low over his face.

"Sure did." I smile as Mouse pounces on a piece of straw caught in the wind. I should have gotten Michelle's phone number so I could send a picture to Claire. And then ask her mom out to dinner. I was a fool to let that woman walk out of my life.

"Mom and Dad are in the kitchen." Colton gestures towards the stately farmhouse with its wraparound porch, a few hundred feet off the road. "Your presence has been requested."

"Do you think they'll ever figure out that I'm the one living there now? And that maybe they shouldn't let themselves in whenever they want to? And that maybe, just maybe, they can't summon me to a meeting in my own house whenever they want?"

Colton leans against the barn door. "Dude. You and

I both know that nothing on this farm belongs to either one of us. It's all part of *the family legacy—*" he makes air quotes and raises his eyebrows "—and privacy means nothing if you're a Carmichael."

I shake my head. "Remind me again why I didn't move out when I had the chance?" I stand and brush my hands off on my jeans as I head out of the barn and towards the house.

"Uh? Because I'm still here. Duh." Colton pushes off the wall to follow me.

As I step out into the sunshine, my gaze settles on the house my family has lived in for the last four generations. Blue sky and miles of open space surround the two-story home. Decades of love, devotion, and hard work are evident in the clean white paint and cultivated flowerbeds, in the porch steps Colton and I helped Dad repair last year, and in the neat trim around the windows. The orchard and its early blooms stretch out on my left. Mom's strawberries on my right. The bleat of a goat greets me as I walk by and a warm breeze rustles the hair at the back of my neck. All I need to remind me why I stayed is stretched out in front of me. This farm is a slice of heaven handmade by each generation of Carmichaels to hand down to the next. I love being here, married to the plants and the soil, tending the animals with the people who know me best and love me anyway, the history of my life etched into every single acre.

I stayed because here at Carmichael Farms, with

my days filled with nothing but work and family, my life is pretty damn perfect. After living through my own personal hell, I have a new appreciation for this simple life and I wouldn't change it for the world.

Ready for more? Click here to check out Inevitably You!

Acknowledgments

First and foremost, thank you to Mr. Wonderful and the Mini Wonderfuls for putting up with me after I spend long days, locked away in my room, living in a completely different world. For laughing when all my words are used up and I have little more than gibberish coming out of my mouth. For loving me in all the ways I love you.

To Melissa—THANK YOU for listening to every single over-thought-out idea and worry I've ever had. I wouldn't be here without you and I know it.

To my early readers—Melissa, Debra, Linda, Candy, and Joyce. OMG THANK YOU for all the awesome advice and hand-holding throughout this process. This book is so much better because of your input. I hope you see your footprints on the final story.

To my friends—Alison, Anya, and Jen. I'm sane

because of you three. Thanks for being an unending font of advice and discussion. I wish we had more time to spend together.

And to the wonderful women in Brooks Books. You might not know it, but you keep me moving forward even on days when I want nothing more than to curl up in bed and sleep the day away.

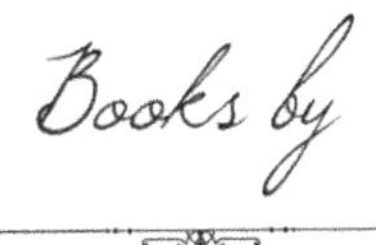

ABBY BROOKS

Brookside Romance

Wounded

Inevitably You

Lexi's story (Title and release date coming soon!)

The Moores Series

Blown Away (Ian and Juliet)

Carried Away (James and Ellie)

Swept Away (Harry and Willow)

Break Away (Lilah and Cole)

Purely Wicked (Ashely & Jackson)

Love Is...

Love Is Crazy (Dakota & Dominic)

Love Is Beautiful (Chelsea & Max)

Love Is Everything (Maya & Hudson)